He ig... ...er mouth with his. . . .

Drew breathed Leah in, conscious only of the feel of her in his embrace.

Leah's mouth opened and, as if with a mind of its own, his tongue dipped inside, robbing him for an instant of any knowledge of where he was or why he did this. All he knew was that he was lost in the intoxicating richness of her mouth.

He barely noticed when her hands fluttered up to his arms. Barely noticed the sparkle of colors dancing across his closed eyelids or the sensation of movement rippling through his biceps.

He knew only that it seemed she had melted into his arms, their connection so intense he felt as if they might merge into one person at any moment.

MELISSA MAYHUE

"An author with a magical touch for romance."
—*New York Times* bestselling author Janet Chapman

(Turn the page for rave reviews of Melissa Mayhue's enchanting romances.)

Healing the Highlander is also available as an eBook.

A HIGHLANDER'S HOMECOMING

"An enthralling page turner. The hero's and heroine's emotional turmoil will pull you immediately into the story. The combination of plot, deeply emotional characters and ever-growing love is breathtaking."

—*Romantic Times* (4½ stars)

A HIGHLANDER'S DESTINY

"Fae and mortal worlds collide in Mayhue's . . . wondrous tale. . . . The characters are well written, the action is nonstop, and there's plenty of sizzling passion."

—*Romantic Times* (4 stars)

"This is one of those series that I tell everyone to read."
—Night Owl Reviews (5 stars)

A HIGHLANDER OF HER OWN

"A wonderful medieval time travel romance. . . . Melissa Mayhue captures the complications and delights of both the modern woman and the fascination with the medieval world."
—*Denver Post*

"Fun and enjoyable."

—*Romantic Times*

SOUL OF A HIGHLANDER

Winner of the Golden Quill Award for Best Paranormal of 2009

Winner of the Winter Rose Award for Best Paranormal of 2009

"Mayhue's world is magical and great fun!"
—*Romantic Times* (4 stars)

"Absolutely riveting from start to finish."

—A Romance Review

Also by Melissa Mayhue

MELISSA MAYHUE

Healing the Highlander

POCKET STAR BOOKS
New York   London   Toronto   Sydney

Pocket Star Books
A Division of Simon & Schuster, Inc.
1230 Avenue of the Americas
New York, NY 10020

This book is a work of fiction. Names, characters, places, and incidents either are products of the author's imagination or are used fictitiously. Any resemblance to actual events or locales or persons, living or dead, is entirely coincidental.

First Pocket Star Books paperback edition March 2011

POCKET STAR BOOKS and colophon are registered trademarks of Simon & Schuster, Inc.

For information about special discounts for bulk purchases, please contact Simon & Schuster Special Sales at 1-866-506-1949 or business@simonandschuster.com.

The Simon & Schuster Speakers Bureau can bring authors to your live event. For more information or to book an event contact the Simon & Schuster Speakers Bureau at 1-866-248-3049 or visit our website at www.simonspeakers.com.

Cover design by Min Choi.
Art by Alan Ayers.

Manufactured in the United States of America

10 9 8 7 6 5 4 3 2 1

ISBN 978-1-4391-9020-3
ISBN 978-1-4391-9037-1 (ebook)

To Liam and Xander,
the two newest heroes in my life!
Welcome to the world!

Acknowledgments

As always, my thanks go out to my family for all their help while I was buried in writing this book.

Many thanks to my wonderful editor, Megan McKeever and to my excellent agent, Elaine Spencer. I feel so very lucky to get to work with both of these talented ladies. They really do make this the best job I've ever had!

But most of all . . .

My most heartfelt thanks go out to the readers. You guys make it possible for me to live my dream!!

Healing the
Highlander

Prologue

MacQuarrie Keep,
The Highlands of Scotland
1293

As the last emerald sparkles flickered away into the night, Leah Noble huddled close to the floor, her eyes clenched shut. Stomach churning in fear, she prayed to any and all gods who might hear her to grant that the magic would pass her by.

"Are you unharmed, lass?"

Leah jumped, startled as much by the unexpected sound of Margery MacQuarrie's voice as by the woman's gentle touch to her shoulder. She tried to nod her answer, but the terror wracked her entire body with violent tremors. Even her voice refused to cooperate when she opened her mouth, a series of pathetic whimpers all that she could manage.

"Oh, my poor lassie," Margery whispered, gathering Leah into her arms, stroking her hair and down her back as if she tended a small child in need of consoling.

It was this overwhelming kindness, following so closely on the heels of a day that had drained her both emotionally and physically, that prompted her complete undoing. Long beyond her control now, her whimpers turned to great heaving sobs as she gave herself over to the older woman's gentle ministrations.

"Och, sweetling, no," Margery cooed. "It breaks my heart to see you weep so for yer loss. Truly, lass, Robbie's leaving is no yer final connection to yer own time and yer own people. He left instructions on how yer to find the MacKiernans of Dun Ard should you ever be in need or want to try to get home again."

A crazed desire to laugh bubbled just below the surface of Leah's panic. Margery had it all so very wrong.

"No!" Leah managed to sputter out at last, fighting to gain control over her bizarre emotions. "I don't want anything to do with whatever Robbie left." She gasped for air in an attempt to stop the sobs that still jerked the breath from her. "I'm not crying because he went back to the future without me."

Margery pulled away from her, lifting one hand to brush damp strands of hair from Leah's cheeks. The older woman's face wrinkled in obvious distress. "Why, then?"

How could she possibly explain her hideous terror and the guilt that gnawed at her heart even now?

After the horrors she'd endured over the last few months, Leah had felt all hope for a normal life was lost to her. Kidnapped by the evil Nuadian Fae, abused, her blood taken daily to build their powers, she'd been demoralized by all she'd suffered. Their plans to use her to breed other half-blood Fae descendants who would in turn be abused as she had been terrified her. But when those same Fae had vowed to track her to the ends of the earth, had sworn she would never escape their control, well, that had been the last straw for her. Added to the unbearable pain she endured every time she tapped into her own Faerie powers of healing, she'd felt as if her sanity were hanging by a frayed thread.

At her darkest moment, when she'd thought her future was lost, her sister's new family had offered her a glimmer of hope. Robert had brought her here, seven hundred years into the past, depositing her in the care of his parents. Without even a hint of a Faerie in sight, Leah had felt safe and secure for the first time in what seemed like forever. It was as if, at long last, she'd found a place to call home.

And then, just as she'd thought herself free to relax, Faerie magic had reared its ugly head once more.

When that emerald sphere of magic had engulfed Robert and the woman he loved, Leah had felt as if her heart were about to burst out of her body. She'd felt the magic's pull, as if it sought to drag her along with the other two. The hair on her arms had risen and her clothing had stood out from her body as if she were being sucked into the magic to return to her own time along with them. The dragging, pulling suction had ceased only when the child, Jamie, had jumped into the circle and the three of them *poof*ed into the future in a shower of magnificent colored sparkles.

How did she admit all that to the woman who had taken her in and even now worried over her?

She owed Margery MacQuarrie honesty even if it was the honesty of a coward. With a quivering breath,

Leah wiped her eyes and tried to own up to her failings.

"Not because they left me behind, Grandma Mac, but because I was terrified the magic would take me along with them. Right back to . . . to all the things I'd thought I'd escaped. And when that poor little boy—" Her voice cracked with another sob as she acknowledged the monster her cowardice had made of her. "When the magic took Jamie instead, I was grateful, as awful as that makes me, grateful it was him and not me."

Leah allowed Margery to enfold her in her comforting embrace, once more giving herself over to the tears that had taken so long to find their release.

"My poor, gentle-hearted lassie," Margery murmured as she rocked back and forth. "You've no a need to take the lad's going onto yerself. While it may be that Jamie took yer place, you must see that he belonged with Robbie and Isabella. Just as you belong here with us."

"Do you really think so?" Leah pulled back from the older woman, searching her face for any sign that Margery simply patronized her with platitudes.

Nothing but sincerity shone in the older woman's eyes. "I do, lass. The magic of the Fae works in its own mysterious way. And though I ken you believe you've no use for that part of yerself," she held up a hand to quiet the protest Leah was about to make, "it is there, nonetheless. Just know, until the day comes you want to embrace it, we'll no ever speak to it again, if that's what you want."

Leah nodded slowly, overcome with gratitude for this caring woman who'd taken her in and treated her as if she really were her own flesh and blood. "It is. I only want to be normal."

"Well then." Margery smiled and rose to her feet, patting down her skirt as she did. "You've naught to worry over. After all, yer Leah MacQuarrie, daughter of Robert, granddaughter to Hugh and Margery. You can hardly be more normal than that, now can you?"

Leah rose hesitantly to stand, mindful of the raw burns covering half her body, the result of her having used her Faerie powers one last time to heal Jamie. The same boy who'd then gone to the future to take her place. The pain would be gone in a few days and her body would return to the way it had been. Perhaps it wasn't such a bad trade for either of them.

Jamie, with his freshly healed body, would have all the advantages the twenty-first century had to offer, plus the love Robert and Isabella obviously felt for him.

She, after a few days to recuperate, would have the rest of her life to live out as a normal person, in the safety of this time and place, without ever having to touch the Faerie magic again.

One

That man was a perfect example of a *Richard* that the nickname *Dick* had been invented for, if ever she had met one. Richard MacQuarrie was a dick of mammoth proportions.

Or maybe an *ass*. Or whatever other appropriately hateful names Leah MacQuarrie could drag up out of her past vocabulary to apply to the man who was turning her nice, quiet life upside down. Too bad no one else here would get the humor of her nickname for her supposed uncle.

"Thank God that jerk's not really related to me by blood," she muttered as she stomped down the hallway.

"Hush!" Margery MacQuarrie hissed as she overtook Leah, a warning hand reaching out to grasp the younger woman's arm. "Yer no to say such out loud. No ever, do you ken? As far as any need know, Richard *is* yer uncle. And dinna you be taking the Lord's name in vain, either, missy."

"Sorry, Grandma Mac." Leah almost smiled, in spite of the current predicament she found herself facing.

She could count on Margery to retain a cool head on her shoulders, always the one to think first and act later. Leah had tried her best to pattern herself after this amazing woman since the day Robert MacQuarrie had brought her here to keep her safe, claiming her as his own daughter. His parents, Margery and Hugh, had accepted her into their home as a part of their family, even though they knew the sixteen-year-old their son had dropped in their laps wasn't really Robert's daughter. Not even learning of her true heritage had deterred their acceptance of her.

For that she loved them as much as if they were her own flesh-and-blood family.

She reached out now, patting the thin, veined hand resting on her arm, feeling her heart clinch as she looked into the older woman's sad eyes. It had to hurt like hell to realize your firstborn was such a waste of skin.

"Don't you worry. We'll think of something." Leah gave the hand a quick squeeze. "I know we will."

Tears pooled in the older woman's eyes, but then, just as quickly as they'd appeared, they were gone. Margery was not a woman to wallow in the hardships life threw in her path.

"We will at that. For now, we'll take our daily tea in my solar, child. Perhaps if we put our heads together, we can come up with a way around all this unpleasantness."

Leah nodded, falling into step behind her grandmother down the hall and up the stairs to Margery's sitting room.

Of course the tea they'd have was no more "tea" than Leah was a "child." It was instead a brew of herbs that Leah had christened "tea" years ago. Real tea wouldn't show up in Scotland for . . . Leah had no idea how many years it would be, but she was sure she'd be long dead before the caffeine-rich leaves she remembered wistfully from her youth made an appearance.

Though it wasn't always easy living in a time seven hundred years before she had been born, it beat the heck out of what Leah had left behind.

Or it had until three days ago when the MacQuarries' older son, Richard, had shown up out of the blue. *Dick*, as Leah decided to christen him, had disowned his family years ago after marrying the woman his younger brother, Robert, had fancied himself in love with. Dick had completely abandoned everything from his past, even taking his wife's family name for his own, no doubt to curry favor with her father, some high-placed lord in King Edward's court.

Now he was back, claiming his rights as eldest son as if he'd never run off and deserted his heritage. Worse yet, he announced on arrival that he also claimed Mac-Quarrie Keep in the name of *his* king, Edward. As if he were some born-and-bred Englishman with not a spot of Scots blood running in his veins!

Before she'd come to this time, Leah had known of the troubles between Scotland and England. She'd read of them in history class. She'd even seen the Hollywood version at the movies.

But nothing, *nothing*, could ever prepare her for the

reality of it. Only living it, day after day for all these years, allowed her to understand what feelings the conflict engendered.

Just as she considered herself well and truly a MacQuarrie after over a decade here, so too she considered herself well and truly a Scot. As such, Dick's actions offended her to the core, both as a Scot and as a MacQuarrie.

And that wasn't even touching the edge of how angry she was with him for what he was putting his mother through.

It took only a moment's study for Leah to recognize the weariness in the older woman's slow step. Once they reached the solar, she shooed Margery over to sit in her favorite chair while she set about heating the water for their "tea."

Margery sighed deeply, closing her eyes when she leaned back against the seat. "If only Hugh had been here instead of off to Inverness when Richard arrived. I should no ever have allowed the boy inside the walls of MacQuarrie Keep."

"Don't beat yourself up, Grandma Mac. Like as not, Grandpa Hugh would have ordered the gates open just as you did. He is your son, after all, and you love him. How were you to know he'd be such a—" Leah cut her rant short, bending over the pot of heating water as if she'd intended not to finish all along. Margery didn't need to hear any more of the negatives already assailing her heart.

"Hugh warned me years ago that my Richard was gone, but did I listen? No. I dinna want to believe the things he told me of my own sweet lad." The old woman sighed again, though this time she sounded more exasperated than sad. "It's beyond my reason at times, lass. It's no like we raised yer own good father any different from his brother."

A warm buzz filled Leah's heart as she poured steaming water over the fragrant herb pouch. At times like this, it seemed to Leah that Margery had pretended to be her grandmother for such a long time she didn't even see it as pretending any more. In fact, Leah suspected that had as much to do with what Margery wanted to be the truth as it had ever had with protecting Leah.

Yet another reason she'd grown to love Margery and Hugh so much.

"Grandpa Hugh will be home any day now. He'll know what to do when he gets here." Leah hoped he would, anyway. He was already past the date they'd expected his return.

Margery snorted inelegantly before lifting her cup to blow across the hot liquid. "When yer Grandpa Hugh hears that his elder son has claimed MacQuarrie Keep in the name of Edward and England, he'll—" She sputtered to a halt as if searching for the perfect description of what her husband might do.

"He'll have a shit fit," Leah finished for her. Hugh might be getting well on in years, but he had a sound mind and hearty temper to go along with it. The old guy was going to be royally pissed when he found out what his son was up to.

Margery took a small sip and pursed her lips, casting what Leah always thought of as the Eagle-Eye look in Leah's direction. "That disna sound like a proper thing for a lady to be saying, lass. You'll want to counsel that tongue of yers while we've so many guests in our home." Another sip of tea was followed by another sigh. "But yer words do have the sound of anger to them, and in truth, I'm no sure they're even half so strong as what yer Grandpa Hugh will be feeling."

Guests? More like invaders. Still, Grandma Mac made a valid point with her advice to watch what she said. In the seclusion of MacQuarrie Keep, she'd grown comfortable and allowed her vigilance to drop.

When she'd first come to this time from the twenty-first century, Leah had worked hard to learn to modify her behavior and speech to conform to what was appropriate for her new life here. For the most part, she knew the expectations.

But *knowing* how to behave and speak like a proper fourteenth-century lady and actually *doing* it all the time were often two totally unconnected activities for her. The patterns of speech these people used still didn't come naturally to her and, unless she stopped to think about what she was going to say, she reverted to being herself. The inhabitants of the keep were used to her oddities and took them all in stride, but Dick and his men? They were a whole different story.

"I canna but believe Richard was of a mind to frighten you and nothing more with all his blether about marriage. I'm sure he's no truly intending to try such a thing."

Glancing up from pouring her own tea at Margery's words, Leah noted the older woman's sudden fascination with the contents in her cup. Well she might avoid eye contact. By now she had to realize that slimy first-born of hers was capable of just about anything. She also had to realize, as Leah did, his comments about handing Leah over to some ally of his in marriage were not an idle threat but a statement of fact. Pure and simple.

Leah shrugged as she made her way over to sit on a cushion next to Margery's chair. "He didn't frighten me." No point in upsetting her grandmother any more than she already was.

Margery's skeptically raised eyebrow was her only response.

"Really. He didn't."

The eyebrow didn't move.

Her grandmother knew her far too well, it seemed.

"Okay. Fine. Maybe he did rattle me a little bit."

How could she not be rattled? They'd sat through a horribly uncomfortable meal with Richard occupying his father's seat at the table as if he had a right to. It probably hadn't been her most clever move to point out to him his error, but the arrogance of his taking that seat had irritated her beyond good caution.

He'd cast that oily, disgusted look of his in her direction and taken that opportunity to inform them both that in order to seal alliances in England, he'd decided his niece should marry.

His niece. Her!

"Hugh will deal with Richard and all his nonsense when he returns, sweetling. Dinna you fret. For now we'll simply—"

"Mistress!"

Margery's words were cut short by Maisey's excited entrance, her wrinkled face pink with exertion.

Leah jumped up from her spot on the floor and hurried across the room to the old maid's assistance.

"Catch yer breath first, dear," Margery cautioned, slowly pushing herself up to stand. "And then you can tell us what has you so a-twitter."

Maisey's sleeves were pushed up over her elbows, a sure sign she'd been cleaning again, though Leah had overheard Margery tell her a thousand times she should leave those chores for the younger girls.

The old maid blew out a breath and grinned, grasping onto Leah's arm for support. "It's our good laird, my lady. He's come home. As soon as I saw him and my lads riding into the bailey, I made straightaway to find you."

Maisey's "lads" were her forty-plus-year-old son and her husband, Walter, who Leah was convinced must be ninety if he was a day.

"Lord's mercy," Margery grumbled, pushing herself out of her chair and heading for the door. "I dinna want to think on what will happen if Richard confronts his father before I've had the chance to speak to him first. The two of them were never . . ."

The rest of her comments were lost as she rushed past and into the hallway, muttering as she went.

Not that Leah needed to hear the words. She had the same concerns about that first meeting between Hugh and Richard. Hugh's quick temper and Richard's snotty attitude of superiority were not going to make for a pleasant reunion. It wouldn't be so much oil and water as it would gasoline and lit matches.

She fought the need to toss Maisey's hand from her arm and dash after Margery. The sweet old lady leaning on her for support had obviously winded herself rushing up here to get them, so she would simply have to bide her time, following along more slowly.

In spite of her best efforts, her impatience must have shown through. They'd made it only midway down the hall toward the stairs when Maisey pulled her hand away and rested it against the wall, taking her weight off Leah.

"Go on with you, lassie. I'll follow at me own pace. You'd best be off to help Mistress Margery. Something tells me she'll need all the help she can get."

Obviously she wasn't the only one expecting the worst from the father-and-son reunion.

With a quick kiss to Maisey's leathered cheek, Leah took off down the stairs at a run.

Angry raised voices reached her ears as she slipped through the large entry door and she quickly realized all their fears had been justified.

In the middle of the bailey her grandmother stood like a statue, her arms outstretched to either side. One hand rested on her husband's chest, the other on her son's, as if by sheer force of will she could keep the men from a physical brawl.

"Stop it!" Margery ordered, her frame all but dwarfed between the two men. "Both of you! You'll stop it right now."

Not good. Margery might be a force unto herself, but the men on either side of her looked to be beyond what reason could control.

Leah jumped over the last step, grabbing up handfuls of skirt so she wouldn't trip as she hit the ground at a run.

"You'll gather these English dogs you've brought with you and you'll haul yer worthless carcasses back to yer . . . *king*." Hugh spat the final word, as if it disgusted him to have it cross his tongue.

"Edward is your rightful sovereign as well." Richard took a step back from his mother, laying a threatening hand on the sword he wore at his hip. "Unless you side with the likes of Wallace and his traitorous rabble. Even the Red Comyn has had the good sense to swear fealty to Edward."

"Aye, that he did. And as I heard word of it, yer king guaranteed in those negotiations there'd be no disinheritance or reprisals. I've no bones to pick nor sides to take in yer fights. As laird of the MacQuarries, my responsibility and only concern is for my people and their safety. And since yer no longer one of my people, *Hawthorne,* yer no welcome here. Now take yer men and leave."

Leah had slowed her steps as she'd neared the men, the tension sparking between them assaulting her senses. But now she felt a need to move closer. The bright red color Hugh's naturally ruddy face had turned concerned her. He was too old to be getting himself so worked up. Seventy-eight might be the new fifty in the century she'd left behind, but in this century, seventy-eight was like living on borrowed time.

When she reached his side, she slipped her hand into his before meeting Richard's scowl. Hugh's subtle squeeze to her fingers reassured her that he hadn't completely lost control of himself.

Richard's lips curled in an oily parody of smile. "In that case, you no longer have a need to concern yourself. I've a document inside, stamped with the seal of King Edward himself, turning these lands over to my keeping, to hold in his name."

Beside her, Hugh stiffened, his hand dropping hers as he crossed his arms. "That I canna allow."

"You have no choice in the matter, old man." Richard turned his back to them, taking no more than a single step before his mother grabbed his arm.

"I'll no have you speaking to yer father in that tone. You may have abandoned all we hold dear, but he's still yer father and you owe him yer respect."

"I owe him nothing. As firstborn, all of this is mine by rights." Richard plucked his mother's hand from his arm, dropping it as if he found her touch distasteful.

"No so long as yer father lives," Margery countered.

"Which may not be all that long," he responded, his fake smile back in place.

Margery's hand snaked out like lightning, a loud *thwack* echoing in the courtyard as her backhand caught Richard along his jaw, snapping his head to the side.

As if she were frozen to the spot, Leah watched in helpless horror while her peaceful world crumbled, crashing down around her.

Richard grabbed Margery's upper arms, giving her a violent shake that bobbled her head forward and back before shoving her away. Her balance lost, she stumbled to the ground.

To Leah's right, an enormous bellow erupted from Hugh and he charged toward his son only to be held in check by two men who rushed forward, pinning him to his spot.

A jolt of air rushed into Leah's lungs, as if she'd held her breath too long, even as the heat of anger scorched through her mind. Slipping past the men who held Hugh in place, she ran to Margery, kneeling down to grasp the older woman's frail shoulders.

"You should be ashamed of yourself! What kind of ass treats his own mother like that?" she yelled in Richard's general direction, focusing her attention on helping Margery to sit up.

He spun on his heel, glaring down at her. "You'd do well to counsel that tongue of yours, niece, before your new husband arrives. Lord Moreland isn't likely to take well to that sort of behavior. It would be a pity to see my old friend forced to spend his wedding night beating some manners into his new bride."

"Husband?" Hugh strained against the men who held him, his face even redder than it had been before. "You've no the right to hand the lass off like some possession to barter. She's no more yers to promise away than these lands."

"And you've no longer any say in the matter, *father*." Though he used the appellation, Richard made it clear he held no love for the man. "The girl should be honored with the situation I've arranged for her. Grateful, in fact. Moreland is a powerful man, though not even his vast wealth can bring back the sons he's lost. Fortunately for our girl here, even though she's well past her prime, she's none too old to give the lord the heirs he desires."

"No!" Leah's breath caught in her chest at Richard's words. This couldn't be happening again. A bevy of emotions threatened to suffocate her, buffeting her with memories of another time, another place, and other faces gloating over her as she was held captive, her life out of her control.

Another bellow of rage from Hugh shook her from the grasp of her haunting memories. Her grandfather had broken free from the men who'd held him, but he made it no farther than two or three paces before they retook him, forcing him down to the ground, his face pressed into the damp earth.

"Lock him away," Richard directed the men who held his father, turning his back and heading toward the keep.

"Richard!" Margery had pushed herself up to stand, one hand protectively laid on Leah's shoulder. "What's gone wrong with you? You canna continue to—"

"Enough!" her son roared, startling her to silence. "I'm trying to be a good son, Mother. Don't make me lock you away with your husband."

Leah remained on her knees, her body shaking so hard she doubted for the moment her legs' ability to hold her weight. Fear sloshed in her stomach like sour wine.

How could this be happening to her again? She'd run seven hundred years into the past to escape the horrible, evil Fae who'd sworn to turn her into nothing more than a brood mare. She'd turned her back on her family and her heritage, seeking shelter in the midst of mortals only to find herself once again faced with the same threat.

"Let's get you inside, lass." Margery held out a hand to help her to her feet.

Leah clasped the older woman's fingers as she rose to stand, all the while keeping her eyes fixed on the ground. Disgust at her own cowardice warred with her dread of seeing the disappointment she feared she'd find swimming in Margery's eyes. Or worse yet, pity.

It had been Margery who'd sat at her bedside, consoling her through the years of nightmares as she'd gradually worked herself free from the terrors of her past. Margery who'd held her in her arms, sharing her strength and love as if she were her grandmother by blood. Of all the people in her world, Margery would be the one to instantly recognize what fear possessed her now.

"Try no to fash yerself over Richard's plans. We'll think of something. Trust me that I'll no allow you to be used in such a way."

Tears threatened at Margery's words, glassing over Leah's vision even as holding them back burned at her throat.

Weak, pitiful coward!

After all these people had given her, all they had done for her over the years, now that they were in trouble, she should be strong for them. Instead, it was still *her* in need of comfort, her being led back to the keep as if she were the only victim here.

Her cowardice, her weakness, disgusted her, even as it washed over her in great drowning waves.

She couldn't face going through this all over again.

Two

It felt as if rivulets of fire ate their way through his leg.

Andrew MacAlister shifted his weight on the horse he rode, trying to find some modicum of relief from the constant pain that plagued him as he made his way across the bailey to the stable. After two days on horseback and a week in Inverness—a week away from the grueling daily sword practices that kept his pathetically damaged muscles limber—he feared for his ability to stand when he dismounted.

With a little luck, the stable would be empty.

"I see you've made it back at last."

Damnation. His brother Colin led his own horse from the back of the stable toward the door. As usual, the only luck he could count on consistently was bad luck.

"And you? Yer leaving, are you?" Drew asked the

question, though from the pack on Colin's mount, the answer was as obvious as the black mood hanging over his younger brother. Still, conversation gave him a reason to remain seated.

"Aye," Colin growled in response, jerking at his reins much harder than necessary. "Our stubborn new sister refuses to lend the smallest aid. Since she will no share what she knows, I go to seek my own answers."

Ellie. Andrew felt a grin spreading in spite of his personal discomfort. Their older brother's new wife was indeed a stubborn woman. Her determination to do what she thought was right was one of the qualities he admired in her.

"I see nothing to spark yer amusement in this, brother. Times are dark and the proper foreknowledge could make the difference in what happens to all of us."

"Ah." So that was it. "We all agreed when Ellie became part of the family that we'd no ask those questions of her, did we no? There's a danger in learning that which we're no supposed to."

Ellie had been sent into their lives last year. Swept from her home, seven hundred years in the future, she had been brought to this time and place by Faerie Magic to find the one man meant for her, their brother Caden. As descendants of the Fae themselves, all the Mac-Alisters accepted the oddities in their world as well as the responsibility being a Fae descendant carried with it.

"Ha!" Colin snorted as he lifted himself up onto his mount. "In more ways than you ken, brother. For now, though, there's a more immediate danger than to fash ourselves over the possibility of altering history. In case you've no noticed in yer travels, Comyn has negotiated our freedom away to the English king and Wallace is forced into hiding with a price on his head. We're at a crossroads in our struggle, and still that irritating woman will no even tell me whether or no Wallace will again lead us to victory over the English or if all hope for Scotland is lost."

Ever the warrior, his brother. Though, without a doubt, he'd be at Colin's side if he weren't a worthless shell of a man, and likely he'd be every bit as frustrated.

"She's no idea, she claims. She's no a student of history so how can she tell that which I ask." Colin shook his head, his skepticism evident. "So I'm off to find the answers on my own."

"Where are you away to?"

"North. To the glen."

If Drew had been standing on his own two feet, the surprise of Colin's answer might have toppled him over. The Faerie Glen!

"None of Mother's stories ever told of the Fae having shown themselves to any but the MacKiernan women, and damn few of them. What hope do you have in going there?"

A line of tension worked in Colin's jaw, his eyes darkening with his emotion. "Perhaps no more than I had with Ellie, but I canna be at peace with the answers I have now so I've no choice but to see if our ancestors will respond to my pleas. Even the prince himself should be concerned for the survival of his descendants."

Prince Pol? The name had been handed down through the generations as the Faerie who was their ancestor, but Drew's read on the ancient story wasn't of a man who cared what happened to anyone. Some unknown millennia ago he'd given his blessing and curse in a fit of anger before retreating behind the curtain of the worlds, never to be seen again.

Colin would be better off counting on Mortal help than on the mysterious prince of their family table.

"Dair and Simeon? Do they ride with you?" The two men, one all but family since childhood, the other family by virtue of his aunt marrying their laird, had become almost inseparable companions to Colin. Warrior blood and honor bound them together.

Drew tried hard not to resent the fact that he could never be one of their number.

"No. This I do alone." Colin reined his horse around, pulling up alongside Drew's mount to face him. "The need to ken the truth of what's to come is my own demon to face."

No one understood personal demons better than Drew. Nodding his acceptance of his brother's decision, he clasped Colin's arm, each man's hand tightening around the other's forearm.

In an attempt to lighten his brother's mood, Drew grinned. "Too bad you dinna think to seek yer answer from True Thomas before his death, aye?"

Colin's face stiffened into the strained mask he seemed to wear so often over the last few years. "Whose answers do you think have stolen away my peace if no the ones I received in the Rhymer's home?"

His brother had consulted the infamous Thomas of Erceldoune? Colin had become one surprise after another.

Rumor had it that Thomas the Rhymer had been taken lover by no less than the Faerie Queen herself, giving him the power to see into the future. No doubt about it, he and Colin needed to find time to have a long talk one day, though, clearly, this was not that day.

"Go in safety, Col. I pray you find that which you seek."

"I wish the same for you, my brother."

Drew watched in silence as Colin rode away, puzzled as to his brother's parting comment.

Colin couldn't know. None of them did.

Drew had carefully cultivated the image his family had of him. That they should all see him as a disappointment, a second son who wasted his time in thoughtless pursuit of pleasure was highly preferable to their learning the truth. No one knew of the countless hours he'd spent searching, the painful experiments he'd endured at the hands of alchemists and those who claimed to be healers, or the vile potions and the disgusting plasters he'd tried.

And no one ever would if he had his way of it.

He'd rather a thousand times over see disappointment in the eyes of his family than pity.

With a long breath, Drew swung his stiffened leg over his horse's back, bracing himself for the fresh wave of pain that would hit when his weight shifted to that limb.

As he'd suspected, no amount of mental preparation could overcome the all-encompassing shock of pain. His leg gave way and he stumbled backward, catching himself against the nearest stall.

The wounds he'd received in the battle to rescue his cousin Mairi and his sister Sallie a decade past should have ended his life. But, thanks to his Faerie blood and the amazing potions his cousin had brought from the future, he hadn't died.

Not literally, anyway.

No, his heart beat on, his chest expanded and contracted with every breath, and he awoke to greet each empty day. But the muscles that had been carved through continued to wither away as the years passed. Under his skin, his scarred hideous skin, the meat shrank and twisted, contracting into hard painful knots.

Scar tissue, his new sister Ellie called it.

The daily workouts in the lists helped, but forego the exercise for even a day and he paid for the lapse with an overall stiffening and intensified pain. Already, despite his efforts, the once-injured limb was shortening, requiring great concentration on his part to avoid displaying the awkward limping gait he noticed in himself when he tired.

The scars on his body were hideous, but what they kept him from doing was even worse. The constant pain and growing deformity slowed him, robbed him of his speed, his flexibility, his fighting skills.

Though the injuries had spared his life, they'd resulted in his living as only half a man. His dreams of finding glory and seeking happiness had been stripped from him at the tender age of eighteen. Dreams stolen by the deceitful Fae who'd endangered the lives of his sister and cousin.

Fae he hated with every shred of his being. Vile uncaring creatures who'd taken from him all that mattered.

With his body as it was, he couldn't follow the warrior's path as Colin did, as they'd spent their youth planning to do together. Any hopes of a loving wife and family were gone on the edge of the sword that had carved into his flesh. A man such as he had become couldn't support a wife and family. He spent his days working his body to exhaustion or scouring the land seeking miraculous cures which more and more frequently these days he feared did not exist.

In time, he'd be forced to retire to his bed, a useless lump of meat to be cared for by someone else.

A burden such as that was not something to expect any woman to shoulder.

"Master Drew! I dinna realize you'd returned."

The young stable boy's feet came to a quick halt only a few paces away.

"Aye, James, I'm back, but no for long." Pushing his weight away from the stall, he tossed the reins in his hand to the boy. "Care for him well, lad. We'll be off again on the morrow."

It took all his concentration to avoid favoring his leg as he crossed the distance to the great stairs leading up to the entrance of Dun Ard.

Argeneau, the alchemist he'd spent the last week with in Inverness, had heard of a potion used at the abbey on Iona. A good night's rest and he'd be off once more, chasing the elusive miracle that might allow him to be whole again.

Three

Was this what Fate had planned for her, no matter how hard she worked to escape it?

Leah huddled in the corner of her darkened room, the unattended fire dying down to embers as she clutched her arms around her legs, her forehead balanced on her knees. Stomach-squeezing fear swirled and melded with hateful memories, growing into a harsh burden too large to fight. The whole of it swarmed thickly around her head and she tightened her arms, as if she could hide from the oppressive weight by shrinking into herself.

The tactic didn't work any better this night than it had when she'd been held captive by the Fae all those years ago. She could not ignore the threat away.

Her wrist tingled and she jerked her head up, her eyes darting to the spot on her arm as if she expected the metal chain that had held her prisoner to be fastened there once again.

"This is crazy," she whispered into the silent room.

It was happening all over again and she was just sitting here, waiting to be a victim once more.

"Oh, no I'm not." She spoke with more strength this time, denying into the dark as she straightened her back and dropped her hands to her sides.

She had been a frightened sixteen-year-old when the Nuadians had kidnapped her, helpless to change her situation. While she might still be frightened, at twenty-eight, she had long ago sworn she'd never be helpless again. She would take charge of her own destiny.

All she needed was to come up with a plan.

"Which sure as heck isn't going to happen if I just sit here on my butt, feeling sorry for myself," she muttered, pushing herself to stand. However many hours she'd wasted moping over this was that many hours too many.

There. That was better already.

"Deciding to take action makes all the difference in the world." A shiver ran down her spine as she uttered the words, but she shook it off.

Okay, maybe not *all* the difference, but it certainly beat waiting passively for someone else to decide her fate.

Someone like *Dick*.

Grabbing up the long metal poker, she leaned down and prodded at the embers in the fireplace before tossing in another stick of wood.

How was she going to avoid Dick's plan to hand her over to some old English guy as breeding stock?

"I could run away," she said decisively, dusting the ashes from her hands. It was what she'd done before. She'd run from her time to this one to escape the Nuadians. She could run again.

Even though this time running away was easier said than done.

Guards were posted throughout the keep and at the gates. And even if she could somehow manage to work her way past them, where would she go? It wasn't as if she had neighbors or family to run to. With Robert's supposed death and Dick's abandonment of the tiny clan, there had been no marriages to seal alliances with other families. She certainly hadn't been any help to them in that regard either. Perhaps if she'd ever indicated any interest in marriage, there might be an alliance for them to rely upon now. As it was, clan MacQuarrie was on its own with no one to turn to for help.

Not to mention, it was a big, empty Scottish countryside out there, with plenty of bad guys wandering around.

Leah scrubbed her fingertips against her forehead, trying to ward off the headache that threatened. She needed to stay calm. Focused. There had to be a reasonable way around this nightmare situation, if only she could think of it.

"I need a brainstorming session." Just like back in high school in the college prep classes she'd taken. The fancy whiteboard and markers might not exist yet, but that didn't mean she couldn't use the process. All she needed was another brain or two.

And she knew exactly where to find them.

She slipped out of her room, and hurried along the darkened hallway. When she reached her destination, she rapped her knuckles quietly against the heavy wood but didn't wait for a response before pushing the door open and calling out as she stepped inside.

"Grandma Mac?"

Margery sat at a small table next to the fireplace, her head bent forward as if to catch the words of her companions, Maisey and Walter.

All three started guiltily as Leah entered, giving her the distinct impression she had been the topic of conversation only moments before.

"What are the three of you up to?" Even in the dimly lit room, Leah could see the lines of concern marking her grandmother's face.

"It's yer grandpa Hugh. He's in need of rest and food to regain his strength after such a long trip, but Richard's put him in the auld tower. There's no even a proper fireplace out there."

"What can I do?" Leah asked, recognizing her grandfather's problem to be more immediate than her own. Her concerns could wait until later.

The auld tower was little more than the crumbling remains of the original building on the MacQuarrie property. Nothing much was left but stairs spiraling up around three floors. Only the lower level was in use anymore and that only for storage. She'd been warned against setting foot in the top tower room for years. With the floors and roof rotting away, it was just plain unsafe. Adding in their frequent rains and no heat, it was an even more dangerous place for a man Grandpa Hugh's age.

"We have to get him out of there. Have you spoken to Dick? Um . . . Richard," she corrected when three sets of confused eyes turned her way.

Margery clasped her hands in front of her on the table, her grip so tight her fingers paled from lack of circulation. "He refuses to see me, sending word by one of his men that he'll consider my request in the next few days. When he has the time."

"When he has the time, my arse." Pounding her fist to the table, Maisey snorted her disgust. "Begging yer pardon, Lady Margery, but that one was always a spoiled little bastard. He's waited the whole of his life to challenge his father. Like two warring rams they are and always have been. We've no time to lose if we're to help our laird, but it's clear we canna do this by ourselves. We need help." Her determined gaze rested on each of them in turn. "From them what would be willing to drive these English-loving bastards out of MacQuarrie Keep before it's too late. From them what has the power to do it."

Her husband nodded his agreement, his pale, watery eyes fixed on Margery, waiting for her decision.

Margery nodded slowly. "What would you say we should do?"

"Send a messenger to bring us aid, my lady, just as we discussed this very evening."

Again Margery nodded. "As you say, my friends. But it will needs be one of us. We canna trust any others with our plan."

If they were limited to sending one of the people in this room, their plan was in danger before it even began.

Walter was ancient. His exhaustion from the journey to Inverness with Hugh showed in every one of the deeply etched lines on his face. Maisey could barely wobble up and down the stairs without a stumble. And Margery? No way Leah was letting her grandmother do something so dangerous.

That left only one option.

"Me," Leah squeaked as all three heads turned her direction. "It should be me," she repeated, her voice stronger now.

"Aye," her grandmother acknowledged after a long pause. "There's little doubt that you would be the best choice to send from the keep. And before this Lord Moreland of Richard's arrives."

"Exactly," Leah agreed, more confidently than she felt.

Richard had informed them that Moreland's party would be arriving any day now. Time had become her enemy as much as Dick and this lord he planned for her to marry.

There was no other choice. Her serving as messenger addressed her own problem as well as her grandpa Hugh's. But that didn't mean there weren't still obstacles she had no idea how to overcome.

"But where would I go? And how do I even get out of here? There are men posted at the gates."

It was as if she'd managed to come full circle back to her earlier idea of running away, smack into the same problems she'd found insurmountable the first time she'd considered the idea.

"There's the auld water passage," Walter murmured, his fingers idly scratching his scraggly beard. "The stairs down have been closed off since Laird Hugh and I tried playing in there as bairns, but I wager we could open it again easily enough. 'Tis no more than a matter of moving the barrels stored on top of the trapdoor."

Margery's fingertips covered her lips, her eyes blinking rapidly, a sure sign the woman's mind was whirling with her plans. "I'd completely forgotten Hugh's stories about that," she murmured.

"What water passage?" This was something Leah had never heard a single mention of, not once in the twelve years she'd been here.

"When the keep was first built, Hugh's grandfather had an opening to the sea put in place. According to the family stories, he may have had business dealings with . . ." She paused and grinned, her eyes lighting as she continued, "Um . . . let's just say they were men of questionable reputation. The passage into the keep is accessible only at low tide. At all other times the opening is below the water level and the passageway itself is filled with water from the loch."

Amazing. It was like something out of a storybook. Next thing they'd be saying there were secret tunnels in the walls no one had thought to tell her about.

"So, okay, we get this passageway opened up, and I can sneak out that way. But that still doesn't answer where I'm to go for help once I'm out of here."

Margery cleared her throat, looking down at her clenched fingers before answering. "We've no family outside the castle proper other than a few shepherds and their families and it's no as if any of them would be a match for the men Richard has brought into our home. Whether or no they'll agree to come to our aid I canna say, but there's really only one place I can think of to ask for help, Leah. The one place yer father said you should seek help if ever you found yerself in need. The MacKiernans of Dun Ard."

"Oh Lord, no," Leah breathed, taking a step backward. Not the Faerie descendants. For all these years, she'd tried to put their very existence out of her mind, as if by not thinking of them they couldn't inhabit her world. As if by not thinking of them, she could cause the Faeries themselves not to exist.

"Through you, they're the closest thing we have to family. By our taking you in, there's a debt of honor they owe us. We have no one else to turn to. They're our only hope, lass. Yer only hope." Margery looked up to meet her eyes at last. "Yer grandpa Hugh's only hope."

So not fair. For herself she might say no. Surely a forced marriage to a Mortal couldn't be any worse than having to put herself back in the hands of the Fae. But how could she refuse anything that might save Hugh MacQuarrie?

She couldn't.

All those years ago, she'd sworn two things after her ordeal at the hands of the Nuadians: first, that she'd never again willingly associate with anyone of Faerie blood, and second, that she would do whatever was required of her to insure her own safety and that of the people she loved.

Now it seemed that in order to keep the second vow, she had no choice but to break the first.

The MacKiernans of Dun Ard it was.

Four

The smell alone was enough to set Leah's stomach roiling, but when she touched the wall to steady herself and the thick, wet slime squished through her fingers, she wanted nothing so desperately as to turn around and race back up the narrow, slick steps she'd just descended.

"I'm a braver woman than that," she muttered, half under her breath. She couldn't allow a little dead-fish stench to stop her now.

"Of course yer a brave one, my lady," Walter replied, hunching down ahead of her in the dark, wet tunnel. "But might I suggest you be watching where you put yer foot, lass. It's fair slippery along this way."

No kidding.

Once the decision had been made that Leah should go, her coconspirators had wasted no time in formulating a plan and putting it in motion. As Grandma Mac had pointed out, there was no time to waste. The longer Grandpa Hugh was kept in the auld tower, the lower his chance of survival became.

So it was that Leah found herself creeping down a dark, wet tunnel sometime in the wee early morning hours when the waters lapping at the back of the castle were at their lowest.

Walter had taken a boat out earlier in the evening, supposedly to net a catch for the next day's meal, a perfectly normal activity that drew no attention from the unwelcome occupiers of their home. The soldiers had been much more concerned with their desire to have fresh fish on their table than with any idea that old Walter might be up to something sneaky.

Leah, her small bundle of essentials slung over her shoulder, had waited impatiently in the back of the big storage room along with her grandmother and Maisey. It had taken the three of them well over an hour to move the barrels around to expose the old wooden covering in the floor. When a faint knocking had sounded from the other side of that wooden covering, the older women had looked as rattled as she had felt.

With the long metal bar Walter had left for them, they pried up the trapdoor to find Walter hunched in the dark below.

"Wait," her grandmother had urged, her hands fumbling about her own neck. "I feel the time has come for you to have this."

With those words, she held out her hand. A length

of ribbon draped across her palm and hanging from the cord, a stone. The sight sent a shock of recognition coursing through Leah, landing in her stomach like a lump of heavy dough.

"But how?" Leah had asked. "It's not possible. I saw with my own eyes, Isabella had that in her hands when the Magic took them." It had, in fact, been that stone from her own mother's necklace that had provided the final piece of the Magic needed to send Robert and Isabella forward in time.

"No this one, sweetling. I've worn this close to my heart from the time I was small child, waiting for the day it would be needed." Margery held up the ribbon and dropped it down over Leah's head to hang around her neck. "This feels to be the right time to pass it along as it was given to me. It's time you were about meeting yer own destiny, lass."

"But . . ." Leah's mind reeled in confusion as the stone slid down her neckline, warming the spot against her skin where it lay. It was a perfect twin to the carved hematite stone she'd given to Isabella all those years ago. The one that had belonged to her mother.

"We must go now, lassie," Walter had urged, spurring her to action.

A quick hug from each of the women and Leah had lowered herself into the slimy stink pit she now traversed.

The tunnel itself was so small, Walter's bulk filled the dark in front of her, his normal tottering gait morphed into a slouched-over parody of a walk as he moved forward in the inky black.

"Only a bit farther, lass," Walter assured her. "Me boat's tied up and waiting just below the opening."

Leah nodded though she knew, in this dark and with his back to her, Walter couldn't see her action. Still, speaking aloud might require that she breathe through her nose, and a nose full of this stench was something she wasn't willing to risk simply to acknowledge his comment.

With her next step, a cool, fresh breeze rustled around her and she craned her neck to see past the old man. Ahead the texture of the dark tunnel seemed to change, as if it softened to a lighter shade of black.

A few steps more and a circle opened in front of her, stars twinkling in the space Walter had occupied only moments before.

"Walter?" she hissed, freezing to the spot as the shock of his disappearance overtook her.

"Squat down and lower yerself over the edge, lass. The boat's just here."

Relief washed over her as she realized they'd reached the end of the tunnel.

Short-lived relief. Clearly the nasty tunnel was a haven in comparison to what she faced now.

The boat Walter encouraged her to drop down into appeared to be little more than a small wooden box, rocking to and fro precariously on the waves that slapped against the castle wall. Walter's bulk alone filled half the thing.

"Come along with you now," Walter urged, reaching up to tug on her hand. "We've a need to move with a purpose if we're to get you far enough away before daybreak to make yer escape."

"Move with a purpose," she repeated weakly, swallowing her fear to drop down off the ledge and into the small craft.

Her feet hit the wood with a *thud* and the boat rocked wildly under her weight.

"Down," Walter ordered, tossing a woolen over her head as she dropped to her knees. "Flat into the bottom of the boat, lassie. We dinna want any who might see me on the loch to realize I've a passenger, now do we?"

That was the last thing they wanted.

Under the cover of the blanket, Leah curled onto the floor of the craft. Hugging her bundle of supplies to her chest, she did her best to ignore the stench of dead fish permeating everything around her.

"I'll just cast me net and see what I come up with as we make our way. Bringing back a nice catch can only add to the authenticity of our ruse, aye, lassie?"

She felt the motion of the craft pushing away from the castle and out into the depths of the loch. Once more the boat rocked wildly as Walter apparently stood and tossed the net. Leah tightened her grip on the woolen that covered her, wishing the boat had handles or, better yet, that life vests had already been invented.

The little boat rocked back and forth with the waves, setting Leah's stomach to rolling with the motion. The rocking increased as the old man rose to his feet at regular intervals and after a while Leah began to wonder whether her greater fear was the boat tipping over or the motion sickness that gripped her.

If only Walter would just sit down and be still . . .

After a particularly violent series of movements, she could stand it no longer. She jerked the cover from her face to gasp in deep breaths of fresh air in an effort to keep herself from losing what little she'd managed to eat that day. Water sprayed against her cheeks and she quickly realized it wasn't the old man's movement at all that set their little boat rocking but the large waves repeatedly buffeting their craft.

Oh, this seriously sucked.

"You should probably know, I can't swim, Walter. I never learned how." Leah wiped her face and peered up at the old man's back. "I'm just saying." Not that she thought there was much he'd be able to do about it if one of those waves capsized their boat. He'd likely not even be able to save himself.

"Dinna you be fashing yerself over a little rough water, lassie." Walter chuckled as he pulled on the oar in his hands. "Old Walter kens the ways of this loch, never you fear. I've bested her waves since long before you were born."

Easy enough to say since she hadn't technically been born yet.

The boat rolled over another mound of water, sending a wave of nausea pulsating through Leah as the spray covered her face.

She closed her eyes, refusing to watch what was to come. Maybe it would be like reading billboards when she traveled in a car. If she couldn't see anything, maybe she could keep the nausea at bay.

Her head pounded as the minutes ticked away and her stomach tightened. It was only a matter of time before she'd be hanging over the side, emptying her guts into the roiling waters that threatened to capsize the box they rode in. Already she could feel the first spasms forming deep in the pit of her stomach, sending little warning burps to her lips.

She pushed the hood of her cloak away from her face in anticipation of the impending embarrassment.

"This be it," Walter called over his shoulder.

His words were followed by a sharp bump underneath her and she sat bolt upright, completely forgetting the need to hide her presence in the boat.

To her surprise, Walter had piloted them safely to the edge of the bank and even now he stepped out into the shallows, pulling the little craft up into the weeds.

Leah couldn't remember a time she'd been so grateful to scramble out onto solid ground, her stomach still a rumbling mass of turmoil.

As the first rays of morning light lit the sky, Walter splashed into the water to pull her bundle from the boat, passing it over to her with a grin.

"I told you you'd nothing to fret over, did I no?"

"That you did, Walter. What can I say? I'm just a worrywart." She gave the old man a hug before tossing the makeshift strap of her bundle across her shoulder and backing away a few steps.

"You're sure yer up to doing this?" Walter's eyes looked even more watery and red-rimmed than usual as he waited for her response.

No matter how she felt at the moment, there was really only one answer to his question. It wasn't like she had any choice. It was her or no one.

She nodded her agreement, not sure she could say the words aloud.

"Then remember to keep to the trees, lass, and step lively. Dinna forget to use yer ears as well as yer eyes and dinna be about trusting anyone. As soon as Richard discovers yer gone, he'll no doubt send men out to search the countryside for you, aye?"

"I'll be fine, Walter. I can do this." Leah forced the words of reassurance as much for her own benefit as for the old man's. Though, in truth, she felt about as far from fine as she could imagine.

"You've the dirk Maisey gave you close at hand?"

Again she nodded, patting the cloth pouch hanging from her waist.

"Then be off with you, lass, into the trees. And may God watch over you." With that final word, Walter climbed back into the little boat and shoved off from shore, heading back into the choppy waters of the loch.

"From your lips to his ears," Leah muttered as she turned away from the sight of his leaving. Standing here alone in the freaking middle of nowhere, she could use all the divine help she could get.

Opening the little pouch at her waist, she dug under Maisey's knife to remove a much-folded sheet of paper, tilting it toward the rising sun to look over the drawing once more. Not that she really needed to see the words below the drawing. She'd committed those to memory when she'd first opened it last night.

The letter had been written by Mairi MacKiernan as an introduction to her family should the day ever come when Leah had need of them. It instructed her to travel north to find the MacKiernan home, a castle called Dun Ard. There was also a small map Mairi had drawn. When Leah reached Dun Ard, she was to ask for Mairi's aunt Rosalyn or her cousin, Blane. Apparently either of them would believe the wild story of where she'd come from and who had sent her.

Thank goodness Grandma Mac had kept the letter all those years ago when Leah had wanted nothing to do with it. Without this familial connection to the MacKiernan clan, there really was no one to aid them.

Folding the paper and returning it to her pouch, Leah studied the area around her. Walter had dropped her far enough from MacQuarrie Keep that she could see no sign of the towers. That was as they'd planned. If she couldn't see them, they couldn't see her.

The little map Mairi had drawn, a mass of squiggles and straight lines, appeared to follow roads, such as they were. Leah would simply have to trust it was the roads of her current time and not some modern-day version. It also showed a starting point from MacQuarrie Keep. Three days' ride to Dun Ard, the letter said.

Too bad she had to keep off those roads. Following them too closely would make her an easy target when Dick's men came hunting for her. Too bad she was on foot. That would extend the time it took to reach Dun Ard. And, strike three, too bad she wasn't starting out from MacQuarrie Keep.

Leah huffed out a deep sigh, noting absently she could see her breath misting in front of her. Just her luck the chill of spring insisted on hanging on so long. As she pulled her cape close around her, her hand brushed over the stone dangling from her neck. She pulled the ribbon from inside her bodice and rubbed the polished stone between her fingers. Just as her mother's had, the carving on this stone felt warm to her skin.

How Grandma Mac had managed to get her hands on this was a story she intended to hear the minute she returned to MacQuarrie Keep. For now, though, she was simply grateful to have it. Just the weight of the stone around her neck made her feel stronger and less alone somehow, as if it were some kind of ethereal connection to her mother.

"Crazy, huh?" she asked aloud, tracing her thumb slowly over the carving once more. "But if you are out there watching over me, I could really use some help right about now. Show me where I need to be. Help me find my way to what I need most."

Almost instantly, a stab of heat shot through her fingers, and she jerked her hand away, allowing the stone to thud against her chest as she examined her fingers. Searching for the red of a burn, she was amazed to find nothing. When she tentatively stroked the tip of her index finger across the face of the stone again, it felt absolutely normal.

With a humorless laugh at her own indulgent flight of fancy, she tucked the stone back down inside her bodice and studied her surroundings intently.

She needed to get moving.

Somewhere out there, she could only hope she'd run into those squiggly-line roads Mairi had drawn for her because there was nothing she could see from here that looked even remotely like that map.

For now, the one thing she did know was that the path to Dun Ard headed north. With the sun rising to her right, north should be straight ahead.

"Then straight ahead it is," she murmured aloud, setting off at a lively pace, just as she'd promised Walter she would.

Five

~~~~~

*H*ow far had she come? A hundred miles? A thousand?

"Ha!" The sound of her own voice startled Leah and she shook her head at her skittishness. In spite of how long she'd been walking, she'd be lucky if she'd managed a solid ten miles in the proper direction. Lord, but she was tired.

After the first few hours, with what felt like hundreds of false starts and doubling back to find her way around rivers too large to cross on foot, she'd finally realized that all of those squiggles on Mairi's map were neither roads nor decoration. They were the bodies of water she needed to make her way around.

Which explained the little arrows and straight lines. All of which would have been an absolutely perfect guide *if* she'd started off from the front gate of Mac-Quarrie Keep.

Which she hadn't.

She stood at the crest of a particularly steep incline, breathing hard, having resorted to climbing on hands and knees by the time she reached this spot. There, below her, off to her right was what looked amazingly like one of the roads she'd sought all day.

"Jeez Louise," she huffed and then laughed out loud. That phrase, one of her mother's favorites, had certainly come from somewhere deep in her memory.

Pushing hair that had come loose from her braid out of her sweat-dampened face, she realized she'd better begin to think of where she'd set up camp for the night. The sun was already sinking low in the western sky so darkness couldn't be too far off.

Pushing away all thoughts of how uncomfortable she was with spending a night out in the open by herself, she forged down the side of the rise, headed for the cover of trees and the river beyond.

Another river. It was amazing that Scotland had any dry land at all, considering how many rivers riddled her mass. But with this one, thank goodness, she'd also caught sight of the road and where there was a road, there would have to be a spot to cross the water.

For tonight, though, she didn't want to be anywhere near that road. Just in case Dick's men traveled it.

Her stomach rumbled with the hunger she'd tried to ignore for the last few hours. "Just a little farther," she whispered, encouraging herself to keep putting one foot in front of the other until, at last, she reached the water's edge.

This would be a great spot for her to camp for the night. Not far from the water's edge, large boulders tumbled together to form an overhang. She was pretty sure that spot would be just right for her to snuggle into, giving her a bit of security while she slept.

While she tried to sleep, she corrected herself.

With the rocks to her back and the water to her front, it felt like she already had some natural barriers in place to protect her from whatever might happen by.

Whatever or whoever.

She dropped to her knees by the boulders and pulled the strap of her bundle over her head, letting it fall to ground at her side. Just a moment to sit and do nothing felt like pure luxury after her day of cross-country walking. What she'd really like, with night approaching, was to build a raging big fire. But, while it would warm her as temperatures dropped and keep away any wild animals, it could also act as a beacon in the dark to any who might already be searching for her.

No fire for her this night.

Instead, she'd rest for a moment more and then she'd pull out some of the bread and cheese she carried with her and put together a cold version of an evening meal.

The very thought of food set her mouth to watering and her stomach grumbled again. As she began to loosen the ties on her bundle, she noticed the filth and grime caked around her fingernails. From the slime in the tunnel she'd traversed early this morning to the dirt she'd picked up climbing that last hill, her hands were absolutely disgusting.

Tired she might be, but not so tired as to touch her food with that filth on her hands.

She pushed herself to stand, the muscles in her legs quivering with exhaustion as she did, and headed the few feet to the water. As she neared the bank, her foot slipped on the marshy ground and she grabbed wildly at the bush next to her. Sliding to one knee, she threw out her arms in front of her. Taking the brunt of fall on her right side, her hand plunged into the foliage covering the ground.

"Crapola," she hissed, pulling her hand up to examine her stinging fingers. She'd slid more than she'd fallen, and she wasn't so much hurt as rattled.

Once again she pushed up to her feet and carefully took the two remaining steps down to the river's edge where the deep waters eddied and swirled.

Well, wasn't that just perfect.

She shook her head as she squatted down and leaned awkwardly over a dead tree stump to scoop up a handful of water. Barely one day on the road and she was already a mud-splattered mess thanks to that klutzy little episode.

"Could have been worse," she murmured, looking back at the deep skid mark her foot had made in the soft mud. Another few inches and she could have gone into the river, a very nasty possibility considering how deep the water here appeared to be and her inability to swim. "A whole lot worse."

The sound of her voice ringing in her ears, she tossed the edge of her cape behind her to avoid letting it drape down into the water. The last thing she needed was a wet cape on a night when she'd have no fire.

Another scoop of water and she rubbed her hands together, realizing as she did so that the stinging in her fingers had intensified. The tips were swelling and turning red, too.

"Double crapola." Obviously there were nettles growing here and, lucky her, she'd found them. After a while, she knew from experience, the stinging would stop and her fingers would be completely numb. No big deal. A minor irritation that would pass before she woke in the morning. Still, it was one more annoying distraction she didn't need.

Once more she leaned over the stump and dipped down into the water, scrubbing her hands together. That would have to do for washing up. At least her hands would be cleaner than they had been.

Pushing to stand, Leah leaned her weight against the stump to support her tired, shaking legs. As she did so, she heard a strange sucking noise and the stump gave way under her hand, sliding forward into the waters at her feet.

She windmilled her arms, pitching her body back, away from the water, but her foot tangled in the heavy cape she wore and the next thing she felt was the shock of the cold water as she tumbled in.

Nothing beneath her feet to push against. Sheer and total panic tightened her chest even as she flailed her arms against the strong current below the surface of the water. Gasping in great mouthfuls of river, she struggled to catch her next breath.

So heavy. She felt the water dragging her down like a great, dark hand pulling her surely toward the bottom no matter how hard she fought it.

She might have screamed; she wasn't sure. All she did know for sure was that no matter how hard she fought, the grasp of the river was stronger than she would ever be.

Her chest burned with the need for oxygen and she gasped again, her mouth filling with as much water as air. Again the inexorable weight pulled her down as surely as if she were in the clutches of some creature from the muddy depths.

This is it, her mind raged as the waters closed over her face. She was going to die and there was absolutely nothing she could do to prevent it.

Or perhaps she was dead already, because what she glimpsed as she went under that last time surely could be nothing if not the face of an angel.

It was around here somewhere.

Drew pulled on the reins he'd held loosely in his hands, bringing his steed to pause as he gathered his bearings. He remembered a spot where he'd over-nighted on his last travels through this area. A protected place back off the road a piece, where the forest followed the bend of the river and boulders appeared to have been tossed about as if the gods had used them in a giant game of chance.

With a click of his tongue, his mount started forward, carefully picking his steps from the beaten track and into trees.

There were of course places he could have found shelter along the way. The MacKiernans were not unknown is this part of the land. There were friends, allies, family, even a small monastery he passed up the day before.

Wisely passed up, he thought to himself as he ducked his head to avoid a low-hanging branch. Out here, in the open, alone, he had no need for falsehoods to explain himself or his actions. No need to speak of where he was headed or why. No enduring the well-meaning advice and counsel his family and friends felt it their duty to inflict on him.

When his family had learned he was headed out yet again, his brother's wife, Ellie, had insisted on showing him some stretches she thought would help him to keep his leg from stiffening. In spite of how ridiculous they had looked to him, after all the time he had spent in the saddle, he just might give them a try this night.

His horse's ears pricked up and the animal tossed his head as they broke through the trees and into the clearing. Drew's attention focused on his immediate surroundings and he brought the animal to a halt.

What was that noise up ahead? Some animal thrashing in the water?

A sharp, crystalline scream echoed through the clearing, coming to an abrupt end.

Not some animal. A woman.

Drew leapt from his horse, ignoring the stumble as his weak leg hit the ground, forcing himself to run in spite of the pain. His world stuttered, shifting into slow motion as he looked to the river.

The woman struggled, her frantic efforts against the rushing current pushing her farther and farther away from the bank. As she sank under the surface, he jerked his sword from his back and tossed it to the ground, eliminating the extra weight in preparation for what he was about to do.

No time to think how bizarre he felt in that instant, as if their eyes had connected somehow.

The shock of cold closed around him when he dove into the river, as near to where he'd seen her last as he dared. Down, down he pushed, to grab whatever he could reach in the murky depths below him where she'd disappeared.

Something brushed against his fingertips and he kicked, propelling himself down until his hand closed around thick, water-bloated cloth. He lifted with all his might, fighting the energy-sapping pull of the cold river as he attempted to wrap his arms around the body.

Not a body! A struggling, living woman who flailed her arms and kicked her feet, pushing in the wrong direction in her desperate attempt to reach air.

He drew her to him, her back against his chest, fighting her and the currents in order to thrust them both up, up toward the surface.

So close now.

His face broke through and he gasped to fill his lungs even as he fought to pull her head up into the open air. He managed to get her face to the surface for only an instant before the churning waters tugged her down again, the weight of her clothing dragging her toward the bottom.

Down they went together, Drew unwilling to let go his hold on her.

Damn the woolen she wore! He clawed at the ties around her neck, succeeding at last in ripping the ribbon from the material and allowing the heavy cloak to fall away as he kicked his legs to propel them back up once more.

She didn't fight him any longer. Her movements had

stilled by the time they broke the surface and a dreadful panic filled his chest along with the fresh sweet air he gulped down.

Shifting his hold, he hooked his arm around her, tucking his hand under her armpit. With the heavy woolen gone, there didn't seem to be much to her.

Four strong strokes and he reached land. Treading water, he managed to shove her up onto the bank face-first, her lower body still hanging into the river as he lifted himself out beside her.

No time to rest yet. Forcing himself to keep moving, he rose to his knees and grasped the limp woman under her arms. He lifted her, scrambling backward to drag her up the bank until her whole body was out of the water.

After the days on horseback, exertion and the cold water pushed his muscles beyond their limit, sapping his strength. His thigh went rigid as a cramp shot through the damaged tissue and he collapsed with the pain, dropping the woman the last few inches to land next to him, her cheek resting on the ground next to his leg.

She hit with a thud and water spewed from her mouth as her body convulsed, racked with coughing.

Thank the Fates!

Drew kept his gaze locked on the woman's face as he kneaded his fingers into his knotted thigh muscle. Though she'd turned to lie on her back with her eyes still closed, she breathed, great gasps of air filling her lungs between fits of coughing.

"You'll breathe easier, lass, if you but move to yer side."

She didn't resist when he rolled her over, but the instant he withdrew his touch, she pushed up to her hands and knees, backing away from him.

"How do you feel?"

"Alive," she croaked, pressing both palms to her chest. "Barely."

Water clustered on her dark lashes as she blinked, knitting them together like a netting of delicately thin leaves found covering the deepest forest floor. And her eyes! Even red-rimmed from her traumatic experience, they glowed like strange, dark jewels, the rich brown of fertile soil in spring.

"I must look awful," she murmured, trying ineffectively to push back errant clumps of blond hair that plastered wetly to her face.

She worried about how she looked? He stared at her fidgeting there, unable to think of any appropriate reply to give her. It was the impossibly ridiculous sort of thing he could easily imagine his sister, Sallie, might say in similar circumstances. What strange creatures women were that their minds could possibly dredge up such a thought so closely on the heels of having nearly drowned. All of them were beyond any man's ability to comprehend.

A breeze stirred through the clearing, biting into his water-soaked clothing and reminding him that nightfall was at hand. As he considered his own discomfort, he realized this strange woman in front of him hadn't been fidgeting as he'd first thought. She was shivering, and quite hard, too.

"We've a need to get out of these wet things or we'll both catch a fever." He pushed to stand and held out a hand to assist her to her feet. "I'll start a fire and then you can tell me how you managed to—"

"No!" She clutched his sleeve, her eyes looking for all the world like those of a frightened doe. "No fire!"

"Dinna be daft, woman. Why would you no want a fire?" Though the day had been pleasant enough, the dark would bring the full chill of early spring with its arrival.

"Because it can be seen by—" She stopped speaking abruptly, dropping her hold on his sleeve as she backed away again. "Who are you? What are you doing out here?"

This was beyond what he might ordinarily tally up to typically confounding female behavior. This woman's fear shone around her like a halo. And why wouldn't she be afraid? Out here in the wilderness with a strange man and none of her own companions to be seen, she'd every right for concern.

"Andrew MacAlister." He bobbed his head respectfully, as if they stood in the great hall of his family home. "I'm traveling on business." Which, no matter how frightened she might be, was all she needed to know about his journey. "We need to dry you off."

The time for niceties had long since passed.

"Then you're not English?" Her hand clutched at some bauble hanging from her neck, her eyes rounded in suspicion. "You're not looking for me?"

So that was it. A runaway. That would explain why there'd been no one around to save her.

"Since I've no idea who you are, I can say with certainty I was no looking for you, nor anyone else for that matter, until I heard yer scream for help." He turned his back to begin gathering bits of fuel for his fire. "And all I search for now is the makings of a good fire to warm us after our wee dunk in the water."

"Wait."

Drew straightened, a pile of broken twigs in one hand, and turned back to face the confounding woman.

"My name is Leah MacQuarrie. Listen, I know my request seems odd. It's just that . . ." She paused, pushing wet bits of hair behind her ear as if stalling for time while she made up her mind whether or not to say more. "There's a chance my uncle may have men out looking for me. If you start a fire, it'll be like setting a beacon out for them. I can't risk having them find me."

More confirmation of his runaway theory. Likely some family dispute he had no intention of entangling himself in. After all, he remembered all too well how dramatic his own sister had been growing up. Though, in truth, he'd be the first to admit that the female in front of him now was a woman grown, not a girl.

Drew nodded, hoping to convey that he might actually be considering her request. They were having a fire this night whether she liked or not, there was no question in his mind to that. Still, for now, distraction might be a better tactic than honesty.

"Have you brought with you dry things you could change into?"

Her forehead wrinkled in her confusion and she blinked several times before answering, as if his change to the discussion was formed of words she didn't quite understand.

"No," she answered at last. "Just some food and a blanket."

"Very well." He strode to his horse and dug into his bags, pulling out a tightly rolled shirt and handing it over to her. "I've only one spare set myself, so we'll share. You take the shirt and I'll have the plaid, aye?"

She took the garment he offered and disappeared behind the boulders, stopping to pick up a small bundle he hadn't noticed earlier.

Good. Untying all those wet laces should keep her busy for a good while. By the time she got out of those wet things and returned, their fire would be well under way.

Six

Not even the most determined silent treatment in the world could hold out long against a growling stomach and the smell of fresh-roasted fish.

Whatever.

Now that Leah was over being angry about the fire, maybe it was time to focus a little more thought on how lucky she was this guy had showed up. This guy and not one of Dick's men.

"That was so good. Thank you. I hadn't realized how hungry I was."

Leah licked the remains of dinner from her fingers and studied Andrew MacAlister across the fire. Discreetly, of course. Wouldn't do to have him catch her ogling, even if he was, without a doubt, the most handsome man she'd ever seen.

Maybe especially because of that.

"I'm pleased you liked it."

He shifted his attention from the food in his hand to smile at her and she darted her eyes away.

That was too close! He'd almost caught her staring.

"Does this mean we're speaking again, then?" His grin widened as he asked the question. "That yer over yer temper about the fire?"

She didn't answer right away, instead taking her time to consider an appropriate response.

When she'd returned from slipping into his dry shirt and found he'd started a fire, she'd tried to argue him into putting it out. He'd turned his back on her, completely ignoring her request, telling her to stop being a silly female and to let him worry about anyone whose attention the fire might draw.

It was the "silly female" crack that had really gotten to her. Even after more than a decade in this century, she still hadn't reconciled herself to accept the pervasive male superiority garbage.

"A fire didn't seem like a smart thing to me. Not when I can't risk being caught before I reach my destination."

Andrew nodded thoughtfully, shifting the woolen blanket he wore draped around his shoulders. "I accept that. Though I dinna suspect dying from exposure would be a much better choice, now would it?"

She looked down at the ground, feeling his soft brown eyes bore into her when he paused, as if he expected an answer she had no intention of giving. If he planned to wait for her to admit that he was right and she was wrong, he was in for a mighty long wait.

Even if he *was* right.

"I'd say the time has come, lass, for you to be telling me what this destination of yers is and why you'd be willing to risk yer life to reach it. Perhaps I can help."

Perhaps he could, but getting his help meant she'd have to trust him enough to tell him everything, and how could she trust someone she'd only known for a couple of hours? Of course, he *had* saved her life and that had to count for something in his favor. Other than starting the fire and calling her a silly female, he'd been considerate and respectful, more big check marks in the trustworthy category.

Tick, tock, Leah. She needed to make up her mind. And, really, what did she have to lose at this point? They sat out here alone, in the dark, in the middle of freaking nowhere. If he were a bad guy, his knowing where she was headed and why could hardly make her situation any worse than it already was.

Looking up, she met his unflinching gaze. Goodness, but he had great eyes.

And that, as stupid a reason as she recognized it to be, was what ultimately aided her decision. She refused to believe that a man with eyes like those could possibly be all bad.

"My grandfather is being held captive in MacQuarrie Keep. I'm trying to reach the only people I know to turn to for help."

"Who are these people?"

"The MacKiernans of Dun Ard."

Andrew froze in the act of stirring the fire, the stick in his hand flipping up a *poof* of embers as it came to rest against the surrounding stones.

"And what makes you think these MacKiernans will be willing to help you?"

"They're honor-bound to help because they're family." She paused, weighing her words. "Family of a sort. They're related to the man my sister married."

She wouldn't even try to explain that none of the MacKiernans would ever have heard of her sister's husband since he wouldn't be born for another seven hundred years. That was the whole reason for the letter.

The letter.

"Oh my God." Her stomach flip-flopped as she thought of the single thin sheet of paper, folded and tucked into the cloth bag she'd worn at her waist. The same bag that had gone into the water with her.

Leah jumped to her feet, dropping the warm cocoon of her blanket as she scrambled to locate the little purse.

"What is it?" Andrew was on his feet, too, pulling his sword from the sheath on his back as he rose.

"Oh no, no, no, please, no," she all but chanted as she dropped to her knees and snatched up the bag from under the bushes where Andrew had spread their clothing to dry.

Without the letter, how would she ever convince the MacKiernans she'd legitimately been sent to them? Without the map, she wasn't even sure she'd be able to find Dun Ard in the first place.

Heedless of the stones and debris digging into her knees, she fumbled with the ties holding the bag shut, her shaking fingers slowing her progress in opening it. Reaching in, she hastily pushed aside the little dagger Maisey had given her, hardly noticing the sting when her thumb slid past its sharp metal edge. Beneath it, her fingers closed on a water-soaked lump that had been her precious paper.

Slowly she pulled the wad from the bag, confirming her worst suspicion.

"Oh, no." Screwed. She was so screwed.

"What's that you have there?" Andrew's question startled her, his voice coming from right behind her.

"My only chance to save Grandpa Hugh's life," she whispered, gritting her teeth in her frustration. This couldn't be happening.

Andrew reached around her, scooping the wet mess from her hand. "What is this?"

"It's a letter, *was* a letter," she corrected, "introducing me to Mairi's aunt. With a map to Dun Ard drawn on it so I could find my way there if I ever had need of the MacKiernans. Maybe if I try to dry it near the fire—" She half turned, reaching out to take it from him, but he grabbed her wrist, dropping the wet lump of paper to the ground as he did so.

It wasn't his action that froze the words on her lips or prevented her leaning over to pick up the letter.

It was the glimpse of his bare chest.

Somewhere along the way, he'd dropped the blanket he'd wrapped around himself and now wore nothing but his plaid. The long tail draped over one shoulder might cover that one side, but that still left a whole swath of bare naked muscles open to her view.

Leah swallowed hard, forcing herself to look away, up toward the night sky. It had been a very long time she she'd seen bare, naked muscles to match the likes of Andrew's. And even then, they'd been in the pages of a magazine, not up close and personal like these.

"Yer bleeding."

He pressed the edge of his plaid to her thumb, applying pressure to the cut.

"It's no big deal. Don't worry about it. It'll stop in a little bit." A fact she took for granted. Her body healed quickly. For now she simply wanted the sting in her thumb to distract her thoughts from the man who held her hand.

So far, it wasn't working very well.

"Who is this Mairi you spoke of?"

"Mairi is . . ." She began to answer, but the words stuck as if her mouth had gone completely dry when Andrew leaned past her to drag his damp shirt from the bush.

She darted her gaze down to her own hand and pressed her forefinger to her thumb, focusing on the stinging throb in the cut. Anything to avoid watching the muscles in his forearm ripple as he tore a strip of material from the shirt's tail.

He caught up her hand again and gently wrapped the cloth around her thumb, tying it off and tucking the ends neatly under the wrap.

"Mairi is . . ." He repeated her words, dragging them out as if they were a question.

That's right. She'd been speaking. Trying to answer his question.

"Mairi is," she tried again, concentrating on her words. Her relationship to those people was hard enough to figure out without the added distraction of his half-naked body. "It's mind-bogglingly complicated. She's a MacKiernan. Her brother's wife is the sister of my sister's husband." There. Could she make it sound any more confusing? Could she make herself sound any more idiotic?

"Mairi MacKiernan?" he asked, his voice so soft she had to lean in closer to make sure she understood the words.

Big mistake. She could feel the heat rolling off him when she did.

"Yes. No," she corrected herself, all too aware of the man next to her. "Not MacKiernan. She's married. Her husband's name is Ramos . . . Ramos, damn!" Her mind had gone completely blank but for thoughts of chests and muscles. You'd think she could concentrate enough to remember something as simple as the man's stupid surname? So what if she'd only known the whole bunch of them for a handful of days? So what if all she could picture in her mind was Andrew's bulging biceps?

"Navarro?" He supplied, his voice still hushed.

"That's it! You've heard of them?" Mairi had told her that she and Ramos had spent quite a while in this time.

"I have."

This was too good to be true. If he'd known Mairi and Ramos, maybe he knew more. "And Dun Ard? Do you know how to get there?" Leah finally forced her eyes up to meet his, all but holding her breath as she waited for his answer.

"I do."

Maybe she wouldn't completely fail Hugh and Margery after all.

"My only hope to save my grandfather is to reach the MacKiernans. The map drawn on that paper was my only way of finding them. With it gone . . ." She allowed the words to hang in the air as she searched his face. "You said earlier that perhaps you could help me. Showing me the way to Dun Ard would be the biggest help I could hope for."

Bizarre how the pendulum of her world had taken a full swing in the span of mere minutes. Leah could hardly believe how quickly she'd gone from trying to decide whether or not she could trust this Andrew enough to tell him anything about herself, all the way to the point where she found herself now—ready to beg him to take her where she needed to go.

Seven

⌒

Curiosity? Morality?

Drew shifted against the boulder that served as his backrest, staring across the flames at the woman on the other side of the fire. She lay on her side, her head propped up on one elbow. Her long blond hair fanned out around her shoulders, glinting in the firelight like a cape of spun gold.

She'd wrapped her woolen around her, covering her from the waist down, but the blanket might as well be invisible. Drew knew all too well what it concealed. She'd forgotten all about the woolen when she'd scrambled after her pouch in search of the letter she claimed to carry. Wearing naught more than his shirt, she'd exhibited a pair of shapely legs which had looked to go on forever.

He licked his lips at the memory.

Lust?

He could not say why he had agreed to escort her to his home any more than he could say why he'd chosen not to tell her that Dun Ard *was* his home.

Lunacy, most likely.

Everything he'd learned about her so far pointed to this woman being trouble on a grand scale. She claimed to know his cousin Mairi and, try as he might to come up with alternatives, that could mean only one thing.

Leah must have come from the future where Mairi lived.

That inescapable fact led to an even more insidious conclusion. . . . The beauty sitting across from him was somehow connected to the Fae. Likely, she was here because they'd sent her.

That could only mean trouble. Trouble and sorrow and many ruined lives followed in the wake of encounters with the Fae. Certainly his encounter with the Faerie Count Servans had ended that way.

He should have recognized the stench of Fae Magic when he'd first ridden into the clearing.

So many *should have*s.

Once he'd pulled her from the cold waters, he *should have* turned his back and continued on, searching for a safer haven in which to spend his night.

Instead of offering to show her the way to Dun Ard, he *should have* beaten a hasty retreat, leaving her as far behind him as possible.

And yet, in spite of all the *should have*s he could list, he'd done none of them. Here he sat, waiting for first light in order to head north, dragging this walking, talking bundle of trouble straight into the arms of the people he loved most.

Sliding down to his back, he propped his arms under his head and stared up into the starlit sky. The crackle of damp wood in the blaze usually soothed him, lulling him to sleep.

But not this night. This night his mind raced with the possibilities of what was yet to come now that he'd agreed to accompany Leah to Dun Ard.

It wasn't just the Fae he needed to worry about.

"Why are the English after you?"

As he asked the question, he looked over to assess her reaction. Though she still held her head upright, propped on her elbow, the wait for her to answer was so long, he began to wonder if she might have fallen asleep.

"What makes you think they are?" she responded at last.

"You questioned whether or not I was English, in the same breath in which you demanded to know if I had come looking for you."

Another long pause, as if the woman debated every word she considered uttering.

"It's complicated."

Her explanation for everything, it seemed.

"No half so complicated as my life will be if I'm caught aiding a criminal wanted by the English. I dinna fancy the idea of dancing at the end of a rope to pay for yer crimes."

"I'm not a criminal." She pushed herself up to sit and, crossing her arms defensively, she glared at him.

Had he struck a tender spot?

"No? Then perhaps you'd care to enlighten me as to why yer wanting to avoid the English." He might have committed himself to helping her, but he'd be damned if he was going to walk into some bees' hive without at least knowing what awaited him.

"So far all you've told me is that yer uncle could well have men searching for you and that yer grandfather is held prisoner in yer family keep. It's no so much information to go on. It's certainly no enough for me to be putting my own life and freedom in jeopardy over."

"Nobody said you had to help me. You offered of your own free will."

"That I did. And I have every intention of helping you reach Dun Ard. But I must warn you as well, the MacKiernan laird may rightly refuse to endanger his own people if the English are involved in this. I would."

"I suppose I should count my blessings that you aren't the MacKiernan laird then, shouldn't I?"

A twinge of guilt gnawed at his conscience, but only for a moment. His family's safety could well depend on what he learned from her, and he intended to learn all he could before showing his hand.

"I'd expect in return for my agreeing to show you to Dun Ard, you'd be willing to warn me of what I'm up against in doing so." He rose to one elbow, catching her eyes and holding them. "That's no complicated. It's only fair."

"I suppose you have a point. You should know." She nodded slowly, uncrossing her arms and dropping her hands to her lap. "My uncle Richard abandoned his family years ago when he married. He went to England because his wife's father is apparently somebody important in the English court. Last week Richard showed up again. Him and a bunch of English soldiers. He claimed

MacQuarrie Keep in the name of King Edward and locked my grandfather away when he tried to stop him."

"And you think yer uncle has men searching for you because . . ." He dragged out the question, waiting for her to continue her story.

"I escaped to go for help." She looked away, lifting a hand to clasp the pendant hanging from her neck as she did so.

"That's it? That's the whole story?"

She seemed uncomfortably nervous, as if there might be more.

"That's pretty much it." She rose to her knees and scooted closer to the fire, readjusting her blanket as she did so. "It's really cold out here."

A change to the direction of their conversation?

Drew laid his head back down on his arms, closing his eyes as he did so. He'd be willing to bet a saddlebag full of silvers that there was more she wasn't telling him.

For his part, he could only hope whatever she kept from him wouldn't make him regret his offer to help any more than he already did.

Eight

If they didn't find a place to camp for the night that suited Andrew soon, Leah wasn't sure she wouldn't simply fall off the horse in a miserable, exhausted heap. Her inner thighs chafed from rubbing against the horse blanket with each step the animal took, and her shoulders ached from holding herself stiffly upright to avoid leaning against Andrew's back.

She'd never been particularly fond of riding and this riding double, especially with a man she barely knew, was one of the most uncomfortable things she'd done in a very long time.

In spite of that, she had to admit it beat walking. They'd gotten much farther today than she would have on foot. And she was headed directly where she needed to go, something she couldn't have been so sure of before, even if her map hadn't been destroyed.

There had been some doubt in her mind last night after Andrew had agreed to show her to Dun Ard. She'd even gone so far as to study the skies, searching out the North Star in exactly the way her older brother Chase had taught her when she was little.

When Drew had headed his horse in that direction this morning, she'd been able to allay the last of her doubts about him.

But that had been many, many hours ago.

As the sun had dipped lower in the sky, she'd heard her inner child ranting *are we there yet* for so long that she could think of nothing else. Nothing except her raw thighs, that is. And her aching back.

The sun had disappeared behind the trees and the sky had turned dusky purple with the promise of night. And still Andrew showed no sign of slowing or stopping.

She didn't need perfect; she simply needed off this damn horse.

"What about over there?" Leah pointed to a tree-covered area to their left. "Surely we could manage just fine there for the night."

"No," her companion grunted over his shoulder. "We'll no be staying out in the open again. I've no wish to chance one of the English patrols stumbling upon us."

He did have a point there. English patrols would be a bad thing. Especially if they'd had any contact with her uncle Richard. But how could they not camp out for the night? What was he thinking? It wasn't exactly like they could stop at the local Holiday Inn.

"What are we going to do then?" Surely he didn't think they'd just keep riding for days on end.

"There's a wee monastery no too far ahead. If we keep up our pace, we should be able to reach it no too long after the moon's rise. You'll be safer there."

A monastery. She recalled her grandpa Hugh having spoken of staying at a monastery when he traveled to and from Inverness. For all she knew, it could be the very same one. She wished now she'd asked him more questions about his travels.

Andrew's comment about *her* being safe at the monastery took her by surprise, like it was only her safety that concerned him and not his own. She felt a little smile curving her lips in spite of her discomfort. First he'd saved her life and now he was acting like her personal bodyguard. If she actually believed in random luck, she'd be tempted to believe that she'd gotten beyond incredibly lucky in bumping into Andrew.

"Do you need to walk about for bit?"

"No." No way. If she climbed down off this huge animal now, she'd likely refuse to get back on. Her thighs stung like crazy and there didn't seem to be any position she could wiggle into that gave her relief.

Thank goodness she'd be healed by morning or she'd never make it to her journey's end.

Andrew shifted in the saddle, straightening his leg, and a flash of panic hit her, as if she were going to slide off her seat. Without thought, she threw her arms around his waist, clenching her fingers into the folds of his shirt.

When he patted her hand, like some grownup reassuring a frightened toddler, she could actually feel her face turning red with embarrassment.

Minor payment for feeling more secure on the horse's back.

Embarrassment be damned. She had no intention of moving her arms away now that she'd latched on to the man. It was the first time all day she hadn't felt like she might topple off if their mount came to a sudden stop, a feeling that had grown more pronounced as she'd grown more tired.

What was that thing her mom used to say? In for a penny, in for a pound? Something like that. Whatever the exact wording, she remembered the meaning well enough and intended to utilize it right now.

Gently, ever so slowly, she laid her cheek against Andrew's back, scooting forward a little as she did so, tightening her hold around his waist.

And why exactly hadn't she done this hours ago?

It felt wonderful. Especially when he clasped his big, warm hand over hers.

Warm and safe and somehow oddly comforted, she relaxed, letting her mind go blank until new thoughts colored the canvas.

"Why wouldn't you help me save my grandparents if it were up to you?" The comment Drew had made last night continued to haunt her. "It's a worthy cause. They're good people whose lives are at risk. They deserve justice."

Long moments passed and she'd begun to wonder if he'd even heard her question.

"I dinna doubt either their need for or their right to justice. But, if it were my people I had to send into battle, I'd be thinking of the risk to them. Is one life worth more than another?" He paused, as if carefully considering his words, starting and stopping twice before he continued. "For myself, I canna partake in battle so I have to think, by what right could I ask another to do that which I would no do myself?"

She refused to accept the logic of his words. Accepting would refute everything she hoped to accomplish. The very reasonableness of his argument irritated her. But not enough to force her to break the physical contact she had with him.

Instead she consoled herself that, as she'd said to him once before, it was her good fortune that it was the MacKiernan and not him she sought help from.

"If you look through the trees just ahead, you can see the light from the monastery."

She jumped when he spoke, grateful he'd not tried to talk her out seeking the MacKiernan's help.

The trees through which they rode seemed to loom over them in the dark but, in the distance, as if below them, she could just make out the flicker to which he'd referred.

"They leave a light on?" How'd they do that?

"A torch burns through the night, attended by a chosen monk, as a welcome to weary travelers."

Weary travelers? She certainly qualified as one of those.

Thank the Fates the monastery was in sight at last.

Since well before sunset, the muscles in Drew's leg had cramped without yield and he knew all too well that his only relief would come once he climbed down off this horse and moved around.

As usual, the big wooden gates stood invitingly open. The main keep was smaller than Dun Ard, though it abutted a chapel, which gave it the sense of size. He knew from a lifetime of visits that this main structure was only a minor part of the property. There were stables and workshops stretching out around the periphery of the property, bordering neat, well-tended gardens, with fertile fields beyond.

Drew directed his horse to the far side of the main stairs, turning the animal so that he might dismount on the side away from the light. If he stopped close enough to the building, he could use the wall to help support the weight he knew his leg would not.

Over the years, he'd learned many such tricks to hide his shortcomings.

The woman behind him lifted her head from his back, though she still clutched at his shirt.

Probably the best thing about the evening so far.

"There's no women here, lass. Best you'd let me deal with the brothers, aye?" He'd never even seen a female traveler here, but surely the monks wouldn't turn her away.

"Absolutely. All yours."

Her pattern of speech reminded him of listening to Caden's wife, Ellie. That in itself would serve to grow his suspicion that she came from a future time, even if she hadn't mentioned his cousin, Mairi.

In preparation to dismount, he covered both her hands with his, gently unclasping and pulling them away from his waist.

That's fair odd.

The bandage he'd placed on her thumb last night had gone missing. He'd want to remember to check that when he got her inside. A slice as deep as the one he'd seen in her flesh should remain covered to keep it clean until it healed. Perhaps the monks would have a salve he could apply to the wound before covering it with another bandage.

With a final pat to her hand, he swung his good leg over and dropped to the ground. As he'd planned, his back hit the wall with a hard thud but supported the weight his leg wouldn't yet hold.

"Are you okay?"

Apparently he was more tired than he'd realized. Otherwise he would have thought to distract her attention while he dismounted. Now he'd simply have to cover his action.

"Uneven ground here," he mumbled, making his way around the horse to the opposite side, giving his leg a few moments to adjust before he reached his arms up to assist her to the ground.

She felt firm and warm beneath his hands, much as she had toward the end of their day's journey when she'd leaned in close, her head resting on his back. As her body came in contact with his, he could almost swear he felt her heart beating against his chest.

What a daft thought! Exhaustion and too many hours in the saddle were certainly taking their toll on his mind.

"Sweet terra firma," she murmured as he released his grasp from her waist, her smile lighting up her whole face.

He paused, eyeing her more critically. She'd tied something around her hair to hold it away from her face, catching it up at her neck so that it flowed down her back and over her shoulder. The flicker of torchlight glinted off individual strands as if a halo surrounded her.

That would never do. Not in a keep full of celibate men.

Digging into his saddle pack, Andrew pulled out his spare plaid and tossed it over her head and around her shoulders, wrapping it around again to take up most of the slack.

"Hey! What'd you do that for?" She peered out the hood he'd made for her, irritation coloring her expression.

To cover you up.

"A proper lady would always be wearing her cloak on a journey."

"Ah." She nodded her understanding even as the furrows disappeared from her forehead. "And since mine is at the bottom of that river, we're improvising. Good call."

He breathed a sigh of relief as he caught up her hand, pulling her forward to the staircase. It wouldn't have surprised him in the least for her to argue even something so simple as whether or not to wear the plaid.

They stopped at the top of the stairs and he reached down to adjust her hood once more, pulling it forward to hide her face better. As far as he knew, these monks weren't around women very often, if at all. No point in flaunting her beauty.

The door opened immediately to their knock, exactly as it had on the other occasions he'd stayed here.

"Welcome, travelers," the elderly monk began, cutting himself short as he made eye contact. "Andrew! So good to see you again! Yer in need of lodging this night?"

"We are, Brother John," Drew acknowledged, allowing the man to pump his arm up and down. "I'd no have expected to find you serving at the door tonight." Normally one of the lay brothers manned the door, not the prior himself.

"Aye, but we've many a traveler out on the road this evening, my young friend. My brothers are attending others' needs. But where are my manners? Come in, come in." Brother John stepped away from the door, gesturing a welcome for them to enter.

The old monk's words didn't sink in until they stepped into the hallway and found themselves face-to-face with the travelers in question.

Soldiers by the look of them.

Drew did a quick mental count. Ten. Unless there were more already in their rooms.

"Brother Marcus is preparing a small repast for all of you. He'll send word as soon as it's ready. And by the time yer finished with yer meal, we'll have yer rooms ready as well." Brother John, ever the gracious host, beamed his gentle smile over those crowded into the hallway. "Until then, perhaps you'd care to make the acquaintance of yer fellow travelers."

When the prior laid his hand on Drew's shoulder, it was as if the elderly monk had instead taken hold of his guts. He knew in that instant there was no avoiding what would happen next.

"I'll begin yer introductions with my young friend, Andrew MacAlister. He's been a frequent guest at the priory on his journeys over the years. If I'm no mistaken this is a first visit for you gentlemen, though, is it no?"

Nine sets of hard eyes focused on the man who was, without a doubt, their leader.

"It is indeed. Sir Peter Moreland," he intoned with the barest nod of his head, his English accent echoing through the hallway. "At your service, good prior. And who might this enchanting creature be?"

Moreland's gaze focused beyond Drew, honing in on Leah. As he'd introduced himself, Leah's grip on Drew's hand had tightened and she'd moved in a step closer to him. When the man turned the attention of all present in her direction, she crowded closer still, so much so, in fact, Drew doubted there was a feather's width between them.

To say that the man frightened her would be, in his opinion, a vast understatement. More interesting still was his own immediate reaction. He didn't like Leah being frightened.

Didn't like it one little bit.

"She might be my wife." The words slipped out with only minimal thought. There could be no better plausible excuse he could think of to be on the road, alone with a woman.

"Andrew!" Brother John clasped his hand, pumping it up and down once again. "When did this happen? You made no mention of it on yer last visit to us. I canna understand why no even yer own sister's husband spoke a word of this when he was here but a fortnight ago. It's no like him at all."

Much more information than Drew cared to share with the men listening so intently to every word.

"Ranald had no knowledge of my plans, Brother John. We're on our way to inform my family even now that we've wed."

"Ah, a clandestine marriage, is it?" Moreland's smirk said much more about him than his words. "Will you make it a regular marriage in the eyes of the church once you reach your family?"

Drew pulled Leah from behind him, enclosing her in the circle of his arm around her shoulders. As hard as she gripped his hand, he wasn't sure he'd ever regain the feeling. Still, she proved her intelligence by keeping her wits about her and remaining silent.

"An exchange of consent is every bit as legally binding as marriage vows taken in the face of the church, are they no?" He met the Englishman's stare without blinking.

"True. Acceptable enough for unenlightened heathens. But the church views it as a sin, isn't that the case, good Prior?" The grin on Moreland's face, as if painted on, did not reach his eyes.

The prior's lips tightened into a thin tight line as he slowly nodded his agreement.

That Moreland's attitude of superiority grated on Drew's nerves he'd readily admit, but that was no reason to make his friends at the priory uncomfortable. Certainly not a reason when only a small embellishment on this already fabricated tale could easily make his friends feel better.

"Dinna fash yerself over it, Brother John. It's of no consequence. My lady and I will be about doing the right thing in the eyes of the church as soon as we reach my home and our laird can make the proper arrangements."

"Brother Marcus asked that you all be seated now." The young novice who'd interrupted to announce the invitation stared around the room as if so many strangers all at one time were a concern to him. Or perhaps it was that so many of the strangers were English soldiers.

Drew was simply grateful for the lad's arrival.

"Excellent. Thank you, Rufus." The prior extended a hand toward the tables at the far end of the room, his hearty smile restored. "It's naught more than some porridge and bread, but it will fill yer stomachs before you retire for the night."

Drew waited, his arm still sheltering Leah, for the others to go on ahead before he followed Brother John into the great hall.

Inside, both the prior and the young novice hustled about, directing their guests to seats at the big wooden tables near the front of the room.

Drew allowed his gaze to scan the room dispassionately, as if he'd lost complete interest in his fellow travelers. With a little good luck, perhaps he and Leah would find themselves seated at a table separately from Moreland.

As usual, *good* luck was nowhere to be found.

Seated directly across from the man, he'd have no rational choice but to continue their conversation.

"And your family, my lady?" Again Moreland had fixed his piercing stare on Leah. "Might I be so bold as to ask, are they aware you've wed?"

"They are indeed, Sir Moreland, and happy for it, too. My father could hardly wait to be rid of me. One less mouth to feed." Leah didn't look at the knight as she responded, instead keeping her eyes fixed on the trencher she shared with Drew. The sad little smile playing over her lips made her words all the more convincing.

Drew could only hope she understood that the farther afield she strayed from the truth, the harder it could be to keep the story straight.

Or could there be some grain of truth to what she said? Now that he thought on it, she'd spoken of an uncle and a grandfather, but had made no mention of a father.

He'd make sure he reminded her of the dangers inherent in inventing stories later. For now, whatever the case, a gentle nudge from him to alter the direction of their conversation couldn't hurt.

"What of you, Moreland? You dinna have the sound of someone from the highlands. What brings you here?"

The knight paused in lifting a cup of wine to his lips, his false smile giving way to a genuine laugh. "Discreetly spoken, MacAlister, if what you're trying to say is that I sound like an Englishman."

Could he have misjudged the knight? It almost sounded as if the warrior had a sense of humor. "That was indeed my meaning."

"Then you are correct. My men and I accompanied my uncle and his party north. We parted company with them at their destination yestereve to continue on our way in a quest for our king."

"What quest could possibly bring you this far?"

Moreland's smile disappeared, his solemn expression a clear indicator of how serious he considered his task. "We've come in search of the traitor Wallace. He and those who hide him. They all will answer to our king for their actions against the crown."

No, he hadn't misjudged the man at all. An English soldier, born and bred.

"We'd heard rumors Wallace and his men stayed to the eastern lowlands." The prior spoke from behind Drew's shoulder where he hovered with the novice at his side.

"Yes, we've heard those stories. And you can rest assured, King Edward has sent men to scour that area as well. All the same, we've no intention of leaving any stone unturned. The traitors will be brought to justice to answer for their crimes." Moreland lifted his cup but once again returned it to the table without it touching his lips. "We've also a rather personal search to conduct, as well."

"A personal search?" Drew studied the man across from him, noting that, beside him, Leah lay down the bread she held, dropping her hand to her lap.

The smile returned to Moreland's lips and he lifted his cup again, this time taking a drink before responding. "My uncle's reason for coming north with us was to take a bride. Unfortunately, by the time we arrived, it appears the girl had gone missing, so we've split our party to look for her while we search for the traitors. Bad form all around, really, for a man Lord Moreland's age to journey all this way only to find his bride's run away the same day he arrives."

A runaway bride? Drew suddenly sensed a need to move forward in this conversation with great caution.

"Your uncle must be sick with worry for his future wife's welfare."

"Ha!" Moreland snorted his derision. "Sick with anger for the trouble of his travels more likely. He's not a man who takes well to disappointment."

Sounded to Drew as if the lass in question had made a wise choice.

"Do you think we might be shown to our rooms soon?" Leah leaned in to him, tugging at his sleeve as she quietly asked her question. "Our long journey is wearing on me, I fear."

"Of course!" Brother John motioned for the novice to remove the remains of their meal. "I will show you there myself."

Drew stood, turning to Leah to assist her to stand and ushering her ahead of him. He stopped a few feet away from the table, tilting his head in farewell to his dinner companions.

"I wish you luck on your search."

Moreland acknowledged the gesture with a like one of his own. "Oh, no fear. We'll find the ones we seek. We've a good description of the woman. Funny thing about that, too." The knight paused to take a swallow from his cup before continuing. "Your own lovely lady is a perfect match for the description we were given."

Nine

"Cozy, much?" Leah stood as she had since the prior had shown them to their rooms, her back against the wall, arms crossed. "These guys bring a whole new level of meaning to the word *austere*."

Drew wholeheartedly agreed, though he remained silent on the issue. The monks were doing the best they could. Brother John had apologized for their lack of "proper" marital accommodations before showing them to the only room they could offer with a bed large enough for two: the room set aside for the abbot's visits.

Standing here in the abbot's accommodations, Drew wondered little that that august man made his home at a larger, wealthier monastery.

Leah cleared her throat and tried again. "The only way I see two people sleeping in that bed is if they're both under the age of five. And small for their age, at that."

The room itself was narrow and cramped, with perhaps the smallest fireplace he'd ever seen. He suspected they'd need the fire to offset the chill they'd likely get from the large, shuttered window opening in the outer wall. Even now the flame of the candle sitting on the tiny desk at the foot of the bed danced and sputtered as a breeze wafted down from the ill-fitting shutters. The bed itself, though roughly half the size of his own at Dun Ard, was still a sight better than others he'd seen here at the priory.

"It could be worse. Most of those men you saw in the dining hall will be sleeping on the floor in a common room tonight."

"I don't really care where they sleep. But *that* bed still isn't big enough for the two of us. Period."

The tremulous huff of breath that followed her declaration told him more than her words and at last he thought he understood her concern.

Drew prided himself on reading people. He'd learned early how rare it was for people to say what they meant. Even more rare for them to mean what they said. Over time, he'd cultivated the necessary skills to look beneath the social games. It was easy enough. He only needed to separate himself from the crowd, stand aside, and observe.

The signs had been there all along with Leah. He'd simply not taken the time to see them. Her discomfort came not from the size of the bed, but in sharing a room with him.

"Dinna fash yerself over the bed space, Leah. You'll no have to share it this night. I'll take the floor." Though he wouldn't be foolish enough to deny the appeal of curling close to her, his body wrapped around hers, his arms encircling her curves.

The thought brought with it an involuntary flush of heat and a tightening of muscles.

She shrugged without making eye contact, an artfully careless gesture he saw right through. Quickly, she moved past him to press her hand down into the mattress, her nose wrinkling in a most attractive manner as she turned to sit on the edge of the bed.

"I guess this whole pretending to be married thing, sharing a room and all, it's not actually so different from sharing a campfire with you. I mean, we were alone together there, too. And the bed is better than sleeping on the ground. I'll give it that much."

"That it is," he agreed, tossing his bag to the floor in front of the little fire. She might aspire to brave and bold, but he could read her easily now that he knew the signs to watch for. "Not so bad at all." For a fact he'd slept in worse places, though he knew from experience the cold stone floor would only add to the aching in his leg.

He dropped to sit, glancing back to see her staring at the door, the bauble she wore around her neck clutched between her thumb and forefinger.

"What else troubles you, Leah?"

"Nothing," she replied hastily.

Too hastily, to his way of thinking.

"I don't suppose these doors have any bolts or locks or anything like that, do they?"

He doubted very much it was the monks she wanted to bar from entry.

"Dinna spare a worrisome thought to the English soldiers down below. You'll no come to any harm at their hands, no so long as yer under my protection. They search for a maiden, no a married woman. Now try to get some rest. We've two long days on the road ahead of us yet."

Rather than reassuring, his words seemed only to agitate her more.

"What makes you think I have any concerns about those men? I'm not worried about them. I don't care who they're looking for. I never even saw any of them before tonight."

She might well not have seen any of the soldiers before this night, but what she'd told him about her uncle made it clear she wanted to avoid any contact with English soldiers. He just wished she'd tell him the whole of the reason why.

The only piece that didn't quite add up was that while her uncle might well send his own men in search of a runaway niece, it wasn't likely soldiers such as those they'd met downstairs would be distracted from their mission on the king's behalf for such a task.

Not unless the task was somehow personal. Personal as in the side quest Moreland had described his men undertaking—to find his own uncle's missing bride. A missing bride whose description fit the woman he'd just publicly claimed as wife.

One look at Leah, her lips clamped tightly together and her arms crossed protectively in front of her, and he knew she'd be sharing no more of her story with him this night.

"Suit yerself, my lady." He turned his back to her, pounding at his saddle bag in preparation for lying down. "Just remember that's it no ever a good idea to stray too far from the truth in the stories you tell. No more than it is to keep yer traveling companions in the dark about what dangers they might expect to encounter."

Whether she was willing to admit it or not, something in what the knight had said downstairs had made her uncomfortable. He'd seen her reaction to the man's words and, though he'd known her only a short time, he realized it was more than her weariness from a day on the road that had hastened her desire to depart from the dining hall.

"Here. Take this." Leah had moved close, his plaid she'd worn all evening cradled in her arms. "I've got the blankets on the cot so you'll need this."

As he reached for the woolen, his fingertips brushed against hers and the resulting tingle reminded him of her injury from the night before.

"When did you lose yer bandage?" He caught up her wrist and pulled her hand down toward him for a closer look.

"I didn't lose it," she denied. "I just didn't need it anymore."

He ignored her attempt to resist him because he had no intention of being thwarted in his inspection of her injury. Silly woman. The cut on her thumb had been deep and he wanted to make sure there was no redness or swelling.

It was bad enough that she'd likely been sent by the Fae and needed to avoid the English for some reason she didn't choose to share. The very last thing he wanted to add to all that would be his having to care for her if she were brought low by a fever.

He turned her hand over, drawing it closer to the meager firelight even as she pulled against him.

Nothing. No redness, no swelling, not even a hint of her thumb ever having been marred with an injury.

He rubbed the pad of his thumb over the now unblemished spot and looked up. Immediately her gaze darted away, toward the ceiling, toward the door, anywhere but at him.

"I told you it wasn't that bad to start with," she muttered.

When she pulled against his hold again, he released her. She stumbled in her haste, sitting down heavily on her cot before she blew out the candle and quickly curled up under the blanket, her head on the pillow.

He studied her unmoving form for several minutes before settling down on his side to stare into the flames.

It wasn't that bad to start with?

Of all the poor character accusations Drew might fully deserve, he could not be rightly accused of being a fool. He'd seen the cut on her thumb with his own two eyes. Her blood stained the hem of his plaid where he'd stanched the flow from the wound.

And now, with barely a day passed since the injury? It might as well never have happened.

Though he knew there could be only one explanation for such a thing, he simply didn't like the explanation presenting itself.

She wasn't merely sent by the Fae for purposes of their own. She likely *was* one of the Fae.

Ten

~

She was lost, hiding in a small dark hole, just seconds away from being found. Panic burned its way into her throat like a hot acid, bubbling up from her chest until she'd thought she'd drown in it. Still the echo of footsteps came closer and closer. She huddled in the dark, taking a backward step that sent her hurtling down into a black void. Falling. Helpless.

Leah awoke with a start, beads of perspiration dotting her forehead as she tried to remember where she was.

A dream. It was only a dream.

Unlike the ones her sister used to have, Leah's dreams were nothing more than her unconscious mind trying to assimilate all her stress and worries. Still, her heart pounded against her chest like an animal trying to escape her body.

So much for rationalization.

She'd only just managed to recapture some small measure of normal calm when she heard the noise.

A rustling sound, soft and quiet, like something dragging over stone.

Her muscles tensed, freezing her in place, terror washing over her as though she were a child caught in a nightmare. Except that the noise she'd heard was real, not a part of the nightmare she'd awakened from.

Barely daring to breathe, she forced open her eyes and slowly shifted the woolen blanket away from her face. An ambient flickering light filtered through the room, cast by the flames burning in the little fireplace.

Straight ahead of her she could see a plain wooden door. Closed. Okay. She knew where she was. This was the room in the monastery. The room she shared with Andrew.

Somewhat reassured, she filled her lungs with a great gulp of air. That had to be it. He must have made the noise. She twisted a little more, peering down toward the fire where he should be sleeping.

Not sleeping.

She shifted to get a better view, pushing the blanket off her head.

What the hell?

If she didn't know better, she'd swear he was practicing yoga poses.

Half-naked yoga poses.

Oh my.

Unable to take her eyes off him, she swallowed, her throat as dry as if she'd been stranded in the desert. If he wasn't the most gorgeous thing she'd ever seen, she didn't know what was. Her heart pounded in her chest again, but it wasn't fear that set it to racing this time.

It was Andrew.

Shirtless, with only his plaid wrapped low around his hips, he stood in perfect profile. The fire sent patterns of light and dark flickering over his back as he slid one foot behind him and lowered his body into the controlled lunge of the Warrior.

If she'd had him demonstrating those poses for her years ago, she might have ended up with a higher grade in that gym class. Or flunked entirely.

After a few moments, he returned to his original position. When he once again stretched out his arms, muscles rippled and she shivered, feeling as if a wave of heat flowed the length of her body.

It was only as he extended the other leg that she heard the noise again, as if his limb wouldn't quite cooperate in the operation. His body shook, like he was off-balance, and she realized his face had contorted in a grimace as he pushed down into the lunge again.

"What are you doing?" The words were out before she could stop them.

His concentration broken, he collapsed to his knee, head bent as if in prayer.

"Go back to sleep, Leah. I dinna mean to awaken you." He sounded winded when he spoke, as if he'd been at this for a long time.

"You didn't wake me. I had a nightmare." She pushed herself up to sit, letting the blanket fall off her shoulders. She was much too warm to need it at the moment anyway. "What were you doing? Was that yoga?"

He didn't answer right away and for a moment she wondered if he'd even heard her question. Instead, he pushed himself to stand and, keeping his back to her, he clasped his hands behind him while staring into the fire.

"I doona ken the name of what I do. Many years ago, I took wounds in battle. My muscles stiffen if I doona work to keep them active."

A logical explanation. Of course anyone at any time could figure out how to bend and stretch their bodies. Her brain must have been deprived of more oxygen in that river than she'd thought to come up with something so ridiculous as to assume he was practicing yoga poses.

And yet, his movements had seemed so fluid, so structured, so . . . classically eastern.

As she mulled over his explanation, he turned to face her, the firelight glinting off his bare chest, highlighting the contours of sheer muscled beauty. Perfection if not for the silvery scar jaggedly cutting a path that began at his shoulder and disappeared beneath the low-hanging waist of his plaid.

She wondered briefly that she hadn't noticed the scar night before last when his shirt had been draped across a bush to dry. Of course, he'd kept his plaid secured over that side of his body, or certainly she would have. It wasn't the sort of thing she could easily miss.

"That must have been some battle." And he must have been one lucky guy to have survived it.

"This?" His hand traced the path the scar took down his left side. "Different battle."

He'd been wounded in battle more than once. Hello? Fourteenth century, she reminded herself. The history books wouldn't call it a brutal time for nothing.

"You should try to go back to sleep. The sun will be up soon and we'll need to be on our way." He pulled on his boots as he spoke without looking in her direction.

She nodded her understanding, still unable to drag her eyes from his bare chest as if she'd never been taught the first thing about manners.

He waited for a moment more and then caught up his shirt from the little stool where it lay. With a flick and a flutter, the linen closed down over the sight Leah found so fascinating and, at last, the spell was broken. She leaned her head back against the wall and stared up at the ceiling, eyes closed, still envisioning him shirtless as if the image had been burned into her eyelids.

Good thing he'd had his plaid on or she might have been tempted to . . .

The sound of the door opening wiped the vision from her mind.

"Where are you going?"

Andrew smiled at her from the doorway.

"The monks rise well before the sun and I've arrangements to make before we leave. You should try to go back to sleep for a little longer." With that, he was gone.

Right. Sleep. Like there was any chance she could sleep now, with all those totally inappropriate thoughts about Andrew and his chiseled naked chest dancing through her head.

Even if she could manage to put that out of her thoughts, there were plenty of other worries to keep her eyes wide open, from how many days of travel remained before they arrived at Dun Ard all the way up to and including what sort of reception she might find when she reached her destination. And to top it all off? English soldiers running around somewhere here in the monastery. Not just any English soldiers, mind you, but ones who had traveled from England with the man Richard had decided she should marry. English soldiers who were looking for *her*, whether they knew it or not.

Maybe even searching right this minute. Searching for a woman who matched her description. And if they discovered her? They'd drag her butt back to Mac-Quarrie Keep before she had the chance to find the help her family so desperately awaited, and Grandpa Hugh would have absolutely zero chance of survival locked away in the auld tower.

No, there'd be no more sleep for her this morning.

Tossing away the woolen blanket, she clambered off the bed and looked around the little room, her gaze settling on the only piece of furniture other than the bed.

The desk, obviously made from solid wood, turned out to be considerably heavier than it looked.

It took some effort to drag it in front of the door, but once it was done, she felt better. Granted, if the soldiers did come and demand entrance, it wouldn't slow them down them for long. Still, it was the best she could do right now.

She stood a few moments longer, staring at her handiwork, as she rubbed the pendant she wore between her thumb and forefinger. If only Andrew were at her side.

"Well, this is stupid," she muttered, pushing her hair out of her face. It was irrational to wish for Andrew. If the soldiers actually came for her, his being there couldn't very well stop them.

For a fact there would be no going back to sleep,

but simply standing in the middle of the room stressing over what was to come was absolutely crazy-making.

She whipped the blanket off the bed and folded it neatly before gathering Andrew's things off the floor and doing the same with them.

If nothing else, she could see to it that everything was in readiness to leave as soon as he returned.

Drew strode the length of the hallway and took the winding steps down to the main level, regret pounding in his head.

The only bright spot in his life at the moment was that his sister-in-law had been right. The stretching poses she'd shown him had helped his leg a little.

Now if he could only find a stretch to soothe his wounded pride.

He would give anything not to have woken Leah. Anything to take back her having seen him.

Though, if she'd had a nightmare as she claimed, it might have been equally upsetting for her to have awakened to find herself alone.

Equally upsetting? Hardly. He was fooling himself to even attempt that rationalization. He hadn't missed her staring at the hideous scars on his chest. She hadn't been able to tear her eyes away from the marks, her mouth hanging open as if there were no words to account for his disfigurement.

And she hadn't even seen the worst of it, not by any stretch. If the woman thought his chest wounds distasteful, the one stretching from his thigh to his hip would send her screaming from the—

Stop it!

He paused in midstep, struggling to clear his thoughts and relax his fisted hands.

What Leah thought was of no consequence to him. He might be hideous but she might well be Fae, and given a choice between the two? There was no question which he found more distasteful.

Resolved, he continued to the great hall, stopping in front of a small wooden box that sat near the door. The silver coins he pulled from his sporran landed with a dull *thud* when he dropped them through the slot into the coffer. Either the priory hadn't seen many guests of late or their guests hadn't felt obliged to contribute to the brothers' good work.

"Blessings on you for your continued generosity, Andrew."

Drew spun around to find Brother John standing behind him. How the old monk could move so silently was beyond his reason, but it wasn't the first time the prior had managed to surprise him.

"You'll be on yer way soon?"

Drew nodded his answer. The sooner they were away from the priory, the better.

"Do you think I might trouble yer kitchens for victuals to carry with us this day?" While he could easily go a full day without stopping to eat, he wasn't so sure about his traveling companion. A simple fare of bread and cheese would enable them to keep moving without the need for a break to prepare a meal.

"It's no trouble. I'll see to it myself. Is there anything else we might do to assist you and yer lady?"

Actually, there was something else.

"I would be grateful for the loan of a mount for my wife." Not having to ride double should increase the ground they could cover each day. "I'll have it returned to you as soon as possible."

In answer, the prior clapped his hands twice and the young novice Drew had seen last night came running down the hall as if he'd been waiting behind a nearby door for exactly such a summons.

"Have the stables make ready our guest's horse and tell the stable master to choose one of our gentler mounts for Lady MacAlister. Hurry now, Rufus. Our guests have a long day ahead of them and are anxious to be on their way."

"My thanks, Brother John."

"No trouble at all, lad. I'll see to it that the kitchens make ready a light repast to carry along with you. It'll be waiting with yer mounts when you and yer lady are ready to depart."

Drew bobbed his head respectfully before taking his leave of the prior and heading back upstairs to the room he shared with Leah.

Other than Brother John and young Rufus, no one appeared to be up and about yet, a fact Drew took as a positive sign. If he could just get Leah up and moving quickly, they might be fortunate enough to be on their way without encountering Moreland or his men again.

He paused in front of the door to his room, sparing only a moment to debate his next action. A knock seemed the only chivalrous way to enter and yet, if she slept, a knock loud enough to wake her risked waking others.

He needn't have worried.

"Who's there?" sounded in response to a light rap of his knuckles against the wood.

"Drew," he answered, pushing the door open as he spoke.

Only the door didn't open more than a crack.

"What in the name of all that's holy?" Bracing his legs, he shoved his shoulder into the heavy wood, his efforts rewarded by a loud scraping noise.

"Hold on for just a minute." Leah's hissed order wafted through the small opening, followed by a distinctly unladylike grunt and more scraping.

Hold on? He didn't think so.

Another shove and the door gave way enough for him to slip through the opening.

Leah stood a few feet away, hands on her hips, her lips pursed in what he already recognized to be her look of irritation. Next to her, still braced against the door, stood the wooden desk that had earlier resided at the foot of the bed.

Drew arched an eyebrow, pointedly looking from her to the desk and back again. "What had you thought to accomplish with that?"

She shrugged, folding her arms in front of her. "I thought it might slow down any unwelcome visitors."

"Ah."

Apparently she'd been more worried about the English soldiers than he'd realized.

A quick glance around the room told him she'd been busy as well as worried. Their things sat on the bed, all packed and prepared for them to leave.

He motioned toward the bundles. "You're ready to resume our journey, then?"

She nodded her agreement, throwing the plaid over her head and flipping the tail around her shoulders in a quick, practiced motion. "Ready."

He carried the bundles, with her padding along quietly behind until they reached the stairs.

"I don't suppose you happened to bump into . . . um . . . anyone in particular while you were down here before?" Her voice was barely more than a whisper.

"I saw only Brother John. None of the other guests stirred in the hall, if that's what yer asking."

"Thank goodness for that," she murmured, sounding relieved.

He completely agreed. For a change, good luck appeared to be on his side.

They hurried along, their footsteps echoing through the deserted hall, into the entryway and out through the great door.

One look at the bailey and he stopped. Behind him, Leah bumped into his back.

There, directly ahead of them, the novice Rufus waited with their mounts, flanked by Moreland and all his men.

"I guess that explains why you didn't see any of those guys inside, huh?" Leah whispered as she peeked around his back, fisting her hands in the material of his shirt.

"How fare you this morning, my friends?" Moreland's deep voice boomed through the bailey. "We've waited our departure to accompany you on your journey this day."

Proof once again that luck was a fickle bitch where he was concerned.

Eleven

*C*ould it possibly get any worse than this?

Leah pressed against Andrew's back, doing her best to appear subtle in her attempts to study the English soldiers surrounding their horses.

Crapola.

Surely Andrew could come up with some excuse to keep these men from riding along with them today. Having them around was bad. Very bad. Because that Moreland guy had to be at least halfway intelligent to be a knight and halfway was probably more than enough for him to eventually figure out that *she* was the woman he sought. He'd already told them she resembled the description he had.

Crapola and double crapola.

As if he read her thoughts, Andrew spoke up, his deep voice vibrating in the ear she held against his back.

"Our thanks, Sir Moreland, but my wife and I would never think to ask such an inconvenience of you and yer men. We ken the importance of yer quest and we'd be naught but a burden to slow you down."

"Nonsense, MacAlister." Moreland stepped up into his stirrup, seating himself on the back of his mount as his men followed suit. "We would be remiss in our duties to our king's loyal subjects if we left the two of you to manage on your own. As you well know, dangers lurk in the wilderness of your journey. My men and I will see to your safety."

Andrew started forward and, reluctantly, Leah let go her grip on his shirt, breaking the oddly comforting connection she'd had with him. As silly as it was, a wave of relief flooded over her when he reached back to grasp her arm and guide her to his side as they made their way down the stairs.

He was only one man. It wasn't as if he could actually make a difference should Moreland and the pack who followed him realize she was his uncle's intended bride.

And yet, with his hand at the small of her back, she felt somehow protected.

"There's no a need for you to slow yer own progress on our account. We'll make my sister's home by nightfall, so we've no so much wilderness to cover in our travels this day."

Leah relaxed into Drew's hold when his hands tightened around her waist possessively. His actions accompanied his words as if he were accustomed to lifting her up onto her mount on a regular basis, giving it no thought as he spoke.

"So much the better," Moreland replied. "Accompanying you to your sister's home will allow for easy entry."

"Easy entry?" Andrew echoed, his hands dropping to his sides. "I'm no sure I understand yer meaning."

Moreland chuckled, his eyes reflecting none of the mirth he vocalized. "But surely you do understand that we intend to search everywhere for Wallace and the traitors who follow him? That means in every keep and castle we encounter. Granted, only those who share the rebels' cause would dare deny us entry, but why strain the good graces of the king's loyal subjects when there's no need? According to the prior, your family is well known in these parts. We see it as an advantageous barter. We'll protect you on your journey and you can repay us through your good will and knowledge of your neighbors' loyalty."

They planned to search every home in the Highlands?

Leah felt like slapping her head at their stupidity. Did they not understand that many of these Scots were so highly territorial they didn't even welcome their own let alone those riding under the banner of King Edward?

No wonder the history books would be brimming with battles.

Andrew apparently shared her concern.

"I canna speak to my neighbors' political leanings. But I'd be surprised if any, even those whose loyalty to Edward is without question, would willing open their gates to yer inspection."

"As if this godforsaken place holds any loyal to our king," one of Moreland's men scoffed.

"God has not forsaken Scotland, my sons." Brother John's soft voice drew all heads his direction as he joined them at the foot of the stairs. "He resides here, in fact, inside the walls of our priory."

"Standish!" Moreland barked.

"My apologies, good brother. I meant no offense."

The man who had spoken dipped his head respectfully in the prior's direction though Leah could find no sincerity in his face.

"None taken." Brother John favored them all with one of his gentle smiles. "Still, Andrew makes a point. In these troublesome times, many a good Highlander is reluctant to open his gates to a band of strangers."

"And ten men—even good ones such as these who follow you, Moreland—ten men are no enough to force yer way through castle walls." Andrew climbed onto his mount as he spoke, then guided his horse closer to Leah's.

Moreland nodded his head thoughtfully, as if he considered their objections. Still, Leah would swear that something in his eyes belied his every action.

That or she simply didn't trust the man.

"I see your concern now. But, truly, you've no cause to worry over us. These are but a small sampling of the men who crossed over the Tweed with me. We broke into smaller groups to search more effectively but, should we run into any resistance, it would take no time at all to reassemble the full complement."

"Well, that settles that, I suppose. Are you quite ready, dearling?"

Andrew reached out to cover Leah's hand with his, giving her a smile that, as her mother used to say, all but curled her toes. She'd give him credit for one thing. The man would make one heck of a Hollywood heart-throb and his acting was absolutely first rate. If she didn't know better, just watching him in action, even *she'd* be tempted to believe they actually were newly-weds.

What the hell had he managed to get himself into?

Drew cast a quick glance at the woman who rode by his side. She sat, back regally straight, eyes fixed forward, as calm as if every word of the story he'd told these soldiers was fact.

But of course she would. It was exactly what he would expect of a Fae.

He couldn't help but wonder if in truth she felt as calm as she looked. He certainly didn't.

By day's end they'd wind around into the valley where MacPherson Hall nestled. Him dragging a passel of English soldiers and a woman on the run right into his sister's home. And not just any woman, but one who was likely related to the Fae.

And though he worried a little about his brother-in-law's dislike of the English, it was his sister's temper that gave him more concern. With Moreland and his men tagging along, he'd have no choice but to carry on his charade about bringing home a new wife. Sallie would make his life a living hell when she finally learned he had lied to her, no matter what his reason now.

He only hoped Leah understood the importance of keeping up their story once they reached MacPherson Hall.

The thought ate at him, his mind conjuring up likely scenarios of what could go wrong, until he finally accepted the fact that he couldn't risk simply *hoping*. He needed to make sure Leah understood what was at stake here.

He reached for her reins, pulling up on his own as he did so.

"Moreland! My lady must stop for a short while to attend to her needs. Here, while we're no so very far from the water, will do her well."

Leah's eyes had widened with her surprise when her head snapped his direction, but she made not a single sound to contradict his claim.

This spot should do fine. Claiming his wife's need for privacy would allow them to walk back through the trees and brush to reach the small loch. Somewhere along the way, he'd be able to make sure Leah understood what they faced.

He eased off his horse, grateful his leg hadn't tightened into uselessness yet, and made his way around to Leah. She reached down to him, allowing him to take her weight and assist her from her seat.

"My thanks, husband. It's been a long ride."

She played her part so well, he could kiss her.

"I assume yer men will be considerate of my lady's need for privacy?" Drew arched an eyebrow and met Moreland's hard stare without flinching.

The knight looked away first. "You may count on it, MacAlister."

Leah gripped his hand as they made their way into the forest, a bit tighter than necessary to his way of thinking. Perhaps that outward calm she displayed wasn't an accurate reflection of how she felt after all.

"How are we . . ." she began, but instantly went silent when he gently squeezed her fingers and shook his head.

Though he didn't particularly trust Moreland not to send someone to spy on them, they'd have a better chance at privacy the farther away they got.

Only their footsteps in the underbrush broke the stillness surrounding them until, at last, he heard the water just ahead through the dense growth.

"We should be fine to speak here, as long as we keep our voices low."

She nodded, taking a deep breath and letting it out slowly before she spoke. "How are we going to get rid of them?"

As if he hadn't asked himself that very question more times that he could count since he'd stood on the courtyard steps this morning.

"I dinna suppose we will. No until we've reached MacPherson Hall. Perhaps once they satisfy themselves that my sister's home disna harbor the rebels they seek, they'll leave us in peace."

"So you weren't kidding? We're really headed to your sister's home? Isn't that kind of . . . Ouch!"

She'd walked ahead of him, leaning forward to push her way through the brambles of bushes separating them from the water they could hear just ahead.

Blackthorn!

"Be still," he ordered, reaching out to loosen her hair from the tree's grip.

He should have recognized them from the little white flowers covering the bushes. What else bloomed so early in the spring? Not a tree, really, more of a large bush, its long, sharp thorns had tangled in her hair the moment she had tried move past them.

"Serves me right," she muttered. "I wasn't paying the least bit of attention to what I was doing. Even I know better than to walk into blackthorn."

He pulled at her hair as gently as possible, working it loose from the bush. She must have jerked back after walking into the limbs, because the hair seemed to have worked its way around the thorns into a nice tight tangle.

"There," he said at last, pulling the final bit free. "And we've no even been forced to leave a lock behind."

"Thanks." She rubbed a spot on the top of her head, a rueful smile playing over her lips. "I've certainly managed not to miss a single hazard in the last couple of days. Should we try to find a way around all this?"

"No." They didn't have the time to hunt for a better way down to the water. The longer they were away, the more likely Moreland was to send someone to look for them. "Here."

He pulled her face to his chest and ducked his head over hers to shelter her. Lifting an arm, he pushed sideways through the brambles like an old ram in search of a mate. One giant shove and a few scratches later they were through to the other side, only a little worse for the wear.

"Like my own personal bulldozer," she laughed, pulling back from him.

Her eyes sparkled with her laughter, a brown so rich he felt for a moment they were deep beyond any end. And her hair. Torn loose from its bindings, it framed her face in gold curls, lying softly against cheeks pink from her exertion.

"At yer service, my lady."

Whatever a "bulldozer" was, he found he was happy to serve as hers, in spite of the inconvenience. Just looking at her like this lightened his heart.

As they worked their way around some boulders to the water's edge, he glanced down to his arm, where an uncomfortable stinging drew his attention. Blood formed a bright red line where thorns had sliced through his sleeve and into his skin.

"Oh, look at your poor arm!" Leah lifted her hand as if to touch his wound, jerking back at the last moment. "You better wash that off. Those thorns have some natural secretion on them that makes the wound really sore."

She spoke the truth, he knew from experience.

Squatting down next to the loch, he scooped up a handful of water and splashed it over the injury. As if the shock of the cold water cleared his mind, he thought once again of why they were here.

"We must speak quickly in case Moreland sends someone to follow us."

"You really think he'd do that? He promised to allow me some privacy." She dropped to her knees next to him looking up into his face. Apparently she found her answer there. "Oh, all right. Of course he would. That's what soldiers do."

"Exactly."

Drew splashed another handful of water onto his arm, giving only passing thought to whether he should take time to bandage the wound, deciding it didn't warrant care right now. Not with more pressing matters at hand.

"I've no idea how long Moreland will remain at MacPherson Hall. But for the time he's there, we'll need to stick to our story. Having him realize we've lied to him willna be good for us or for my sister's family, you ken?"

She nodded her understanding, her eyes large and serious. "I suppose so. The last thing I want is for him to figure out who I—" She cut off her words, clamping her mouth shut, her eyes darting guiltily up to his.

Again the suspicion crossed his mind that she hid as much from him as she'd shared.

"The last thing I want is to bring trouble down on the heads of my family. So we're agreed, then? You'll continue yer pretense no matter what happens. I need yer oath on it because you'll find when you meet my sister, she can be a wee bit . . ."

The distinctive crackle of a careless footstep beyond the bushes into the forest stopped him in midsentence.

He had no doubt that Moreland's spy approached. But rather than jump guiltily to his feet, perhaps, with a little luck, he could turn this into an opportunity to convince the Englishman the story they told was true.

A little luck and Leah's complete and unquestioning cooperation.

"Dinna fash yerself over meeting my family, dearling." He raised his voice as he grasped her upper arms, praying she would understand they had an audience. "They'll grow to love you even as I do."

Crushing her to him, he ignored her surprise as he covered her mouth with his. He breathed her in, conscious only of the feel of her in his embrace.

Her mouth opened and, as if with a mind of its own, his tongue dipped inside, robbing him for an instant of any knowledge of where he was or why he did this. All he knew was that he was lost in the intoxicating richness of her mouth.

He barely noticed when her hands fluttered up to his arms. Barely noticed the sparkle of colors dancing across his closed eyelids or the sensation of movement rippling through his biceps.

He knew only that it seemed she had melted into his arms, their connection so intense he felt as if they might merge into one person at any moment.

The sound of a man clearing his throat nearby brought him rudely back to reality.

He broke the kiss slowly, gazing down at Leah's upturned face, her eyes closed, her full lips parted. Only a second round of throat-clearing, obviously more forced than the last, kept him from losing himself once again in the woman in his arms.

Looking up, his eyes met those of Moreland. How the knight had managed to get so close to them was beyond his ability to reason at the moment.

Moreland looked almost embarrassed, but not enough to avert his stare.

"Your pardon, MacAlister. I'd no wish to intrude on an intimate moment, but we were concerned when you and your lady did not return."

"We were . . . um . . . detained," Drew responded, peeling Leah's fingers from his arm while he spoke and pushing himself to stand. His heart still pounded in his chest so hard he was surprised those around him couldn't hear it.

"Yes. I can see you were."

Leah's cheeks flooded with pink as he helped her to her feet. He'd give her credit. She acted her part very well indeed. For his own part, he refused to allow his mind to think on what had just happened between them.

Moreland's usual smirk was firmly in place by the time he turned on his heel and headed back the way he'd come.

"Are you ready, my lady?" Drew asked, more for Moreland's benefit than Leah's.

"I am, my husband," she responded, her dark eyes unreadable before she looked down.

They followed Moreland at a discreet distance, neither of them speaking as they skirted the blackthorn bushes they'd forged through on their way to the water's edge.

When they reached the clearing, the soldiers had already mounted up and made ready to leave, their quiet conversations a low hum in the background.

"Yer oath, Leah. You've no given it yet," he whispered, her soft hair brushing against his cheek as he leaned in close.

"I swear it," she whispered back.

He grasped her arm, pulling back immediately when she winced at his touch as if in pain.

"What . . ." he began, but she silenced him with a soft finger to his lips.

"It's nothing."

She turned, placing her foot to the stirrup, and he fit his hands around her waist, lifting her to her seat.

Only then did he see it. A thin red line cutting across her sleeve.

Once in his saddle, he drew his horse up alongside hers. "Leah?"

She shook her head. "Forget it. I told you, it's nothing."

How could he have missed her wound before? Though the material of her clothing showed no sign of damage, the trace of blood on her sleeve clearly indicated an injury like the one the thorns had left on his arm when they'd sliced through his shirt.

Exactly like it.

Cautiously, he reached up to run his fingers over the tear in his skin, anticipating a sting of contact that didn't come.

Pulling the shirt from his skin, he peered through the hole torn by the thorns to find his flesh smooth and unmarked.

By the saints!

He felt as if the air had been sucked from his lungs with the realization of what had happened. Any question he'd had about Leah was a thing of the past now. There was no longer any doubt.

The woman traveling at his side was definitely Fae.

Twelve

Leah's stomach knotted into a hard, sick little ball, so tightly wound, she hardly noticed her aching muscles or the sting in her arm.

After hours of riding, they at last made their way down a brush-covered hillside toward a valley stretching out below them. On the other side, up a steep incline, the rays of the setting sun shone against a rather imposing castle battlement.

MacPherson Hall and Andrew's family awaited her.

The guilt eating at her twisted her stomach another notch tighter.

Poor guy. First he'd risked his own life to jump into that loch to save her, then he'd offered to show her the way to Dun Ard. Since then, he'd just had one problem after another, all thanks to her, not the least of which was the crowd of English soldiers he led right straight into his family's home.

Somewhere, somehow, she meant to figure out a way to pay him back for all he was doing for her and for all the trouble he put up with as a result of it.

But first she'd have to make it through meeting his family and pretending to be his new wife.

And no doubt, somewhere along the way, he was going to demand an explanation for what had happened when she'd touched him back there next to the loch. An explanation she'd like for herself as well as for him.

Her face heated again at the memory of the moment and the knot in her stomach dropped several inches lower.

It made no sense at all. He'd only been playacting for Moreland's benefit. She'd known that from the first moment. His touch, the kiss, all of it was no more real than their pretending to be married.

And yet . . .

The feel of his lips on hers had taken her completely by surprise. It was like nothing she'd ever experienced or even imagined. When he'd held her in his arms, it had been as if her brain had ceased to function properly.

Obviously. Otherwise she never would have clamped her hand over that cut on his arm. On her arm now, thanks to her cursed Faerie "gift."

How the hell was she going to explain that little episode?

She wasn't. Not unless Andrew MacAlister believed in Faeries.

That thought drove the knot right back up into her stomach.

Maybe when they reached Dun Ard the MacKiernans would be able to help her come up with something. They were, after all, Faerie descendants. Surely they had experience in inventing rational explanations for all the bizarre things they must have done in front of normal people.

Clinging to that hope seemed her only reasonable course of action as they neared MacPherson Hall.

Now if she could only come up with some reasonable excuse to give herself for her reaction to Andrew's kiss.

"Who goes there?"

The wall guard's shout postponed her having to deal with that particular issue. At least for now.

"Andrew MacAlister," the man at her side shouted back. And then, belatedly, "And friends."

Almost immediately the clanking of chains sounded and the enormous wood and iron gates slowly lifted, allowing them entrance.

Men filled the bailey by the time they passed through the wall tunnel, each one armed with a sword or an axe or some other outrageously sharp-looking implement.

Leah shivered at the sight.

She'd seen plenty of armed men at MacQuarrie Hall over the years, but nothing like this. These men spreading out to form a circle around the new arrivals behaved as if they'd trained to defend their home. Their actions left little doubt that they meant business.

The English soldiers they rode with appeared to be approaching the situation with equal seriousness.

"What's this, little brother?" one of the men called out as they came to a stop. "What worry have you brought into my home?"

Andrew moved his horse even closer to hers before answering, reaching out to grasp her reins as if he feared being separated from her.

Or perhaps that was only her fear.

"Hold yer men, Ran. These are soldiers, for a fact, but they've acted in good faith providing protection to us on our journey this day."

The man called Ran snorted his disbelief, crossing his arms in front of him.

"Protecting you from what? There's none here what would wish you harm. Yer claim makes no sense."

Leah laid a hand on Andrew's forearm, feeling it tense under her touch.

"I'd ask you to welcome Sir Moreland and his men as you do me. They mean no harm to any here."

"We bring no threat to any of King Edward's loyal subjects." Moreland's voice rang out across the bailey, greeted with complete silence.

"Drew!"

Leah looked to the woman who called. Small in stature, with fiery red hair, she stood at the head of the staircase, but not for long. In a heartbeat she was down the steps and at Ran's side.

"What's going on here? You confront my brother and his friends like they're some pack of criminals? What's wrong with you?" she demanded loudly. "If Drew says they're friends, that's what they are. Bid them welcome to our home as such."

Ran nodded and the men in the bailey lowered their weapons. A moment later, the soldiers did the same.

Next to her, Andrew slid off his horse. Before his feet hit the ground, his sister was at his side, throwing her arms around him in a hug.

"My thanks, Sallie."

He murmured the words so quietly, Leah strained to hear them and his sister's reply.

"You've no a need to thank me. You ken that."

One arm slung over Sallie's shoulder, he made his way around the horses to Leah's side, where he lifted his hands to help her dismount.

"And who might this be?" Andrew's sister asked as she stepped back, a warm, welcoming smile lighting her face.

His eyes locked on Leah's and she felt the weight of his impending answer like a lead ball in the pit of her stomach.

"My wife," he said as he lifted her down. "This is my wife, Leah. And this . . ." He held her eyes for a second longer before turning toward the woman he introduced. "This is my sister, Sallie."

Sallie's mouth opened once and then closed, as if she considered what she'd heard and worked at processing the words before she was able to respond. In no time at all, she appeared to have made a complete recovery, and the smile that had graced her face returned, even larger than before.

"Well, Drew, you've plenty of explaining to do and that's a fact. But for now, I'll get my new sister inside while you and Ran can see to settling yer friends for the night. Come with me, Leah."

Sallie put an arm around Leah's waist and urged her forward, toward the great staircase. Leah took one last look over her shoulder as the bossy redhead hustled her forward, just in time to see Andrew wink at her.

No, not Andrew. *Drew.* The name his sister had called him. Leah rolled it over in her mind and realized it was perfect for him. As his wife, it would only make sense for her to call him that as well.

"I've so many questions, I hardly ken the place to start," Sallie rattled on as they made their way up the stairs toward the door that would take them into the keep. "But I've no doubt yer weary after a day spent on horseback in the company of all those men."

"I am at that," Leah responded, grateful for any excuse that prevented her having to answer all those questions without Drew at her side.

"Jane," Sallie beckoned to a young woman as they entered the hall. "We need the large guest chamber made ready for the night. And tell Cook to prepare something to send up for our guests before they retire. Hurry now."

They crossed the entryway to a winding stone staircase, where Sallie took the lead. Midway up the steps Leah's legs began to tremble with the effort of climbing the narrow stairway. Whatever nervous energy had carried her through her arrival here had completely deserted her.

As they moved into the hallway of the second floor, a door ahead of them flew open and three small bodies headed their direction.

"Patsy says Uncle Drew has arrived!" the tallest child exclaimed as the boys skidded to a stop in front of Sallie.

"That he has, Duncan. He's out in the courtyard with yer da. You and yer brothers may go down to see him if you—" Sallie stopped talking, shaking her head as the boys raced off, pushing and shoving at one another in their haste, not waiting for her to finish. "They'll be the death of me yet, those three will."

The smile on her face clearly belied her complaint.

"Your sons?" Leah latched onto a subject she hoped would delay any personal questions directed at her as Sallie continued down the hallway.

"Aye. Duncan, Angus, and Connor. The only thing they like more than a visit from any one of their uncles is an excuse to escape their bedtime. They'll be terrorizing the whole of the castle until they're rounded up again. Patsy!"

A young woman popped her head out of a doorway just ahead. "My lady?"

"They've taken off for the courtyard. You'd best go after them. Likely you'll have to clean them up again before putting them to bed."

Patsy bobbed her head and hurried away as Sallie pushed open another door and led the way inside.

The chamber seemed smaller than it really was, dwarfed by the enormous bed centered against the far wall that seemed to suck up all the space in the room.

"I'll just get this fire going and we'll have it warm for you in no time." Sallie knelt in front of the fireplace as she spoke. "You'll want to get out of those dirty things, no doubt. I'll have the maids bring up a bathing vessel and water as soon as they . . . ah, here they are now."

Two young women, their arms piled high with linens, rushed into the room and set about making up the bed.

"There. That should chase away the chill."

Sallie rose to her feet, dusting her hands together. Behind her the fire had roared to life, its flames licking up toward the chimney casting a flickering glow across the room as the serving girls hurried through their task.

"Now. While we wait for the maids to finish their work, you can satisfy my curiosity. How did you meet my brother? And how long have you known him? All of this comes as such a surprise, though a happy one, indeed."

Leah's tongue suddenly felt three times its normal thickness as she tried frantically to think of answers. Why hadn't she thought to speak of this with Drew? Any story she might invent could easily be found out since she knew so little of the man's life.

"Where is she? I want to see her for myself!" An older woman flounced into the room, hands on her hips.

Whoever she was, she'd saved Leah from having to come up with a response, and for that alone, she already liked the woman.

"My maid tells me yer brother has shown up on our doorstep, bringing with him a new wife. This is the one?"

The woman marched closer, thrusting out her chin in what felt to Leah a most belligerent manner. She might have to reconsider her initial genial thoughts about this woman.

"It is," Sallie answered. "Leah, this is my husband's mother, Anabella. Anabella, my new sister, Leah."

Anabella MacPherson made a great show of circling Leah, peering down her nose like someone inspecting market goods gone bad a day or two past.

"You dinna have the look of anyone I ken," she

huffed, circling one more time. "Did you bring any animals with you?"

Animals? Leah looked from Anabella to Sallie, who shrugged her shoulders as if the whole conversation had gone beyond anyone's ability to control. "Only the horse I rode in on."

"Hmmmm . . ." The older woman continued to study her as if she were examining some new species of insect until at last she stepped back and folded her hands at her waist. "Well, she disna have the look of any of yer departed relatives, nor does she come with a pack of nasty beasties determined to dirty our home. This one will do, I suppose."

"Och, well, thank you for that blessing, Mother MacPherson," Sallie responded, sarcasm dripping in her tone. "I'm sure Drew will be pleased to hear he can keep her now that she's passed yer muster."

"Dinna you take that tone with me, missy." Anabella squared her shoulders, looking deeply offended. A moment later she turned her gaze back on Leah. "And where is it you come from? Who are yer people? How did you come to wed Andrew when we've none of us heard a word about you before?"

"Exactly the things I was trying to ask when you interrupted us with yer nonsense about animals and dead women."

The two women glared at each other briefly and then turned the full force of their stares on Leah.

"Well?" Sallie encouraged. "Tell us everything. How did you meet Drew? When?"

"Your brother is a good man." Not at all what the women had asked, she knew.

"We've neither of us questioned the lad's virtue. Now, speak up, lass, we've no all night to spend on this."

Anabella's rebuke left no doubt in Leah's mind that her time for avoiding conversation was at an end.

"Tell us everything," Sallie encouraged. "We're dying to hear it all."

"I hardly know where to start." Leah paused, once again struggling to find something appropriately vague to say.

"At the beginning, woman! As Sallie says, we want to hear it all."

"Are you badgering my bride, Sallie?" Drew stepped into the room, the smallest of his sister's boys in his arms, the older two trailing along behind. "Leave her be 'til she's had a wee rest, aye? Here." He handed the giggling child over to Sallie. "This, I believe, belongs to you."

Sallie took her son and placed him on his feet with a gentle shove forward toward his brothers.

"You had to ken we'd be wanting to hear all about how you met. It's no like you've said a single word about her to give us any hint before showing up here, wife in tow."

"No like you said a single word," Anabella echoed.

"I'm well aware of what I have and have no said with regard to Leah. There'll be plenty of time for yer questions later. For now, we've had a hard day's journey and would appreciate the opportunity to refresh ourselves before we have to face yer interrogation on the morrow." Drew stepped between the two women, placing a hand on each of their backs, urging them toward the door. "Besides, Ran could use yer help with Sir Moreland, I'm sure."

"Sir Moreland? We've a knight in the hall? You've brought a knight to visit?" Anabella asked, patting her hair with a fluttering hand as she hurried ahead. "Ranald kens nothing about the etiquette of welcoming high-born strangers properly, Sallie. He'll be wanting our assistance, no doubt."

"That he will," Drew answered, the grin breaking over his face in total disagreement with his serious tone.

"We're no done with this," his sister chided as she allowed him to push her into the hallway.

"I'm sure we're no," he agreed, shutting the door and turning to lean his back against it. "You ken now why I felt the need to warn you about my family?"

She did indeed.

"I have no idea how to answer their questions. As soon as they began to ask, I realized I don't know enough about you not to trip myself up in any story I might invent."

He shook his head as if it was of little importance. "Leave that to me. We've bigger concerns at the moment."

"Like what?" She could hardly imagine anything more pressing than the two women he'd just evicted from their chamber.

"For one thing, Moreland has asked Ran's permission to camp his men here for a while."

Not good. Not good at all.

The longer she was around Moreland, the more likely she felt it was he might discover the truth of her identity. Besides, his actions made no sense to her at all. If he were on some great quest to track down rebels, why on earth would he delay his men by staying here?

"A while," she repeated. "How long do you suppose that is, exactly? And if he's already assured himself the men he seeks aren't here, why would he want to stay here and delay his quest?"

"I canna say for fact, but my gut tells me he's staying because of you."

"Me?" she squeaked.

That couldn't be a good thing. Drew himself admitted it was only conjecture. But if he were right . . .

"Why would he do that?" She asked the question, though she feared she already knew the answer.

She hadn't managed to convince him she wasn't the woman he sought.

"An excellent question, indeed. But only one of many questions I'm pondering this day." He walked past her and sat on the edge of the enormous bed, patting a spot beside him in invitation. "Perhaps you'd like to have a seat."

Without a doubt she'd like that. But she wasn't going to.

Unbidden, the memory of his lips on hers as they'd knelt next to the loch crept into her thoughts and heat flamed across her face.

Not next to him. And not on a bed. That wouldn't be proper. Not proper and certainly not prudent. Not at all. She'd already done an excellent job of proving just how little self-control she had around the man.

Instead she sank to the floor in front of the fireplace, holding out her hands as if she wanted to warm them. What she really wanted was to stop them from shaking, but since that didn't seem like something she could change at the moment she dropped them to her lap and clasped them tightly together.

"The time has come and passed for us to keep secrets from each other. I need yer honesty now, Leah."

"Honesty?" Her voice cracked on the word, giving her away as surely as if she'd had a giant neon LIAR tattooed on her forehead.

"I ken what you are," he said, his voice little more than a rough whisper, his eyes boring into her as if he could read the secrets in her soul.

How had he figured out she was the runaway Moreland hunted? If he turned her over to the knight now, all would be lost. She'd have failed the MacQuarries when they needed her the most. Please not now. Not when she was so close to reaching the people who would help her. Could help her. Might help her.

Might toss her out on her butt.

The doubts zinged around inside her head like that little orb of metal in the pinball machines she used to love, each new thought stoking her panic.

"It's not what you think."

"No? Then best you tell me what it is I should think, eh?" He got up off the bed and walked to where she sat, dropping down at her side, facing her, his body so close she could feel the heat rolling off his skin.

Or was that simply the fire behind her?

She couldn't be sure of that any more than she could drag her eyes from his.

"Okay. You're right. No more secrets. I admit it. I'm the one Moreland is hunting for. But it's not as though my family wanted me to marry. I told you about my uncle coming back from England and taking over my grandparents' home, tossing my grandfather into the tower under lock and guard." She stopped to take a breath, puzzled by his look of confusion. "My grand-parents support my decision not to wed. It's Richard who arranged this marriage to seal some alliance with Lord Moreland. He wants me out of the way because my grandfather intended that I should be heir to Mac-Quarrie Keep, not him."

Confusion hardened into anger on Drew's face and she fought the need to put distance between the two of them. What had he expected her to tell him? He'd said he already knew.

"I dinna care about Moreland or the lord he serves. That yer the one he seeks was no really in question to me from the moment he described his quest and spoke of yer matching the description of the woman he sought. From the way he watches yer every move, I've little doubt that he suspects you to be the one he's after, as well. I'm thinking that's why he's arranged to stay on here. No." He leaned closer, his voice taking on the same intensity reflected in his eyes as he continued. "I want yer honesty about *this*." He turned his arm toward her, pulling the torn cloth from the spot on his bicep that had borne the cut of the blackthorn hours earlier.

The cut that even now stung her own flesh.

"Oh, crapola."

How could she have allowed this to happen in the first place? She was always so careful never to touch any wound, never to lay her hands on any person with an illness or an injury. Always.

Not always. Proof of that confronted her now.

When his lips had touched hers, strong and warm, she'd lost the ability to clearly think of anything. She hadn't even tried to think . . . just allowed herself to be swallowed up by the feel of him. It was a feeling so all-consuming, so completely foreign to her, she had nothing for comparison.

"That wasn't supposed to happen." Even to her ears her words sounded ridiculously lame.

"I'm sure it wasn't. But it did. My skin is as unmarked as the day I was born. How? How did you do it?"

He was so close. Her heart raced and it felt as though she couldn't pull enough air into her lungs to feed her body the oxygen she needed.

"I don't know how. It's like a curse I can't control." To her horror, her throat tightened and her eyes prickled with the threat of oncoming tears. She held her breath, opening her eyes as wide as possible but the urge was too strong to deny.

It was so ridiculous to allow him to get to her like this. There was no reason for it. No reason at all. So what if he'd seen something she couldn't explain.

Wouldn't explain.

Because explaining would require that she admit to the horrible creature that lurked in her ancestry and that felt too much like defeat after all these years of striving to be nothing more than a regular Mortal. After all she'd gone through, all she'd done to deny her heritage, this was beyond unfair.

She closed her eyes and dropped her head, hoping to hide the tears that filled her eyes.

But he was having none of it.

With a finger under her chin, he gently lifted her face, looking directly into her eyes.

"No tears, dearling. Dinna do this. I dinna mean for you to weep." He lifted his hands to cup her face, gently wiping one escaping tear from her cheek. "I want only yer honesty."

Dearling. The endearment gripped her heart, squeezing, building the pressure behind her eyes. What on earth was wrong with her? It meant nothing. It was just a word. Likely he'd simply gotten so used to their charade that he didn't even realize what he'd called her.

Her breath hitched in her chest, forcing a hated little hiccup of a sob out against her will.

"Ah, for the love of all the saints," he grumbled, crushing her to his chest, awkwardly patting her back as the unwelcome noises continued to bubble up unbidden.

"I don't do this," she hiccupped into his shoulder, too far gone to stop herself now. "I don't ever do this. Everything has just been so horrible. That hateful Dick showing up and Grandpa Hugh out in the tower, cold and sick and maybe dying, and that awful boat and then thinking I was going to die in that stupid river and then Moreland and, and I'm so tired and my legs hurt and, and . . ." She stopped, trying to catch her breath, fighting to stop the sobs before they consumed her completely.

He murmured to her, soft, unintelligible words of comfort, his fingers combing through her hair as he held her close.

She had been absolutely honest when she'd told those two women that he was a good man. A kind man.

And that kindness pushed her completely over the edge. Her emotions demanded their release, and, as though a dam were bursting in her soul, she utterly, completely surrendered herself to the tears.

What had he done? Leah lay against him, so delicate, so defenseless in his arms, her body shaking with great heaving sobs.

Her despair completely his responsibility.

When he'd made his way up to their room, his nephews playing and laughing at his feet, he'd thought only to confront her with what had happened at the loch this afternoon. In her hands lay the gift, the magic he'd scoured the land in search of all these years. He wanted to know only how she'd managed to heal his wound. More to the point, he wanted to know if she could heal the rest of his body.

But he'd never intended this. Never intended to cause her such pain. In his haste to find the answers he sought, he'd completely ignored all she'd gone through in recent days. He'd completely disregarded her emotional state at his own peril and now he was paying the price for that lapse of good sense.

What did you even do with a woman so distraught? It was beyond his experience.

So he let her cry. Let her wash it all from deep inside. He held her, for how long he had no idea. Murmured to her as if to a child. Stroked her head, letting her silken hair slide through his fingers. Held her until her body stilled and her sobs subsided into nothing more than shaky, watery little sighs.

Sliding one arm under her legs, the other behind her back, he rose to his feet, lifting her as he stood. Her head lay pillowed against his shoulder, one slender arm hooked loosely around his neck as if she'd exhausted herself.

Across the room he carried her, depositing her gently on the big bed before lying down next to her, her back snug up against his chest.

She fit the curve of him like the wooden carving he'd seen in the markets of Inverness. It had appeared at first glance to be a smoothly honed statue carved from a single piece of wood, until the seller had shown him how the whole split apart into two perfectly fitted halves.

Within minutes her breathing deepened and slowed as sleep took her.

He brushed a strand of hair from her face, marveling at the delicate curve of her cheek. Physical desire coursed through him, but stronger still was his overwhelming need to protect her.

She held the answer he'd sought for so long. The means to the healing he needed. He would know her secrets and they would make him a whole man. First thing tomorrow morning.

In the meantime, he would do everything in his power to spare her another breakdown like tonight's. From devising whatever story would satisfy Sallie and her nattering mother-in-law to preventing Moreland from discovering her true identity, he would do it all.

In short, he'd do whatever was necessary to keep her safe.

He tightened his arm around her and she snuggled against him, her silken hair catching against his roughened cheek.

Of course he felt protective. She was the means to his salvation. It only made sense when he thought on it. The Fae had stolen his future from him, so it was only right that it should be a Fae who gave that future back to him.

The Fae in his arms.

Thirteen

As if she would never experience a peaceful sleep again, Leah awoke with a start, disoriented and frightened. She lay in a strange room, in a strange bed, enfolded in the arms of a strange man.

No, not a strange man. Drew held her, his slow, steady breaths puffing over her cheek as he held her close. Relief drove out the panic that had at first threatened to crush her.

Relief that was, in and of itself, strange beyond her ability to comprehend. Never, never in a million years, would she have expected to react to any man like this.

After the trauma she'd endured at the hands of the Nuadian Fae twelve years ago, she'd decided celibacy was her only option. First, the very thought of a man touching her had made her physically ill. Second, even if she could have stomached their touch, the ones she'd met in this century viewed women as little more than brood cows, vessels to bear their children.

Considering that had been the Nuadian Fae's plan for her, to use her to provide them with a stable of gifted half-Fae children, she'd long since determined that celibacy would work especially well for her because she never wanted to have children. She wouldn't be used by Fae or Mortal as nothing more than a baby-maker. Not ever.

In spite of all her determination, all her big talk about avoiding men, here she was, somewhere after sunrise, cuddled up against a strong male chest as if she belonged here.

And *that* was perhaps the strangest piece of all. She felt exactly as if she did belong here. Right here, with Drew's warm body curved around hers, one large arm covering her protectively as if he needed her close by.

Oh, Lord. Pretending to be this man's wife had apparently gone straight to her head. Her imagination really was getting the best of her.

And so what if it was? It felt wonderful, no matter that it was all a fantasy. After everything she'd been through the past few days, who deserved a few moments of unfettered fantasy more than she did?

No one.

Drew was, without a doubt, the most gorgeous man she'd ever met in either century. He was kind, considerate, and brave. Almost perfect, in fact.

She turned her nose into the arm he wrapped around her and breathed in deeply. A faint scent of lemon and mint clung to his skin and his clothing. Just as she'd imagined. He even smelled good.

With a sigh of contentment, she relaxed back against him, luxuriating in his embrace as she let her imagination run free.

It took a moment for her to realize the finger stroking down the side of her cheek, gently tucking a loose curl behind her ear, was actually real and not part of the fantasy she'd allowed herself to drift into.

"Are you feeling more yerself this morning?"

His voice rumbled against her back, sending a shiver down to her toes.

That his first waking thought was concern for her set her heart beating faster until she realized she still lay in his arms, that he was gently tracing her hairline with one finger.

What he must think of her! The heat of embarrassment flowed out from her chest, flooding up to her neck and face. Should she move away or simply answer as if awakening in a man's arms was completely normal?

"I'm fine. I guess I just needed a good rest."

And maybe a brain adjustment. Something that would prevent her from getting herself into such an inappropriate situation again.

"Good." His breath feathered over her ear before he pulled away to sit on the far edge of the bed. "Then you'll have no problem now telling me what you did to heal my arm."

Heal his arm? Her mind floundered to play catch-up. What happened to the Drew who'd held her only moments before? That Drew was worried about *her*, not about what had happened between them back at the loch.

She pushed herself up, kicking her feet free from the shift that had tangled around her feet while she slept. "There's nothing to tell." Rising from the bed, she brushed at the impossible wrinkles in her clothing, keeping her back to Drew.

"I already ken what you are. I just want to understand how you did it." His voice, so low and quiet, rumbled around her as if she still touched him.

It was the second time he'd said that to her in as many days. The last time she'd thought he was talking about her being the woman Moreland hunted, but she'd been wrong.

With a sinking stomach, she turned to meet his gaze head-on. "And just what is it you think you know about me?"

"Yer Faerie," he said, rising to his feet. "And you've the gift of healing. A gift I fully intend to have you make use of to heal my injuries."

"Faerie?" She felt as if she'd been slapped in the face. "I'm no such thing. And you're crazy if you think for one minute there's anything I can do to heal you or anyone else."

She wasn't one of those horrible creatures. Her father might have been Fae, but she refused to be one. She'd renounced all that too long ago to pick up that burden again.

His expression changed then, his eyes going distant and hard. Without another word, he rose to his feet and headed for the door.

"Where are you going?" How stupid had she been to yell at him? There was nothing stopping him from marching directly down the hall to Moreland's room and telling him the woman he hunted was right here.

"If yer no even going to make at attempt at honesty, we've nothing further to discuss." He spoke with his back to her. "I'll send one of the maids up with fresh clothing and a bath."

Then he was gone, slamming the door behind him.

Damn him! Who did he think he was? How dare he be angry with her? It was him doing the accusing, trying to make her admit to being some disgusting, vile creature. She was the one who deserved to make an angry exit from the room.

One little kiss and she'd ruined years of careful living. She'd been so wrong about him. So foolish in letting herself get carried away with what a wonder he was. He wasn't kind or considerate or any of those things. He only wanted to use her, just like everyone else.

"Well, that's not happening, bud!" she fumed. "Nobody's using this girl."

If he thought she was going to admit to being something she hated as much as she hated Faeries, he had another think coming. Just because her father had been a Faerie didn't mean for one second that made her one. She refused to let it be so.

And Drew MacAlister was an arrogant fool for trying to force her to admit otherwise.

What a fool he was.

Drew stormed down the hallway, doing his best to bring his anger and disappointment under control. His leg hurt like hell and the woman who had the power to change that couldn't tell the truth for lying to him.

What had he expected? That simply because he'd saved her life, kept her from the men who hunted her, brought her into the home of his family, somehow those actions would convince her to share with him the power she held?

Well, if he had, he'd been seriously mistaken. She chose to repay his actions with lies.

But lies or no, he would be healed. He'd simply have to come up with a way to convince her to help him as he'd helped her. For that reason—and that reason alone!—he determined to stay with her as long as it took.

It certainly wasn't as if he had any interest in the woman other than her ability to heal his body. He didn't. Not the slightest bit of interest.

A laugh of derision bubbled up from deep inside, all but choking him.

It was all good and well for him to rationalize his need to keep her close, telling himself that his attraction to her meant nothing. All good and well, indeed.

Even though he had lain there half the night, sick with wanting her, trying to convince himself he felt nothing for her.

"No a Faerie, my arse," he grumbled, making his way down the narrow stairs.

Maybe it was those Fae powers that drew him to her. That made him want to possess her. That made him feel so helpless when she stared at him with those big brown eyes, so unable to stand there and demand the answers he needed.

"Fool!" he muttered.

Stepping off the bottom stair, he came close to running right into his sister.

"Now there's a face to frighten small children. Good thing mine aren't about at the moment." Sallie laughed, fixing her hands on her hips in that bossy way of hers. "What could possibly have you in such a foul mood on a lovely day like this? You slept the morning away as if you were a fine gentleman. And you with yer beautiful new bride upstairs at that."

"Leah isn't . . ." He was so close to confiding in his sister he could taste it, but he stopped himself, recognizing as he did that Moreland stood just inside the doorway to the great hall.

Sneaky bastard was listening in on them, no doubt. He might be angry with Leah, but he wouldn't let his anger endanger his family. Or Leah.

With a deep breath, he tried again. "Leah is exhausted from our days on the road. Could you have a bath sent up to our room for her?" Reaching out, he captured his sister's arm, pulling her close as he lowered his voice. "And a change of clothing. She looks to be about yer size."

Sallie nodded slowly, her eyes panning over to the doorway where Moreland had stood only moments before.

Not for the first time he congratulated himself on having such an intelligent sibling.

"I'll see to it. And you? Where will you be?"

"The lists," he growled, turning and heading for the door.

He needed the workout more than ever. A morning

spent crossing swords with a skilled opponent, driving his mind and body to the point of exhaustion, that perhaps would serve to drive back the demons which threatened to overwhelm him.

The physical pain left by days on horseback, the anger that threatened to loosen his tongue, the unreasonable need he had for the woman in his bed—they were demons all.

And they were growing.

Fourteen

⁓

Surely it only felt as if every eye in the room were on her as she entered.

Leah made her way down the aisle between the tables in the great hall, eyes fixed on her feet, her hand on Drew's arm. Silly how that physical contact made her feel as if she could handle this. Especially silly since he was barely speaking to her.

Which was fine. Absolutely fine. She didn't care one little bit. After all, she wasn't speaking to him either. Him and his stupid Faerie accusations.

Drew shifted his hand to her shoulder as he held out the seat for her. She had just begun to relax when she made the mistake of glancing up at him.

His eyes were a soft, serious brown that never failed to make her think of a cup of hot chocolate. At this moment, they beckoned to her in a way she couldn't understand, as if inviting her to lose her very soul in their swirling depths.

She broke her gaze as quickly as she could, but it wasn't soon enough. She'd already leaned toward him, without even realizing she'd moved. Her breath hitched in her lungs for a second and she could swear her heart beat so hard the ties on her shift bounced with each beat.

One long, deep breath and she took her seat, her hands locked together in her lap to stop their trembling before someone noticed.

Before *he* noticed.

Stupid, stupid girl. So what if he was drop-dead gorgeous? So what if he had the ability to melt her insides with a single look? He'd accused her of being a Faerie and then gotten angry at her when she wouldn't admit to being that which she hated most in the world.

She lifted her hands to the table, placing them flat in front of her. This was ridiculous. She needed only to make it through one meal before excusing herself to go back upstairs to rest for continuing their journey tomorrow. Soon enough she'd reach Dun Ard and then wouldn't have to deal with Andrew MacAlister ever again.

Dun Ard, where instead of being accused of being a Faerie, she'd be surrounded by them.

Drew seated himself next to her and placed one large hand over hers, his fingers curling around hers before he turned to chat with Sallie's husband.

She stared at his hand holding hers, willing herself not to start the trembling anew as the heat of his touch flowed into her body. The move shouldn't have surprised her. He was playing the part of attentive new spouse for the benefit of everyone present.

Exactly the role she should to be playing as well.

If she were truly meeting her husband's family for the first time, she'd likely feel an overwhelming curiosity about who they all were. She'd want to learn all she could about them. About him.

That was it then. That was her role to play.

Straightening her shoulders, she lifted her head to look out over the room, demonstrating, she hoped, a casual, natural curiosity.

Her plan came to a screeching halt as her eyes met the unabashed stare of Sir Peter Moreland seated only a few chairs down from her. The smile he sent her direction felt as false to her as did his lifting his cup in acknowledgment.

Crapola. She could hardly wait until he and his men set off to make some other people's lives miserable.

Showing much more confidence than she felt, she nodded his direction, forcing a little smile as if she actually appreciated his attentions.

When the serving maid brought the trencher she and Drew would share, he surprised her yet again. Though he released her hand to make room for their meal, he captured it again almost immediately, bringing their joined hands to rest on his thigh.

Touching him so intimately reminded her vividly of waking up wrapped in his arms this morning, and heat filled her face, unbidden, uncontrollable.

"Tell us all how you came to meet."

Although Sallie addressed the question to Leah, it was Drew who answered.

"Pure happenchance, little sister. The work of the Fates. Leah had fallen into a loch where I was passing by and I pulled her from the waters."

The truth? An absolutely brilliant move on his part.

"It was as if I'd found my own golden selkie."

"More like a drowned rat," she added, smiling in spite of herself as she remembered the moment he described.

"Never." He corrected her quietly, gazing into her eyes as if no one else were in the room, before he continued his story.

"I knew from that first moment she was special, and before long, I came to realize she held the whole of my future in her hands."

So much for sticking to the truth. Damn him, but he'd made her heart race again with that stupid story of his.

"Is that where you've gone?" Sallie smiled first at her brother and then at Leah. "All these times you've taken off with no word to any of us. Left us to think yer out carousing and gaming, and the Fates only know what else, when in truth you'd gone courting."

Drew only chuckled in reply, scooping up a bite of porridge with a piece of bread.

"If yer life with Leah is only half so full as yer sister has made mine, then yer a lucky man, indeed, Drew." Ran caught and held his wife's gaze for a moment, his love for her shining on his face. "Lift yer cups as we toast our brother's marriage. May you both have an eternity of happiness together."

Tears threatened, pooling just behind Leah's eyes. To hide her reaction, she grabbed for her cup, swallowing a great gulp of the unfamiliar ale. How stupidly ridiculous of her. She never fell for this mushy stuff. Of all the things life had taught her, the biggest lesson was that there was no such thing as a fairy-tale happily-ever-after.

As if to prove her point, Moreland chose that moment to speak.

"Will you resume your journey to your home on the morrow, MacAlister?" Moreland lifted his cup to his lips, his eyes boring into Drew.

"I canna say. We've no yet made our decision as to when we'll continue on. After so many days of travel, I suspect my lady would be best served with a break in our journey."

"Besides, you canna go yet," Sally interrupted. "Leah and I have no even had the chance to sit and talk, let alone to bond as sisters should."

And they wouldn't have such an opportunity, if Leah had anything to say about it. Even if time wasn't of the essence for her grandfather's survival, as far as she was concerned, that *bonding* opportunity Drew's sister sought was reason enough to leave as soon as possible. Drew might have skated through the story of their meeting tonight, but Leah had no doubt his sister would want plenty more details. Details she didn't have. Details that didn't exist.

Moreland nodded thoughtfully, that now familiar insincere smile playing at the corners of his mouth. "Take your time, my good man. I've decided that we'll remain here as long as you wish."

Drew's fingers tightened around hers. "Pardon?"

"I have decided that my men and I will wait here until you're ready to travel, so that we can see you safely to your home."

Would they never be rid of the man? Leah stuffed a bite of bread into her mouth, her stomach churning at the idea of spending the rest of her days under Moreland's scrutiny.

Surely Drew would do something, say something that would convince the knight to change his mind.

"As I said, we've made no decision as to how long we'll remain at MacPherson Hall. I canna ask you to set aside yer quest indefinitely to accompany us on a journey that holds no danger. Should we feel the need, Ran has men who can ride along with us."

If anything, Drew's grip on her hand had grown tighter.

"But I'm afraid I must insist, MacAlister. It seems the least we can do to repay everyone's kindness to us. Besides, you told the prior you planned to wed properly in the church when you reached your home. My men have all agreed it's been far too long since we've had the pleasure of attending a wedding feast."

From bad to worse. Leah somehow managed to stifle the groan bubbling in her throat. Barely.

"There's to be a wedding, you say?" Anabella piped up from her spot at the table. "Must we pry every single detail from you, Andrew? You'd said no a word to any of us about a formal wedding."

"There are many things I've no said to you, my lady," Drew replied stiffly.

Leah had no doubt he felt as trapped as she did at the moment.

"Well, Sir Moreland, I can only hope yer men are quite comfortable in their accommodations because, wedding or no, I've every intention of keeping my brother and his wife here for as long as possible."

Leah forced down another bite.

Where had all her choices disappeared to? It wasn't even like she could sneak out of here and make her way to Dun Ard on her own. She had no idea where she even was, let alone where Dun Ard was in relation to this place.

She had only two options: Stay here wasting precious time her grandpa Hugh didn't have, all the while risking being found out, or leave with Moreland's men in tow. The soldiers would expect to end up at Drew's home, but she needed to travel to Dun Ard as quickly as possible and he'd promised to take her there.

Two options—stay or go. No matter which she chose, she wasn't getting any closer to finding help for her grandparents.

Neither option was acceptable.

"Are you ready?"

Leah all but toppled her chair when Sallie touched her shoulder. So lost in dissecting her dilemma, she hadn't even realized the woman had moved from her spot.

"Ready?" she parroted back, at a complete loss as to what she was supposed to be ready for.

Crapola. She should have been paying attention to the conversation.

"To retire to my solar for the afternoon with me and Anabella. Even a mending basket holds more interest than watching these men attempt to prove their prowess in the lists."

Drew gave her hand one final squeeze before releasing his hold. Apparently he was ready to have her go.

Without another word, she rose to her feet and followed Sallie out of the hall and up the stairs.

"Lady MacPherson?"

Leah looked up as one of the maids hurried toward them carrying a small child in her arms.

"Ah, lovely, Patsy!" She held out her arms to the child and the little girl laughed and reached for her. "Come to Mama, my sweetling."

Inside the solar, Sallie offered a chair to Leah just before she plopped herself down on a large rug, placing the little girl in front of her.

"I do so look forward to this part of my afternoon. AnaMairi is trying to walk and while it may be work for her, it's play for me. She gives me the perfect excuse to leave the mending to Anabella." Her laughter seemed to fill the room with joy as her daughter awkwardly pushed up to her feet.

A red-haired porcelain miniature of her mother, the child had a laugh that echoed Sallie's.

"You're fortunate to have such a wonderful mother-in-law."

Again Sallie laughed. "Anabella? Wonderful? Oh, no. Not at all. She's actually a horrible, hateful old woman, and you'll do well to ignore almost everything she says to you. Still, I freely admit, I'm quite fond of her."

Leah leaned forward in her seat as she watched Sallie play with her daughter. The woman's comments made little sense to her.

"You like horrible and hateful?"

Sallie laughed, head back, the sound tinkling off the

stone walls like musical notes. "No, my dear sister, I dinna enjoy those things in the least. But here's the secret to that. There's good and bad all around us. What you find depends on what you expect to find. I see beyond the bad with Ran's mother because I choose to find the good. In the beginning, I simply enjoyed having an equal to match wits with me. But now, after years of looking for the good? Every single day I see a woman who would walk through fire for each and every one of my children and that, more than anything, has ensured my love for her."

A spark of envy twinged through Leah's heart. This was a family as it should be. It was what she'd experienced with her sister so many years ago, what she'd enjoyed for over a decade as a MacQuarrie. It was what she risked losing if she couldn't find a way to Dun Ard to ask the help of the MacKiernans to save her grandpa Hugh and Grandma Mac.

"Yer love for who?" Anabella swept into the room, a small basket of yarn tucked under her arm, an imperious frown wrinkling her brow.

"Quit yer eavesdropping, Anabella. Yer setting a bad example for Baby Ana." Sallie still smiled, cuddling her daughter to her. "Want to go to yer mémé, do you?"

The child clapped her hands together and Anabella bent to pick her up, her expression completely changing as she swept Baby Ana into her arms.

"You see what I mean?" Sallie asked quietly, taking the seat next to Leah by the fire.

Leah did indeed.

She selected a garment from the basket and took the needle Sallie offered, quietly starting to work.

"We are going, are we no?" Anabella spoke from her spot on the rug, Baby Ana grasping her fingers while her little legs wobbled back and forth.

"Going where?" Sallie looked up from the stitching in her lap as she questioned her mother-in-law.

Leah held her breath in that instant, already sure she knew what was coming.

"To the wedding, of course. My first thought when I heard the news was how much I'd like to be there when Andrew arrives home with a wife."

"Now, Anabella. It's no a good thing gloat over what happens to yer friends."

The older woman snorted derisively, spurring a fresh spate of giggles from the child at her side.

"She may well be yer mother, lass, but she's no my friend. Never has been. No even when I was married to her brother." Anabella snorted again. "Most especially not while I was married to her brother."

Her back to Anabella, Sallie rolled her eyes for Leah's benefit. "I'll speak to Ran on it, to see what he thinks about our going."

Leah clamped her lips together to keep from telling the two of them what a bad idea it would be for them to travel to the wedding. Awful, horrible, bad idea. Because there wasn't going to be any wedding. It would be inexcusable to drag this entire household heaven only knew how far, for absolutely nothing.

Trouble was, she wasn't in any position to tell them that. She'd given her oath she wouldn't.

"You see to it that you do speak to him, my dear."

Sallie wiggled her eyebrows and grinned before she answered. "But, I could have sworn, Mother Mac-

Pherson, no two nights past, you were complaining of pain in yer knees and back and announcing to all who'd listen that you'd no be caught dead on a horse again."

"I may have, at that, but mark my words well, Marsali Rose, this is one of those moments in life I willna be denied, no matter what physical burdens it requires of me. To see Rosalyn's face when Andrew rides into Dun Ard announcing he's brought home a bride? That's a sight worth any amount of aching bones."

Something in the older woman's chatter had caught her ear. "Wait. What did you say?" Surely it couldn't have been what she thought she'd heard.

"Pay no attention to her," Sallie reassured, a hand to Leah's knee. "I told you no to listen to half of what she says. She meant nothing against you, did you, Anabella? It's only that she and my mother have always had this wee rivalry stemming from bad blood between them that dates back to a time when they were but girls themselves. Dinna take her words to heart."

As if she cared one bit what that grumpy old woman thought of her. Her concerns were much larger than her own little ego. Perhaps she'd only imagined she'd heard the words because the name was in her thoughts.

"Did you say Dun Ard?"

"Aye." Anabella laid Baby Ana on her stomach on the rug and rose to her feet, a hand at her lower back. "Dun Ard is the seat of the MacKiernan clan. Andrew's home."

Rosalyn. It was the name Mairi had told her to ask for. Mairi's Rosalyn was Drew's mother?

No wonder he knew the way to Dun Ard. It was his home.

A heat rose to Leah's face and her heart pounded in her chest, but this time it had nothing to do with embarrassment or fright. She couldn't remember the last time she'd been this angry.

He'd all but lied to her! Here she'd gone out of her way to confess everything to him and he'd hidden this most important of all information from her. Even knowing her grandfather's life was on the line, he'd not told her he was a member of the family whose help she sought. He'd said nothing. Nothing!

Then, as if to plop the proverbial cherry on top, he'd had the unmitigated gall to accuse *her* of being Fae. Him, of all people. Knowing all the while what *he* was.

Oh, did she ever have a thing or three to say to Mr. Andrew MacAlister, not a single one of them fit for the ears of Baby Ana.

Dropping the mending back into the basket at her feet, she slowly rose to stand.

"Where exactly would I find these lists you mentioned?"

Fifteen

~～

Thrust. Withdraw. Defend.

Drew sent a silent thanks to the Fates for his wickedly good ability to wield a sword. That gift allowed him to participate in sword training without putting any real thought into it, even with an opponent as worthy as Moreland was turning out to be.

Moreland. The man had quickly become a thorn in Drew's flesh.

There was no way he could allow the knight and his men to accompany them to Dun Ard. His laird might well insist that the MacKiernan retain their neutrality in the troubles that rocked their land, but it was words only. They all of them knew it.

Half the men living at Dun Ard had fought against the English at one point or another. Hadn't Colin been held for ransom by an English sympathizer just last year? Hadn't the laird himself been taken captive by the same man?

Drew held no illusions as to what might result from a company of English soldiers marching into Dun Ard.

As if the patterns his feet followed were written somewhere in his unconscious, he feigned a move to his left, then twirled to his right to strike.

Moreland stumbled backward but quickly regained his balance, following with a nod of respect, which Drew returned.

Here they could be civilized. Here the threat was lessened. But at Dun Ard, where his brother and the men who'd followed him into battle against the English lived, things might well be different. Especially once Moreland realized they'd deceived him.

No. Under these circumstances, he could not lead these men to his home. He would not.

This time the pattern his feet followed led him to drive straight in, backing Moreland up a step or two. Automatic. Done without needing to think. It simply happened as if the hand of the Fates guided his own, allowing nothing to distract him.

"Andrew MacAlister! I'd speak to you now, if you please."

Nothing except Leah's voice. Her presence drove everything else from his mind.

"I'm somewhat occupied here, dearling. Can it no wait?" He ducked and twirled, lifting his sword at the last second to deflect Moreland's blow.

"Now," she insisted, her arms crossed beneath her breasts. She had the look of a woman who intended to say more, but, for the moment, her soft mouth drew down into a line as hard as her glare.

"Yer woman's learned to sound like a wife quickly enough," Ran quipped, laughter from the men gathered around drowning out other comments.

"Now," she repeated.

He could ignore her demand. Could allow her to wait and fume, but then he risked her speaking what was on her mind. From the looks of her, that seemed anything but an intelligent course of action for him to take.

"You'll excuse me if I end our round early?"

Moreland nodded his assent, his usual smirk surprisingly absent. Drew passed the practice sword he held to one of the waiting men, each of them eager to try his mettle against the English knight.

Once outside the practice yard, he stopped to grab up his shirt, wiping the perspiration from his face and chest before approaching Leah.

She'd stepped a short distance away, and though she maintained her resolute silence as he approached, her eyes sparkled dangerously with her anger.

Whatever had set her off must have been something to have witnessed indeed.

"I can only assume it's a serious matter that brings you out here?"

"You bet your ass it is. You lied to me, you hypocritical bastard," she hissed.

This definitely was not shaping up to be a conversation he wanted to hold within hearing distance of an eager audience.

Taking her by her upper arm, he led her out into the center of the bailey, far enough from everyone that they couldn't be overheard. Far enough into the open, no one could approach without his notice. Far enough the walk might give him a chance to bring his own temper into check.

More than her anger, her accusation caught him unawares.

"I'm no a man who perverts the truth to anyone, least of all you. You'd best be explaining yerself."

"Me?" Her cheeks had turned a mottled red. "If anyone has any explaining to do, it's you. Why didn't you tell me Dun Ard is your home? What did you think? I'd be so happy to be shown the way there, it would never occur to me that you'd lied about it?"

So that was it. He should have guessed one of the women would let it slip sooner or later. His money was on the ogress herself, Anabella.

"You accuse without just cause, my lady. You never asked if Dun Ard was my home, only if I could show you the way to get there."

Not a lie. At most, no more than a sin of omission.

"That's a fine line of crapola, and you know it. I told you why I needed to find the MacKiernans. I told you my grandfather's life depended on it. I told you who had directed me to them. You had every opportunity to tell me you *are* them. Especially when you were telling me you wouldn't help me if you were them." She gulped air as if her indignation could not wait. "Not to mention the unmitigated gall it took for you, *you* of all people, to accuse *me* of being Fae and then have the nerve to get angry when I wouldn't own up to it."

Proof that she well knew his family's bloodline. Progress at last.

"Does that mean you are admitting what you are now?"

The sound she made in answer was something like the growl of a trapped boar. Best he keep his hands away lest she decide to take a few of his fingers.

He shrugged, noting that Moreland and two of his men watched them closely. "Nevertheless, I've no ever lied to you. No yet."

Her eyes narrowed suspiciously as he spoke. "What's that supposed to mean? *Not yet?*"

Perhaps this wasn't the best time or place, but he'd have to break the news to her sooner or later. Might as well get it over with.

"I canna take you to Dun Ard, Leah. Surely you can see the danger it would present to my family."

"What?" Her voice actually rose an entire octave. "Danger to your family? My grandpa Hugh is going to *die* if I don't get help. Die as in dead. I can't think of much worse danger than that."

Somehow he had to make her understand that there were many more lives than just one old man's at stake here.

"Do you see that man over there?" He nodded his head in Moreland's direction. "He obviously suspects our story. Wherever we go, he's determined to go as well. I've kinsmen at Dun Ard who fought at Wallace's side against men like Moreland. Can you no understand what could happen if I lead him to Dun Ard and he realizes we've been lying about who you are? I'd be putting my entire clan at risk. Yer grandfather's life wouldn't be the only one forfeit."

Her lips tightened back into that thin, hard line. "My whole family is already at risk. Without your clan's help, they have no hope."

Impossible. She was absolutely impossible to reason with.

"Would you truly have my people fighting hardened soldiers like these?"

"I would. You have no concept of what Hugh and Margery MacQuarrie have done for me. I'd have anyone, anywhere, do anything necessary to save my grandparents. Anything."

He hadn't much time to convince her. Moreland and his men even now headed in their direction.

"And what of you? What are you personally willing to risk?"

"I already told you. Anything."

"Aye? Well, lassie, are you ready to offer up the rest of yer life, married to me? Because if we lead that man to Dun Ard, in order to convince him yer no the one he seeks, we'll be forced to speak our vows on the steps of the church to see him gone without a battle. I'm convinced he'll leave with no less."

Her eyes opened wide, the anger instantly replaced by an emotion he found hard to read. Fear? What in the name of the Fates could the woman fear in him?

"Even that," she stated at last. "For Hugh and Margery, I'd even go so far as to wed you."

"MacAlister!"

Time was up. Moreland and his men approached.

He grabbed Leah's shoulders, pulling her close as he bent his head to hers.

Only to give Moreland pause and to give himself time to think. Certainly he had no other reason.

Her lips were soft to his touch. Soft and warm, like her body that leaned into his embrace. Those lips parted on a tiny sigh and his tongue darted inside, as if the taste he'd had once before had only whetted his appetite.

The world around him ceased to exist; his only thoughts were of the woman he held in his arms. Of her hands that fluttered up to cup the sides of his face. Of her heart pounding against his chest. The taste of her, the feel of her.

"MacAlister!" Moreland called again, shattering the spell.

"I've had quite enough of that man today," Leah murmured, her lips hovering under his.

He couldn't agree more.

"As you wish, my lady."

With one arm behind her back and another behind her knees, he swept her from her feet in a movement that didn't even require him to move his lips from hers.

"MacAlister!" Moreland called a third time, only feet away.

"Apologies, again, Sir Knight. I've found myself embroiled in a marital dispute that requires my immediate attention to resolve." He grinned at Moreland as he turned on his heel, striding toward the main keep.

"You know exactly what that man is going to think we're headed to do right now, don't you?" Leah linked her hands behind his neck and laid her head on his shoulder.

"Exactly what we want him to think, my lady."

It felt right to hold her in his arms, as if she belonged there. As if he had every right to be carrying her thus.

Good thing, come to think of it. Once they entered the gates of Dun Ard, the die would be cast and her in his arms was something they'd both better get used to.

Oddly enough, he had a sneaking suspicion that it might not take a great deal of effort at all.

Sixteen

No turning back now. His path might as well be written in stone.

Drew braced his feet against his stirrups, stretching his leg in an attempt to find some relief. They'd been hours in the saddle this day, with more to come. He normally made the journey between MacPherson Hall and Dun Ard in one long, nonstop stretch. Traveling as slowly as they did with this large group would require at least two days.

A full day on horseback always aggravated his leg.

Spending his last two nights on the hard stone floor hadn't helped much either.

Once the decision to travel to Dun Ard had been made, something had happened between him and Leah. Some indefinable shift in their relationship. Whether it was the knowledge that riding into the courtyard of

Dun Ard, a pack of English soldiers in tow, meant a formal marriage, or something else, he couldn't be sure. He knew only that he felt different around her now.

If anything, his attraction to her had grown. As a result, each of the past two nights he'd taken his blankets and slept across the room from her. Foolish, perhaps, but the only way he could be sure he kept his hands off her.

She would be his wife.

It was the only way to guarantee that Moreland and his men would leave Dun Ard. And the English leaving was the only way Drew could insure the safety of everyone there.

He glanced over his shoulder at the wagons and horses that followed.

The first wagon was piled high with all it took to transport a household for an extended period of time: foodstuffs, clothing, whatever the women had determined needed to go. Once his sister had set her mind to making the journey, she'd been a veritable whirlwind, impressing him with her ability to organize everything so quickly.

If only the wagons could travel as fast as Sallie made things happen.

Leah rode in the second wagon along with Anabella, Sallie, and two youngest children. As he watched, Leah lifted her hand in a little half wave.

He marveled at her calm. He'd been so sure of her reaction when he'd confronted her with what would have to happen if they went to Dun Ard. As sure as he'd been of his own. And yet, neither had been even close to what he'd expected.

To his surprise, she'd agreed to the wedding without argument. As for his own feelings, amazingly enough, he wasn't the least bit hesitant. In fact, now that the decision had been made, he found himself viewing the coming event with growing anticipation.

Ahead of him, his two older nephews rode on horses next to their father, the whole lot of them surrounded by Moreland's men.

Drew swiveled his head to note the positions of the soldiers. Seven, eight, nine . . .

Ten. There'd been ten before, hadn't there? He was certain of it. And yet, a second count confirmed it was nine who accompanied them now.

"There's a small glen no far ahead. Close to the water, sheltered by trees. A good spot to set up camp for the night." Ran kept an eye on his boys as he spoke, pulling his horse closer. Moreland joined them almost immediately.

"We'll respect your knowledge of the area, MacPherson." Moreland directed his mount forward, passing the word to his men to prepare to stop for the night.

"Leg bothering you?" Ran looked straight ahead as he asked.

Of all his family, only his brother-in-law actually spoke of his injury. The others seemed to take pains to avoid the subject, as if they feared upsetting him. It was his suspicion that his brother-in-law harbored guilt deep in his soul over the side he'd been on in the battle that cost Drew full use of his leg. Not that Ran had any reason to feel guilt. He'd been a pawn as much as Drew. More so, in fact. The Faerie responsible for it all had controlled Ran's every move.

Drew shook his head, denying his pain even as he pushed back the memories of that time. Nothing to be gained in adding to the weight Ran carried. He of all men knew well the burdens memories of the past brought with them.

Another glance back to the wagon where the women rode showed him Leah watched him still.

There was one bright spot in this convoluted situation. At least his marriage to Leah would eliminate the problem of his injury. As his wife, she could hardly refuse to share the secret of her healing ability.

"That's it!" Ran called out, urging his mount to catch up with Moreland. "The entry to the glen is through those trees, there on the right."

It was as Ran had said, a perfect spot to make camp for the night.

Drew directed his horse away from the others, turning so he could dismount next to a large tree. He counted on using his mount's body to hide the stumble he knew would come when he dismounted. Once he could place his weight fully on his leg, he made his way to the wagon to assist Leah down.

She came immediately into his uplifted arms, hooking her hands behind his neck as he swung her down.

"Whatever possessed me to trade riding horseback for a seat bumping along in that torture wagon is beyond me, but, truly, I have learned my lesson this day."

"Perhaps it had something to do with the horse you rode belonging to the priory. I sent it back as soon as we reached MacPherson Hall." The steed and a healthy donation to thank the prior for his generous assistance.

"All the same." She paused, one hand still cupping his neck. "I'd rather crawl the entire way on my hands and knees than to climb back in that thing."

He stared down into her eyes imagining her on her hands and knees and he was lost, his mind wandering off, filled with visions that did not stop there.

"Drew? Will you agree?"

Damnation. He'd completely missed what she'd said, lost in the deep, molten pools of her eyes. Lost as if he'd been beckoned to enter and lose himself in wicked play.

"Drew?" she repeated, sliding her hand to his cheek.

"Yes," he agreed, with not the slightest idea of what her request might be. Her touch turned his skin hot with wanting her and he cared for nothing else in those moments.

"Oh, good," she breathed, stepping back from him and placing her hand on her neck as she stretched her head from side to side. "Riding with you will be much better than what I endured today, I can assure you. Oh! I'd better go help."

Ride with him? He really must start paying attention to Leah's words when she spoke. Easier said than done when she insisted on putting her hands on him. Now, thanks to his inattention, he'd have to spend the whole of tomorrow with her body pressed against his.

He could almost guarantee he'd be remembering those hands-and-knees visions before the day was out.

The early evening flew by as he tended his horse and gathered wood for the fire. The next thing he knew, their meal was done and his fellow travelers began settling down for their night's rest, preparing for another day's journey with the sun's rise.

"I've readied our bedding." Leah waited for him, the wavering light from the firepit dancing over her face.

The time he'd both looked forward to and dreaded all day had finally come. Though he'd avoided close contact with Leah for the last two nights, there was hardly any way he could keep his distance now. Not with everyone around expecting them to behave as any normal man and wife would.

A glance to his sister and Ran offered little solace. They lay close together, their young daughter cuddled against her mother's side.

Leah held out her hand and he made his way around the fire to join her. Her fingers were cold in his grasp, betraying her outward calm.

They lay down together on their sides, her back against his chest, just as they had lain three nights ago. Just as they would lie for years to come once they married.

The scent of her hair filled his nostrils and he pulled her close, burying his nose in the golden locks. He held her there, feeling her body relax against him, listening to her breathing slow.

He had no idea how long he lay that way, too conscious of Leah in his arms to find the elusive sleep he needed.

Too long, that much he knew.

When the pain in his leg demanded he change position, he rolled to his back. To his surprise, she followed, rolling toward him and fitting her head into the crook of his arm.

Little more than smoldering embers remained of the fire, the light it cast negligible. Only the faint glow of he moon allowed him any sight of her at all. Her lips, parted in sleep, were an invitation if ever he'd seen one.

An invitation he couldn't quite force himself to ignore.

Gently, he lowered his lips to hers, barely brushing against her warm skin. Beneath his touch, she moaned, pressing her body against his.

He pulled his head back, fighting the need that swept over him. The urge to take her might be strong, but he hadn't lost all sense of propriety.

Not yet, anyway. Come this time tomorrow, after a day spent with her body rubbing against his, he might not have the strength to say the same.

Without a doubt, he'd gotten himself into more trouble than he'd bargained for when he'd pulled her from the loch's icy grip.

But as she moved again, tossing one slender arm over his chest and snuggling against him, he also had no doubt that, given the chance to do it all again, he'd make the same choice.

Eagerly.

Seventeen

───⟋⟍───

Leah had never considered herself a delicate, nervous type of female. She preferred to think of herself as a strong woman, one who could handle just about anything Fate could toss her way without blinking. Even during the past two days of madness as the entire household at MacPherson Hall readied themselves to travel, she'd managed to maintain her calm and keep that self-image intact.

But in this last half hour or so, circumstances had done their best to shatter that notion of her self-image.

She stood in the MacKiernan laird's solar at Dun Ard with Drew at her side, his arm around her shoulders. Moreland accompanied them, like the proverbial ball and chain.

Truly, she was growing to despise the blighted man, based solely on his annoying persistence.

Waiting for the MacKiernan laird to meet with them, she tried to clear her mind. If she thought too long about where she was, she feared she might be physically ill. She stood in the den of Faerie descendants she'd managed to avoid for the last decade. This was it. She'd finally reached the people who had the power to help her save the MacQuarries. Soon she would know whether or not they also had the will. Her mission was complete.

Sort of. She wouldn't actually be able to ask the laird for the help she needed until they could manage to get rid of Moreland.

That, as much as the tension she felt flowing off Drew, had set her nerves on edge. Still, she thought she was doing a pretty good job of hiding it.

"All will be well, dearling. Dinna fash yerself so." Drew's whispered attempt to comfort would seem to contradict her impression.

"No fashing going on here. I'm totally fine," she whispered back, working hard to convince herself that just because her knees felt as if they might buckle under her at any moment, that didn't mean she wasn't fine.

"Fine, are you? My mistake. It must be some other woman who trembles at my side."

How she could find such a smart-ass even the least bit attractive was beyond her.

At the thought, her heart started to pound in time with the flutter in her stomach.

She was likely making the biggest mistake of her life. To admit that attraction, even to herself, was far from smart.

They were only playing at this husband-and-wife thing. Drew might have thought to keep her away from

Dun Ard by threatening her with an honest-to-God marriage at the church's door, but he'd seriously underestimated her if he thought she would let a little thing like getting married stop her from getting help for her grandparents.

Besides, they both knew that once they were married and Moreland had taken off, she and Drew could have the marriage annulled. No big deal.

Even if it did feel like a big deal.

She just had to keep her wits about her.

After they'd agreed that marriage would be the only way to get rid of Moreland, the only way to convince him she wasn't the woman he hunted, Drew's attitude had changed. Nothing she could exactly put her finger on, but a change nevertheless. Whether it was their confrontation about his having kept his identity from her or the situation forcing him into a marriage he didn't want, she couldn't say.

What she could say was that from that moment, it felt as if he actively sought to keep a distance between them, even going back to sleeping on the floor rather than sharing that big bed with her. She'd offered to put a bolster down the middle between them and still he'd refused to sleep near her.

Until last night.

Although, in truth, he'd had no other option with everyone watching. It was expected. And he'd played his part to the hilt, holding her close all through the night.

A shiver went up her spine at the memory, and the arm he had around her shoulders now tightened.

As much as she hated to admit it, it would be easy to get used to having him around. Too easy.

"Thank you for yer patience. Do be seated."

The older of the men who entered the room beckoned toward the waiting chairs and they sat. Obviously the laird they awaited, he wore his authority like an invisible garment. Not haughty or arrogant, simply in charge.

One of the men who accompanied him stood to the right of the laird's chair while the other two took up positions farther back, flanking their laird.

"Welcome home, Drew. It appears you've got yerself a bit of explaining to do, cousin, but we'll wait for yer lady mother to arrive for that story." The MacKiernan laird turned the full power of his icy blue stare toward Moreland. "For now, perhaps yer guest would be kind enough to explain the presence of English soldiers in my courtyard."

Moreland, to his credit, dipped his head respectfully. "Sir Peter Moreland. I'd like to assure you, your lairdship, no concern is necessary by any except traitors to the royal house and those who shelter them."

Once again Drew's hold tightened on her hand.

"I'm sure I dinna need to tell you, Moreland, these are turbulent times in our land. The MacKiernan learned long ago the best way to protect our people was to avoid taking sides in political battles. You'll find no traitors in the lands I control, of that I can assure *you*."

"I'm pleased to hear it, your lairdship. In addition to searching for rebels, we also seek a runaway. A young woman who is promised to wed my uncle, Lord Henry Moreland. Beyond that, my men and I are here to honor the friendship struck with your young kinsman and his bride. We desired only to see them safely to the end of their journey and to celebrate their formal union with them."

The laird continued to hold the knight in his piercing stare. "Since we've had no unaccompanied young women unknown to us arrive here at Dun Ard and my cousin and his bride are now safely with us, I can assume that you and yer men will be on yer way soon?"

Moreland's perpetual false smile, the one Leah had rarely seen reach his eyes, returned to his lips.

"Soon. My men and I will stay until after MacAlister and his bride are formally wed. To show our respect, you understand."

"Of course." The laird nodded thoughtfully before sending a smile of his own the knight's direction. "We'll see to quarters for the lot of you. How many might that be?"

Moreland chuckled, holding up a hand. "No, I wouldn't think of imposing on you, your lairdship. You need quarter only myself and my squire. My men will be camping outside your gates in preparation for the arrival of the remainder of my army. And I assure you, good sir, their number is much too large to impose upon your hospitality."

He was assembling all of his men here? That couldn't be a good thing.

"Very well. It will be so. If that's all, sir knight, I'd ask that you excuse us now. It seems we've family matters to discuss to ready ourselves for a wedding celebration."

One of the men behind the laird moved to the door, holding it open for Moreland's departure.

At the door Moreland paused as if he'd forgotten something of importance. "I should like to add, your lairdship, as an aside I'm sure you'll find humorous, the description we were given of the missing woman matches that of MacAlister's new bride."

If Leah had thought her knees weak earlier, she hadn't known what weak knees really felt like.

She did now.

"You'll find there's no a lack of fair young women to be found within Scotland's borders, Moreland. Within our own walls, we've many who could fit such a description."

"I don't doubt that, your lairdship. But even you'll admit the coincidence a strange one when I tell you they also share the same given name. Leah. The woman we seek is Leah MacQuarrie of MacQuarrie Keep. Which reminds me." At last he turned, a predatory smile lighting his eyes. "I don't believe I ever learned your bride's surname."

"Noble," Leah replied before Drew could answer. "And I can give you the names of my parents and siblings if you'd like."

"Not necessary, my dear. I apologize if I've offended. It's simply that I find the coincidence fascinating."

"No offense taken, sir." No offense, perhaps, but a buttload of stomach-churning anxiety. Not to mention guilt.

For a woman who disliked Faeries as much as she did, it was impossible to ignore the profound irony in her situation. Standing here in a roomful of Faerie descendants, she felt threatened by only one—a plain old Mortal.

Perhaps there was more to what Sallie had said about finding the good and evil you seek than she'd consid-

ered. She'd found evil in the Fae because she'd looked
for it there.

"If that's all?" The laird paused for an instant, his
gaze still on Moreland until the knight nodded. "Very
well. Simeon, please deliver Sir Moreland to the care of
our chamberlain to see to his accommodations and then
find Lady Rosalyn and bring her here to join us."

The young man at the door bowed his head before
escorting Moreland from the room.

"Noble, eh?" Drew cocked an eyebrow as he whispered. "That was an interesting choice."

Interesting, indeed, but not in the way he thought.
After all these years, using her real name had felt as
much a lie on her tongue as if she'd claimed her name
was Smith.

"You warned me once to stick close to the truth. I'm
only doing as you advised."

Drew looked as if he would question her response
but the door opened and a woman swept in, her gaze
fixing on the two of them as she made her way to Drew's
side. He was on his feet instantly, accepting the kiss she
placed on his cheek before she seated herself in the
chair he'd vacated next to Leah.

"Sallie tells me I've a new daughter." She took up one
of Leah's hands between her own, catching her gaze and
holding it.

Her eyes were the same penetrating blue as the
laird's were, and being caught in their snare made Leah
feel the need to squirm.

This was Lady Rosalyn, the woman Mairi had told
her to find if she ever needed help. And yet, here she
was, on their first meeting, doing her best to deceive

this woman who could mean the difference between life and death to Grandpa Hugh.

Rosalyn looked from her to Drew and back again before she spoke. "And it appears Sallie has the right of it." With a pat to Leah's hand, Rosalyn sat back in her seat, apparently satisfied by whatever scrutiny she'd performed.

"Yer mother may be well pleased, but you've explaining yet to do, little brother." The man at the laird's side spoke up for the first time. "Dragging an army of Englishmen to our doorstep is no a good thing, in case you've no realized it."

Drew, who had moved to stand at her side as if on guard, now placed a hand on her shoulder. "We had no choice. Moreland insisted. I believe he suspects Leah is the woman he seeks."

"And is she?"

Drew moved directly behind her, both hands on her shoulders now. No doubt he was concerned she'd forget their agreement not to broach the subject of rescuing her grandparents until after they'd married and Moreland had taken his men and left Dun Ard. He had no need to worry. She might not be an expert on reading people, but it didn't take an expert to realize this tension-filled room was no place to throw out a request for a risky rescue mission.

"She's my wife, Caden," Drew insisted stubbornly. "Once we formalize the marriage at the door of the church, Moreland and his men will leave."

The man who'd stood silent behind the laird stepped forward, his long brown hair sweeping over his shoulder as he dipped his head. "It's been my experience that

English soldiers dinna leave anywhere peacefully. No matter what they promise."

Drew's fingers tightened on her shoulder. "I may no have yer experience in fighting the English, Dair, but I've dealt with many a man in my journeys. This one will leave when he's satisfied that he's wrong."

Dair shrugged and stepped back, as if he'd spoken his piece and was done.

"If yer the MacQuarrie lass," the laird began, but Rosalyn interrupted.

"It's of no matter, Blane. No now. Andrew claims her as his wife and that's all we need to concern ourselves over." Rosalyn rose to her feet, pulling Leah to stand with her. "The four of you lads can stay and blether on for as long as you like. My new daughter needs a proper welcome to her new home and a good rest after days of travel. As for me, I have a wedding celebration to arrange."

Leah looked to Drew, who nodded his reassurance before she allowed Rosalyn to lead her out into the hall-way.

As the woman said, they had a wedding to plan.

Eighteen

⁓

Leah lay alone on the bed in the little room where Rosalyn had left her. The sun had long since gone down and still there was no sign of Drew.

She pushed up off the bed and crossed to the fireplace, staring into the dancing flames.

Maybe he wasn't coming at all. Maybe his family wouldn't permit them to share a room until they said their formal vows.

Maybe he'd completely forgotten about her now that he was home.

Dropping to her knees, she wiped an errant tear from her cheek.

Stupid girl. Obviously an evening spent in her own company wasn't a good thing for her. It allowed her overactive imagination to take flight from reality.

Besides, it shouldn't matter whether he showed up or not. It was ridiculous of her to even fret over it. If they'd put Moreland in some other part of the keep, there was no need for him to pretend they shared a room. After all, he'd brought her to the place she needed to be, just as he'd said he would. The least she could do was let him get back to his normal life.

Normal? That might be stretching things a bit. As normal as possible with an English knight in the castle and his growing army camped outside the gates.

Soon enough they'd go through the wedding performance for Moreland's sake and get rid of the obnoxious knight. Then she'd be free to return to MacQuarrie Hall with men at her side to rescue Grandpa Hugh and Grandma Mac.

If the MacKiernan laird agreed to help, that is. And from the we-don't-get-involved speech he gave Moreland this afternoon that was feeling like a pretty big *if* at the moment.

Only the door swinging open saved her from dissolving into a puddle of self-pity.

"Come with me. I've a surprise for you." Drew stood in the doorway, his arms filled with a bundle of fabric, a half grin decorating his gorgeous face.

"What?" She stood, unable to tear her gaze from him. His hair hung in damp tendrils at his neck, as if he'd just climbed out of a bath.

The grin grew larger. "If I tell you what it is, it willna be much of a surprise now, will it? Come on with you." He reached out as he took the three steps toward her, grasping her hand when he reached her. "Dinna be a spoilsport."

He looked happier than she'd seen him in days so, what the heck, she followed along after him like a good little wife.

Guest, she censored her thoughts. Like a good little *guest*.

Halfway down the hall, one of the doors opened and Moreland peered out, pulling back into his room as they passed with a silent nod their direction.

So much for the theory he'd been put in another part of the castle.

"There's just no getting away from him, is there?"

"Put him from yer mind, dearling. Think instead on yer surprise."

"And how am I supposed to do that when you won't tell me what it is?" she grumbled.

He only laughed, saying nothing as he led her down the stairs and through the kitchens, out into the night. The moonlight showed her they were in a garden, one she'd want to come back and investigate tomorrow in the daylight.

"Down this way," he said, pulling her along behind him.

Ahead she could make out a building, the light of fires inside glowing through the doorway.

Not even if she had thought about his "surprise" for a week would she have been prepared for what lay inside the little building.

"Wow." She stopped at the doorway, words failing her.

Massive iron kettles steamed in one of the largest fireplaces she'd ever seen outside a castle, their moist heat radiating out and embracing her.

"It's a bathhouse. My brother Caden built it himself," he told her, pride brimming in his voice as he led her farther in.

"And the surprise part?"

He chuckled as he directed her behind one of the half walls to where a large wooden tub brimmed with steaming water. A stool sitting next to the tub held a bar she could only assume was soap.

"I thought you might like a proper bath. Here." He handed her the bundle in his arms, which turned out to be a large drying cloth and a clean shift.

Oh, would she ever!

"The water's fresh and hot. I filled the tub myself just before I came to get you. You take as much time as you like and I'll wait over here on the other side of the wall, to make sure yer no disturbed while you bathe."

If she hadn't thought him superior among men before, she did now. Clasping the bundle to her chest, she rose up on her tiptoes and kissed his cheek before hurrying to the tub.

This was going to be a little slice of heaven.

This had turned out to be a large helping of sheer hell.

Drew leaned his head back against the wall, listening to the woman on the other side. Her sigh of contentment when she'd stepped into the water had been almost more than he could stand, especially with the touch of her lips still tingling on his cheek.

The little splashing sounds she made fired his imagination with visions of her settling into the tub. Her hair flowing down her back, her skin wet and glistening in the firelight, her head thrown back, lips parted in her way.

This was not a path for his mind to be wandering down. Not yet. Better he should concentrate on how to respond to Blane's impending decision concerning Leah's dilemma.

He'd told his laird all that he knew after she'd left the room. Her running away from MacQuarrie Keep to find the MacKiernans, his suspicion she'd been sent by the Fae, everything.

Almost everything.

His laird had kept his own counsel but his brother had freely shared his concerns, not the least of which had to do with the impending marriage.

"You canna wed the woman for no other reason than to keep her safe from this Moreland," Caden had insisted. "You canna sacrifice yer own happiness for her safety. Neither of you will be happy. Think on it, Drew. What you do is forever. How will you feel when yer true Soulmate appears?"

Easy for Caden to say. He'd found the one he was destined to share his life with.

"*If*, brother, not *when*," he'd responded. "I willna live my life on *if* any longer. I sacrifice nothing. I freely choose marriage to Leah." He'd meant it.

That was what he hadn't shared.

For reasons beyond his understanding, he not only chose to wed Leah, he wanted to do it.

Another deep sigh from beyond the wall brought him back to the present and set him to grinding his teeth.

He rose to his feet, slowly, allowing his needy body the time to adjust before he began to pace. Time. His whole life was about time.

Two days' time and Leah would officially be his wife.

Two days' time and he'd not need to wait impatiently on the opposite side of the wall.

Two days' time and his pain would be relieved—both in his leg and in his loins.

"I'm almost done," she called.

"No hurry," he answered.

Two days' time.

More splashing on the other side of the wall. As if he could see through the stone, he imagined her stepping from the tub. Imagined her wrapping the drying cloth around her lovely curves. Imagined her walking around the wall and dropping the cloth before wrapping herself in his arms.

Two days' time.

Unlike in his imagination, when she actually did step around the wall, she wore her shift, not the drying cloth. Even that was enough to set his heart pounding in his chest.

Her hair fell over one shoulder, its length encased in the cloth he'd imagined covering her body.

"I guess I'm ready." Her smile dazzled when she looked up at him. "That felt wonderful. Thank you for thinking of it."

He nodded his acknowledgment as he reached for her hand, not even aware of the words he mumbled.

They walked back to the keep in silence, her with her thoughts, him wondering if there was any possibility those thoughts might include him.

A torch burned at either end of the long hallway, casting their shadows dancing over the stone walls as they made their way toward their room.

A small noise, the sound of wood against stone, as they passed down the hall alerted him that Moreland watched them once again.

The knight was not an easy one to convince, but Drew was willing to give it another try. More than willing, as it turned out.

At their room he paused, his hand on the knob. When Leah looked up, a question filling her eyes, he braced an arm on either side of her, backing her up against the heavy wooden door as he did so. Ducking his head, he brushed his lips over her cheek, enjoying the feel of her soft skin against his face.

"He watches."

She acknowledged his warning by wrapping her arm up and around his neck. Her fingers playfully circled his ear as she turned her head to touch her lips to his.

He pulled her close, one arm at her back. His other hand cradled her head, as much to keep her near as anything else.

When her tongue traced his lower lip, he was lost.

She smelled of the balm and mint soap she'd used, the scent soothing his soul. Her body close to his filled a void he hadn't realized was there.

And the taste of her! Her mouth was an addiction gone wild.

Whether the door down the hall closed or remained open no longer registered in his thoughts. They were filled entirely with the woman in his arms.

He pushed against the door, stumbling through when it opened, holding her against him still. He had no idea how he managed to shut the door, though the slamming registered vaguely in the back of his besotted brain.

Thank the Fates for the small room.

Mere steps and the bed hit the back of his knees.

He tumbled down onto the mattress, taking her with him, neither of them breaking the kiss that had begun in the hallway.

He rolled them over, pushing up the skirt of the thin shift she wore in the process. The heat of her bare leg against his ignited his growing desire. As if his skin had taken on a new sensitivity, sparks shot through his thigh where it touched her.

Her breath caught, her hands capturing his shoulders as he buried his face in the crook of her neck. His fingers worked at the ties of her shift, loosening the opening until he'd freed the tops of her breasts.

Full and firm, they beckoned to him, and he followed their siren call. His tongue traced the top of one rounded beauty and Leah moaned beneath him, her hands finding their way under his shirt, burning into his bare back.

This moment was perfect. She was perfect.

Not perfect.

He forced himself to stop, his forehead resting between her beautiful breasts as he gasped to reclaim his breath. To reclaim his wits.

They might have represented themselves to be married, but in his mind, in his heart, in his soul, he knew they were not.

Until she made that final commitment, he would not dishonor her, no matter how much he wanted her.

And none but the Fates could possibly understand how very much he wanted her.

Summoning what little reserve he had left, he lifted his head to look into the dark pools of her eyes. In his need for her, his imagination ran wild for an instant, trying to convince him he could see into the depths of her soul, could see there within those depths, her, waiting, beckoning him to join her inside.

Though there was nothing he wanted more, it was not to be. At least not now.

He lightly kissed her chin and then her forehead, his ego boosted to realize her heart pounded as a match to his.

"We forget ourselves, my lady," he whispered, rolling off her to rise to his feet.

"Over here," he directed, taking her hand to help her up and leading her toward the fire. "Sit." His ability to speak in more than one or two words seemed lost as he motioned to the little stool near the fire.

A little frown wrinkled her brow, but she complied wordlessly, sitting down as he indicated with her back to the fire.

He dropped to his knees behind her, and pulled away the towel that covered her hair. Gently he combed his fingers through her tangled curls, letting the strands glide over his hand. Even wet it felt soft to his touch and he fought the need to bury his face in it.

He wanted more. So much more. But for now, he'd force himself to settle for this.

Only one thought made this moment bearable. Over and over in his mind, perfectly timed to the pounding of his heart.

Two days' time.

Nineteen

~

She hardly recognized who she'd become.

Leah lay on her back, staring sightlessly up at the canopy, fingering the stone that hung from her neck.

Tomorrow would be her wedding day.

All those years ago, the day before she'd left her own time she'd spent at her sister's side, making preparations for Destiny's wedding.

"Are you sure this is really what you want? There's time to stop it, you know. You don't have to do this if you don't really love him and all," she'd said. Her greatest fear had been that her sister was marrying Jesse to make sure his family would transport Leah back in time to keep her safe.

Destiny had laughed. "Trust me, I've never wanted anything more."

"How can you be so sure?"

Her sister had clutched both her hands over her heart. "I feel it here. I want him so much I can hardly breathe. All I can think about is being with him. Just the thought of being away from him hurts. And when he holds me?" Again she laughed. "Lordy, Leah. The man curls my toes. It's everything Mom used to tell us and more. Remember her stories about how we'd each find our Soulmate one day? Jesse is mine. I'm absolutely sure of it."

"Okay, then. If he's what you want, I'm totally happy for you. How you can stand to have any man's hands all over you, though, is more than I can imagine, but I'll take your word for it."

Destiny had wrapped her arms around Leah then, hugging her close. "Oh, baby. You only feel that way because of what those Nuadian bastards tried to do to you. You won't always feel this way. I promise. Your Soulmate will come along when you least expect it, just like Mom always said. This wonderful, scary, confusing bliss-jumble will happen for you one day, too. I just wish I could be able to be there with you when it does."

On that day, at that moment in time, she'd believed with all her heart that her sister had been completely wrong. She would never, ever want a man to touch her.

Now she wasn't so sure.

Last night, for the first time in her life, she'd had a taste of that wanting Destiny had tried to describe to her.

"And it sucks," she grumbled, pushing herself up out of bed. At least it sucked when the man she wanted stopped dead in the water like Drew did last night, leaving her weak with the wanting.

She ran her fingers over the face of the stone one last time, feeling as if it somehow brought her closer to the sister she hadn't seen for so long. Sighing, she leaned down to gather up the bundle of crumpled blankets Drew had slept on last night. Again.

"I am such a ditz," she chided aloud.

Having him sleep in her bed, after what had happened when they returned from the bathhouse, would only have led to one thing.

And that's where the part of her she didn't recognize reared her loud self up, all demanding and needy. That one thing was exactly what she'd wanted so badly last night. What she wanted right now.

If she closed her eyes, she could almost feel his hands on her body. His lips, hot against her skin.

"Hormone meltdown." Had to be. No other reasonable explanation came to mind. Leah Noble MacQuarrie just did *not* behave this way.

She tied back the curls that flew wildly around her face this morning. If she'd only taken the time to comb them as they dried, she wouldn't have this problem. Of course, once Drew started messing with her hair last night, doing his own version of drying it in front of the fire, the only thing she could think of was how good it felt to have him touch her.

Unmanageable curls were a small price to pay for that experience.

She'd just dropped her shift down over her head when a knock sounded at her door.

"Leah? Are you up?"

It was a woman's voice she didn't recognize, that much she realized right away, surprised by what sounded distinctly like a Texas accent.

An even bigger surprise awaited when she opened the door.

The woman looked so much like her sister Destiny, her legs felt as if they might not hold her.

"Are you okay? You just went white as a sheet," the woman exclaimed, taking her arm and leading her back into to the room to sit down. "Put your head between your knees for a sec. Should I go get Drew?"

"No!" Drew was the last thing she needed. "Who are you?"

"I'm Ellie. Caden's wife? Caden is Drew's older brother, so I guess that makes us sisters-in-law." Ellie squatted down in front of her, running her hand over Leah's head like she might pat a dog. "You want me to fix you some tea or something?"

"No." Tea? They couldn't possibly have tea. Tea didn't exist here yet. The shock of her surprise was wearing off at last. "I'm sorry, did you say what you wanted?"

Ellie chuckled. "I did not. I was too busy worrying about whether you were going to pass out on me or something. I saw Drew on his way out to the lists and he told me I should come get you so you could spend some time getting to know the other ladies here. They're working on your wedding dress. Would you like to join them?"

Plainly, it seemed wrong to say no. They were, after all, doing something for her.

"I'd like that."

She studied Ellie as they made their way out into the hall and to the room where the other women waited. Now that she really paid attention, she could see lots of differences between this woman and her sister. Ellie's hair was much longer than Destiny would ever have worn hers and her nose was a little more upturned. Her eyes were a different shade, too.

Though her initial reaction had likely been no more than her having her sister on her mind only moments before this woman arrived, there were definitely similarities.

"Here we go," Ellie announced, holding open a door. "Look who I've brought to join us!"

Leah had barely taken her first step into the room before the squealing started.

"No, no! You can't be in here!" Anabella jumped to her feet, placing herself firmly in front of whatever activity was in progress behind her. "What's wrong with you, Elenora? We're working on her headpiece. You ken that to be bad luck."

"Perhaps Leah would enjoy seeing the garden, Ellie. Why don't you show her the way there," a smiling Rosalyn leaned around Anabella to offer.

"Sorry," Ellie offered as she ushered her out of the room and toward the stairs. "I should have remembered how they get about stuff like that. Would you like for me to show you the garden? The herbs are all up and fresh and the fragrance is really quite nice."

Actually, the garden was a spot she had wanted to explore.

"I know my way there. I saw it last night on the way to the bathhouse. If you have other things you need to be doing, I'm not going to be the least bit offended."

"Oh!" Ellie shook her head, crossing her hands over her heart. "I'm so glad you found the bathhouse. Isn't it just the best? I swear it's probably my favorite indulgence."

Leah could well understand its attraction. The only thing that might have made it better last night was to have had Drew wander around to her side of the wall.

But, clearly, that was a fantasy for another time.

At the bottom of the stairs, Ellie put a hand on Leah's forearm, flashing what appeared to be a grateful smile. "I did promise Bridey—the cook, that is—that I'd spend some time in the kitchens going over details for the feast. Are you sure you won't mind if I abandon you?"

"Not at all." She never minded spending time on her own. Well, she hadn't before she'd met Drew. "It's out this way, right?"

"Through the kitchens. I'll walk you that far. I feel bad sending you off on your own."

Ellie escorted her all the way to the back exit where she paused, her face lighting as if she'd had the most wonderful idea.

"Oh! I know how to keep you company. Baby!"

At the woman's shout, what had to be the largest dog Leah had ever seen bounded around the corner, sliding to a stop in front of them.

"Baby might look a little intimidating at first, but he's a total sweetie. Keep a good watch on Leah for me, big guy. You two are going to get on just fine." With that, she hugged the dog's massive neck and disappeared back into the kitchens.

Leah eyed the dog for a moment, ultimately deciding he didn't look like he planned to attack. Though she'd swear he seemed to be grinning at her as she started out to find the lovely bench she'd passed last night.

It would be the perfect spot to sit quietly and indulge in that fantasy about Drew appearing on her side of the wall down in the bathhouse.

Drew leaned his head back against the wall of the shed, eyes closed for a moment while he caught his breath. But only for a moment. Any longer and someone might think him weak. He might think himself weak.

Though there were only four of them training in the lists this morning, it had been a good session. His body was exhausted, but he knew from experience that the workout would pay off for him long into the evening, with hours of lessened muscle pain.

He opened his eyes and glanced down to the bench where he sat, catching up his shirt to wipe the sweat from his face before turning his attention back to the arena where his brother Caden pitted his skills against those of Alasdair Maxwell.

Dair felt more like another brother than a family friend, having spent more of his life at Dun Ard than at his own family's home. As they'd grown up together, he, Dair, and Colin, his youngest brother, had been inseparable. They'd planned to become knights together, battling the enemies of their country to protect Scotland's freedom while Caden would one day take over from Blane as laird.

They'd had it all figured out.

But Drew's injuries in the battle to save Mairi and Sallie from the Faerie masquerading as a duke had changed all that. Dair and Colin had gone on to follow that dream, just without him.

Drew hardened his heart against the stab of pain, consoling himself with the idea that there could yet be time to join them once he was healed.

"Good practice."

Drew's thoughts were pulled back to the present when the man he'd trained against, Simeon Mac-Dowell, sat down beside him, offering the wineskin he held.

Drew accepted the offer, tipping his head back for a long drink. Sim had joined their family just over a year ago when his aunt Catriona had married their laird. There had been some initial suspicion since Sim had fought for Catriona's brother, Austyn Wodeford, who supported the English, but it hadn't taken long for him to win them over. It helped that he'd played a major role in aiding Blane and Colin in their escape to freedom when they'd been held for ransom last year.

Drew liked him. Sim was a quiet one, but he fought hard and Drew honestly believed that once Sim gave his loyalty, he could be trusted no matter what.

"I've no had the opportunity to extend my congratulations on yer marriage. She looks to be a good woman. For yer sake, I pray it's so." Sim absently scratched his chin, pausing as if he had more to say.

"You ken yer welcome to speak yer mind freely with me."

The other man shrugged, staring at the ground at his feet. "It's perhaps naught, but I feel I should tell you anyway. The English you brought to Dun Ard, Moreland? Though I've never seen him before, I have met the man he serves, his uncle. Lord Henry Moreland spent time at Wode Castle on two occasions while I was there. He had alliances with Wodeford."

Not surprising, really. Those Scots who allied themselves with the English for profit and personal gain were known to have a network of ties within England.

"I tell you only because I ken that this knight suspects yer woman to be the one he seeks. The one who's to be bride to his lord. No!" Sim held up his hand to stop Drew from saying anything. "I'm no asking you to confirm or deny his charge. It's of no matter to me. That she's yer wife was all I needed to hear. I ken you spoke of the situation with yer brother and the laird, and whatever the three of you decided is what I support. I only want you to ken what manner of man you deal with."

"And what kind of man is Lord Henry Moreland?"

Sim shook his head, lifting his eyes as he spoke. "The worst kind. With his violent temper, he's a twin for Austyn, if ever one lived. His men gossiped of the death of his second wife, a young lass who gave him a girl-child instead of the son he wanted. Rumor had it, no long after the birth she and the babe plunged to their deaths from the tower of Moreland's castle."

Drew could think of no good response to the story, his mind a jumble of anger and concern. If *this* was what

Leah's uncle planned for her future, he was grateful he would be the one to wed her instead.

He held the wineskin out to Sim, who took it as he rose to his feet.

"I only thought you should be aware of this." With a careless shrug of his shoulders, Sim strode away toward the keep.

After last night, he had no alternative but to acknowledge his attraction to Leah was more than a simple dalliance. It was even more than his needing her to heal him. It went much deeper somehow.

He'd had to fight all his worst personal demons last night to force himself off that bed. Taking his pallet to the floor, he'd slept not one wink. Instead he'd lain awake, listening to Leah breath, his soul at war with the demon Guilt.

By bringing Leah to Dun Ard, he'd given her no option but to marry him, with no regard for what feelings she might have. Granted, it was no lie that the marriage was a necessity to save her from Moreland's finding out who she was. Still, he'd known she was desperate to save her grandparents and would agree to anything. He'd been equally confident Blane would refuse the help she sought, not willing to put the people of Dun Ard in harm's path, distant relations or not.

So why had he pushed her to this resolution?

For himself and his desires, plain and simple. He wanted her gift of healing to make him whole. And after last night, he confirmed what he only suspected before.

He wanted her.

No matter what she wanted.

He stood, dragging one hand across his face and into his hair, as if he could wipe away the stain of guilt that colored his soul.

No, he couldn't. But after hearing Sim's story, at least he could console himself that marriage to him was the lesser of two evils Leah faced.

Even if she never loved him.

Twenty

Leah paced back and forth in her bedchamber, impatiently waiting for Drew to return. He'd suggested she go ahead and retire for the night since he had no idea how long his meeting with the laird and others might last.

Though he hadn't gone into detail, she suspected he would be speaking to his family of her need for their help. Knowing that might be the case and knowing she wouldn't be there to speak on her own behalf drove her crazy.

Retire, indeed. No chance she'd be sleeping any time soon.

What she needed was a good book.

Books were probably the one thing Leah missed most from her own time. The ready availability to grab up a book and get lost in the story, transporting her from whatever troubles bothered her to someone else's fantasy, now that had been a loss, though one she'd been willing to live with.

One she was still willing to live with. There might be no handy paperbacks here, but there were no Nuadians after her either, and that was a trade-off she could support.

There were books in this time, just not the stories she loved. They were more manuscript than book, often what she'd consider small works of art. Learning to read the perfectly shaped, decoratively drawn letters had been a challenge, but she'd made it a priority and Hugh and Margery had been amazingly supportive. Hugh still surprised her at least once per year with some new text he'd managed to lay his hands on for her.

Even the people of Dun Ard must place some value on the written word. She'd seen a few books in the laird's solar when they'd first arrived. Likely those belonging to the laird were religious in nature, as so many books were in this time, but there might be at least one book of poetry.

An enticing thought, indeed.

What harm would there be in her making a quick visit to the laird's solar? The men were off somewhere discussing her entire future, so surely no one would mind her borrowing a text she could return tomorrow morning.

Decision made, she slipped quietly out into the hall, all too aware that behind a door midway to the stairs, Moreland slept. Lurked, was more like it. The man had become the bane of her existence in the last few days. He was always there, always watching, as if just waiting for her to screw up so he could pounce with a snotty *aha*!

Moving as quickly and quietly as she could, she hurried past his door and down the stairs, making her way to the laird's solar.

She found the door closed when she reached her destination. She lifted her hand to knock but, casting a quick glance to her right and left to make sure the hallway was empty, placed her ear to the wood instead.

A deep murmur of voices greeted her, too blanketed by the heavy wooden door for her to make out any words.

Crapola. She should have realized if Drew was meeting with the laird, that meeting would be taking place in the laird's solar.

Turning away from the door, she considered her options. Going back to her bedchamber was likely the smart move. But sitting in that room alone, waiting, staring into the fire was driving her up the wall.

What about the gardens? She'd spent a lovely hour or so there today even if Ellie's dog had insisted on sitting right next to her as if on guard duty the entire time.

Deciding she'd hit on the perfect compromise, she set off down the hallway and through the kitchens, out into the gardens. She briefly considered whether or not she should have gone back for a wrap of some sort, but as soon as she stepped into the night, she knew she would be fine as she was.

Though it was cool, it wasn't so cold as to drive her back indoors. A late-afternoon rain had left the air smelling fresh and clean in a way she always loved.

Clouds formed a haze over the waning moon, but

there was enough light for her to find her way to the bench as long as she stayed to the path. For the moment, though, she simply stood her ground, enjoying the feel of the evening breeze lightly playing over her face. Yes, coming out here had been a very good decision.

She'd made it almost all the way to the bench when she heard the noise. A footstep perhaps, or . . . looking up ahead she realized the spot she'd hoped to enjoy was already occupied. When she stopped, hesitating, trying to decide whether to turn around, the decision was made for her.

"Join me, Leah."

Rosalyn MacAlister beckoned to her, patting the seat next to her in invitation to the spot that had been Leah's intended destination.

"I'm so pleased you've discovered my favorite hideaway." Rosalyn hugged Leah's shoulders as she sat down. "At last we'll have the peace and quiet to chat for a bit."

"You're sure you don't mind my interrupting you?" If she were escaping to this lovely spot, she certainly wouldn't appreciate having someone disturb her.

"No at all, child. I've those questions I've wanted to ask but never the time and place to ask them."

Oh, no. The infamous mother-in-law grilling. It would be hard enough if she were truly here to marry Rosalyn's son, but as an imposter? Not a comfortable situation. Not in the least. Still, she'd given her word to Drew that she wouldn't speak out before he felt it was safe to do so.

"I'll answer anything about me that I can. Ask away."

What else could she say? After all, this woman was to be her mother-in-law.

"Drew has shared the truth of who you are with us, lass. I'd like to ask about yer father."

He'd told them? And he hadn't told *her* that he'd told them? She'd be having a thing or two to say to him later this night.

"A few years back," Rosalyn continued, "we had a visit from a group of Tinklers. During the course of their stay, one of the women happened to mention yer father to me. She told a story of Robert's death. Him and his bride both."

Leah had almost forgotten the Tinklers who had brought Robert back to MacQuarrie Keep, wounded, dying. Of course they would have believed the story Grandma Mac had given everyone, that Robert had died from the wounds he suffered when he'd been taken prisoner. It wasn't like she and Grandma Mac could have told anyone the truth, after all. Who would believe Robert and his wife along with the child Jamie had all been swept seven hundred years into the future?

Come to think of it, this woman sitting at her side might.

"Yes. Robbie and Isabella both. She wasn't my mother, in case you're wondering." Just in case she was doing the math. If she knew Isa was Robbie's bride, she'd quickly realize Leah couldn't be their daughter.

"So I gathered. Oh! Look up there! Quickly!" Rosalyn grabbed her hand and pointed to the sky, where a shooting star blazed a short streak through an exposed patch of black before disappearing. "It's a sign of things to come, that. Proof of a Faerie promise delivered."

A Faerie promise? Leah barely had time to consider what shooting stars and Faeries could possibly have to do with one another when Rosalyn switched tracks again.

"Speaking with that Tinkler, that was the second time I heard tell of Robert's death. Now, I was a party to the first story, so it's well I ken what really happened, and it set me to wondering, was it the same this time as the first? Is he really dead or has he gone back to . . ." She paused, allowing her words to hang in the air above them.

"He's gone back." Why she'd open up to a complete stranger, one of Faerie blood at that, was beyond her. "Him and his bride."

"How lovely." Rosalyn nodded her head before dropping it back to gaze up at the sky. "Robert was a good man when I knew him. A good friend to my nephew, Connor."

"They're still good friends." Leah felt almost as if the choice of whether or not to volunteer the information was beyond her control.

"I canna say I'm surprised, but it is good to hear all the same."

Rosalyn patted her hand and they sat quietly together for several minutes before she spoke again, her voice barely more than a whisper.

"You come from that time, aye? You've the Faerie blood in you, do you no, lass?"

"No more than you."

Rosalyn chuckled, patting her hand once more, her voice returning to normal. "Well said, daughter. Well said."

Daughter. Whatever "truth" Drew had told them, he obviously hadn't shared the real one. No wonder he hadn't said anything to her about it yet.

"Is it worries that bring you out here this night? You've no call to fash yerself over the wedding tomorrow. All is in order. Cook started preparations yesterday so even the feast is well on its way to being done. Ellie and Sallie have done wonders in organizing everything in record time."

Was she suffering from nerves? Yes. About the wedding? In part, maybe. She denied it all the same.

"I'm not worried. I just needed to get out of the room for a while. I felt like the walls were closing in on me."

Again Rosalyn chuckled softly. "Aye, it's the worries of any new bride. I went through the same myself on the night before my own wedding. Though I'd known Duncan for nigh on thirty years before he finally realized he wanted to wed me, and though I had no a single doubt in my heart that he was my own true love, I still spent the night before my wedding sitting out in this very garden, looking up at the stars for reassurance."

Leah dropped her head back, allowing her gaze to rake the sky. Good thing she wasn't looking for stars to reassure her. Even the small patch of black she'd seen before was covered over now.

"Though I dinna sit on this bench," Rosalyn picked up her conversation as though the long pause had never happened. "There was naught but a stump here back in those days. My Duncan made this bench for me with his own two hands. We spent many a night sitting on it, staring up at the stars together. After he died, I brought it here from Sithean Fardach so I could sit upon it each night when I come out to converse with him."

Wait. What? "Converse with who?"

"Duncan, of course." This time Rosalyn laughed, a hearty, happy sound. "Before you think yer new mother is addle-brained, rest assured I do it only because it makes me feel as if I still have him to talk to. To share my burdens and my joys. Like this. Duncan!" She called out the name as if she'd just spotted an old friend walking by. "Do you see her? This is to be our new daughter. Drew's wife. I told you, did I no? They're slow as a summer day, but eventually, they'll each find their intended and be as happy as you and I were."

How low did she feel right now? Did worms have underbellies? Here was this sweet lady, sitting out here mourning for her lost love, believing her son was to marry the woman of his dreams. Lower than a worm's underbelly, whatever came lower than that.

"Drew puts a great deal of effort into trying to convince everyone around him that nothing matters to him but drink and gaming. I ken differently. You do as well, do you no?"

"I believe he cares about his family." And that he was a man of great integrity. And trustworthy. And handsome beyond belief.

"He's been through a lot, that lad has. He was but a boy when he near gave his life trying to save his sister and his cousin Mairi from evil men who thought to use them for their own evil purposes. When they brought Drew home, his body hacked and bleeding, I thought for sure I'd lose him. But he's a fighter and he survived.

And in spite of the scars he hates so, he's grown to be a fine, strong man."

The scars. She'd seen that horrible scar on his chest. No wonder his mother had thought he might die. From the looks of it, he was lucky he hadn't.

"He's a good heart, that one," Rosalyn continued. "Caden's all about responsibility to Dun Ard and Colin's all about defending Scotland and honor, but Drew . . ." She paused, patting Leah's hand once more. "Drew is all about heart. No matter what he pretends, his feelings run deep. Perhaps deeper than those of his brothers. He's spent the last ten years thinking himself less than a man because of the scars marring his body. I'm so grateful he's found the woman who was able to see through that exterior to heal the scars on his heart."

The woman was killing her.

No. Her own conscience was killing her. No matter what she'd promised Drew, she couldn't do this. Not to his mother. Not to herself.

"Rosalyn, I've another motive for coming to Dun Ard with Drew."

"Aye?"

"My grandparents, Hugh and Margery MacQuarrie, they're being held captive in MacQuarrie Keep by their older son, Richard. He left the family long before I came to live with them. Abandoned them to live in England with his wife and her family. He even uses his wife's family name. He's claimed to be holding MacQuarrie Keep in the name of Edward, King of England. I came here to seek help from the MacKiernan laird to rescue my grandparents. I came because your niece, Mairi, told me if I ever needed help, you guys were the ones I should turn to. You were family." Once she'd started, the words tumbled out, one over the other like spring thaw from the mountains. She couldn't have stopped herself if she'd tried. "I don't know if that's what Drew has said to you, but there it is."

Rosalyn turned to her then, embracing her fully, hugging her tightly as if she comforted a lost child. Crazy as it seemed, Leah felt like a child in need of comfort at that moment.

"Drew told us of yer grandparents' troubles. Even now we await Blane's decision on the matter. It's up to him as laird to consider all sides and weigh what's best for all concerned."

She wanted to argue, to say something, anything, to convince Rosalyn that what really mattered was Hugh and Margery. But being here, being accepted as she had been, made her all too aware of the difficult decision facing the MacKiernan laird. His people meant as much to him as her grandparents did to her.

"In the meantime," Rosalyn patted her back with one hand after she broke the hug, "we'll sit here together and enjoy the peace of the night for a bit. Rest assured we'll no let these ills cloud our celebration of yer marriage to Drew. Yer going to have the happy start to yer lives together that you deserve. There will be plenty of time after to fuss and fash over what we can and canna control. Until then, just rest easy in the knowledge that Drew works to yer benefit, representing yer case with our laird."

And just how effective did she think that would be? A man who didn't support her cause, arguing her side of it?

"Drew told me once he'd refuse my request if he were laird and it were up to him. That he wouldn't risk one set of lives for another."

"He told us that as well, so it's all the more good fortune for you he's no the one to be making that decision. Drew's no a man of violence. He believes in using his mind to avoid a fight if there's any way. All the same, while he spoke his piece as a member of the family, he puts his beliefs aside and fights on yer behalf for what you want, for no other reason than that you want it."

How could that be possible? She'd never met a man, Mortal or Faerie, who'd sacrifice what he believed best simply to be nice. It made no logical sense.

"Why would he do that, Lady Rosalyn? If he believes what I ask for is bad for the people of Dun Ard, why would he argue my case before the laird?"

A gentle smile played across Rosalyn's face and she shook her head. A small movement to be sure, but one that clearly relayed her amusement. On the receiving end of that look, Leah felt the only thing missing was for the woman to ask if she could be any more dense.

"As I said, he kens it to be what you want. And because he loves you so, he wants to see to yer having what makes you happy."

That was utterly ridiculous. Drew didn't love her. His mother obviously didn't understand that this was all a sham for Moreland's benefit. He couldn't love her.

Which still left unanswered why he'd fight for what she wanted when it went against what he believed in.

"Surely you dinna doubt his love for you?" Rosalyn reached out, lightly touching Leah's cheek before an even broader smile touched her lips. "But of course you

do. Yer to be married on the morrow and yer filled with
the silly doubts of a new bride. Well, daughter, let me
put yer mind to rest. I ken my son, better perhaps than
anyone. I see the way he looks at you. I see how his eyes
follow you when you leave the room. I read his feelings
in his face. Trust me, lass. You dinna have any need to
question his feelings for you. Drew is a man in love.
And yer the woman he's in love with."

Twenty-one

It was exactly as he'd suspected.

Sir Peter Moreland slipped silently back into the shadows of the trees, blending with the night as if it were a part of him. He had no need to hear any more of the women's prattle.

When he'd spied Leah sneaking down the passageway from her bedchamber, he'd followed. At first he had thought she would attend the gathering in the laird's solar, but she'd veered away from that room and ended up out here.

What a stroke of luck it had been for him that Lady MacAlister chose the same spot this night. He couldn't have arranged a better rendezvous if he'd planned for a fortnight.

As a boy, he'd squired at his uncle's estate, serving an old knight, Sir Barret. The man rarely spoke to anyone. Peter had quickly learned that when the knight did speak, his words bore listening to. One of the more lucid tidbits of knowledge he'd shared had related to women, just like the ones sitting on the bench yards from him now.

Barret had confided once that the key to avoiding many a battle lay in learning the secrets your enemy held. And the best place to learn those secrets? From the women of the castle.

Every clever conversation, every devious maneuver he'd tried had failed to produce the evidence that the woman sitting before him was Leah MacQuarrie, the woman his uncle had traveled to Scotland to wed. But put her alone with another woman and within minutes he had all the proof he needed.

The question now was what did he do with his new-found knowledge?

She and MacAlister presented themselves as husband and wife already, and with their formal wedding tomorrow, the die was cast.

The scenario worked well for him, as long as he managed all the cards in his hand. Many a fortune had been lost in overplaying.

Lord Moreland was old and his health failing. With both his sons lost in service to the king, the rightful line of succession fell to Peter. As long as his uncle didn't remarry, and have sons, that is.

Simply not finding the missing girl had rankled at his sense of how to play this particular political hand. Coming back without her might lead his uncle to believe he hadn't tried.

But bringing her back already wed? Now that would

put a fair wrinkle into his uncle's plans. And should he still decide he wanted her, which considering the woman's looks wasn't out of the question, a good long waiting period would be required. Her marriage would be no impediment. Considering his lordship's connections with King Edward, there'd be no problem in having her wedding to the Scot put aside. And if that failed, they could simply eliminate MacAlister. Marriage to a widow would be no problem.

Since Lord Moreland's goal in marrying was to produce a male heir, he'd need to make sure any child she carried resulted from the proper bloodline. It could take months to verify the woman wasn't already carrying MacAlister's child.

His uncle's last wife hadn't survived the aftermath of bearing a female child. Peter knew all too well the rumors surrounding Elspeth's death, though he couldn't be sure whether or not the gossip was true. What he did know to be true was that if having a daughter had been unacceptable to his uncle, having another man's spawn would be beyond inexcusable.

That fact alone would necessitate a delay of months and that led to his uncle's real problem. Time. Or more accurately, lack of time. From all indications, Lord Moreland didn't have a lot of time left. The rigorous hardships of traveling so far north to claim this woman as wife, and the trip back once they were wed, both would take their toll on the old man's failing health.

Peter tapped a finger to his chin, considering his next course of action.

Waiting seemed the prudent course. Waiting for an opportune time *after* the happy couple were wed.

At some point after the wedding, he'd snatch her up, take her back to MacQuarrie Keep, and deliver her to his uncle exactly as he'd been charged to do, proving his worth and his loyalty to his uncle once again.

No matter what happened after that, it could only be good for him.

Whether his uncle rejected the woman after hearing she'd married another, or chose to marry her anyway in spite of the time it would take to clear the way, it was all good for Peter. His only wait then would be for his uncle's demise.

To be honest, he doubted his uncle was strong enough to make it back home no matter which option he chose.

All the better for him. After the years of abuse and insult he'd suffered silently at his uncle's knee, he, better than anyone, deserved the inheritance.

It was as if God himself had decreed it so.

Peter smiled, turning silently to make his way back to his room, already planning the changes he would make when he was named Lord Moreland.

He, unlike Uncle Henry, had nothing but time.

Twenty-two

The hour had grown late by the time Leah and Rosalyn at last parted company. Rosalyn had told her stories about Mairi and Connor and his wife Cate, so many stories that she felt like she really knew those people for the first time.

And then there were the stories about Drew. It was as if she were able to see him as the mischievous little boy his mother described.

Drew, whom his mother claimed with certainty was in love with her.

Could it be possible?

Leah turned the likelihood over in her mind as she made her way back to her bedchamber.

Wouldn't that just be the final touch to the farce she'd been living? This wonderful, caring man who'd saved her from drowning, guided her where she wanted to go, protected her, even lied for her, to have him fall in love with her? The guilt would be more than she could stand.

She already owed him more than she could ever repay. How did one go about repaying love?

No. In spite of what his mother said, it wasn't possible. She was letting her vanity get the better of her. He wasn't the type of man who'd fall willy-nilly in love with some bedraggled woman he'd plucked from a river.

He was drop-dead gorgeous. He could have any woman he wanted.

And yet . . . his mother had said he didn't see himself that way at all. She'd said that he saw himself as less than a man because of the injuries he'd received. Granted, that scar down his chest was scary-looking, but how on earth could he think it diminished his beauty in the least?

Because the mind is powerful and controls a person in strange ways, forcing one to behave and think in a manner no reasonable person would expect.

Better than anyone, she should know. It had taken her years to get past what had happened to her in her youth. The idea that Drew thought of himself as less of anything dug at her heart.

He deserved better than that.

She pushed open the door between the kitchen and the hallway just in time to bump directly into Drew.

"Where the name of all that's holy have you been? When I found you missing from our bedchamber, I searched every inch of the keep, all to no avail." His cheeks were flushed a deep, mottled red and his eyes glittered with his emotion.

Could Rosalyn have had the right of it?

"Slow down a minute. I was out in the garden visiting with your mother."

He locked his fingers around her upper arm, leading her to the stairs and up toward their room, lecturing as they went. "Yer no ever to do that again without letting me know where you've gone. Do you ken what I'm saying to you? No ever."

She hadn't experienced anything like this since she was a little girl. They'd lived across the street from an elementary school and she'd gone over to the school grounds to play on the equipment. She'd seen her mother coming from the top of the slide and could tell even from a distance, her mom was furious.

It had been one of the few times her mom had ever spanked her, and even though it had been only one quick whack to her bottom, it had been devastating to her five-year-old psyche to have her mother that angry with her.

It had been her sister who had explained. Leah had huddled in her bed in the room she shared with Destiny, crying, feeling sorry for herself.

"Mom's so mad at me. She hates me," she'd sobbed.

"Don't be such a baby, Leah. She loves you to death. That's why she was so angry. She was terrified when she couldn't find you, that's all."

Destiny had been right, of course. She'd gone out to the living room and climbed into her mom's lap for cuddles, just like nothing had ever happened.

It was fear that had made her mother so angry. Fear formed out of love.

Oh, Lord. Maybe Rosalyn was right.

"I'm sorry you didn't know where I was. I didn't mean to frighten you, but I couldn't very well tell you where I was going when I didn't have any idea where you were."

"Frighten me?" he scoffed, pushing open the door to their room and leading her inside. "I was no frightened. Only concerned when I could no find you."

He wasn't frightened, huh? Just like he wasn't embarrassed now that she'd caught him being frightened.

"I'm sorry," she repeated, softly this time, reaching up to cup his face, fanning her thumb over his cheek. The day's growth of beard sent tingles through her skin as she rubbed her thumb back and forth.

The move she'd intended to sooth his emotions set hers on fire as if the feel of him was all it took. Whatever had been wrong with her last night, whatever had stripped her of her reason and made her want him, whatever it was, it still had control of her.

It apparently controlled him as well.

With an arm around her waist, he dragged her to him, crushing his lips to hers, holding her as if he'd never let her go.

"I couldna think straight for worry that Moreland had taken you away," he whispered when he broke the kiss. "I doona ever want to go through that again."

What could she say to take away the hurt she heard in his voice? *Sorry* seemed lame. *I won't do it again* would be a lie because she had no intention of spending every minute of the next few days in this room.

There was no good response. Instead she wrapped her hand around the back of his neck. Running her fingers up into his hair, she lifted her head the bare inch that separated them and resumed the kiss he'd broken before speaking.

His arms tightened around her and she felt her feet leave the floor but his tongue had dipped between her lips and that really was her only concern at the moment. That and the feel of his arms as they held her.

Then she was on her back, the soft bed beneath her, his hard body covering her.

His big hands cradled her head as he deepened their kiss, making her want to crawl inside him in her need to be close to him.

Her skirt slid up when his knee pushed at her, and her bare skin burned at contact with his. She lifted her legs, locking her ankles behind his back and he moaned into her mouth, rocking his pelvis against her.

A whole new level of need fired through her body.

From the rock-hard feel of him, his need was every bit as great as hers.

It was no effort to slide her hands down to his waist. A couple of tugs later and the bottom of his shirt came free from his plaid, offering her open access to his bare back.

Muscles rippled under her touch and her shift was lowered. Hot breath feathered over her sensitive breasts just before his tongue began to draw circles around her nipples.

His head shifted and he took her breast into his mouth. For an instant, she felt as if he were pulling her very being deep inside his own body.

An errant memory of a book she'd once read about the Wild Woman mythology wafted through her mind. Now, right now, for the first time in her life, she felt she understood what it meant to actually be a Wild Woman. No longer a child, not yet a Wise Woman, but that magical step in between.

At this moment, more than anything, a Wild Woman was the only thing in the world she wanted to be. His Wild Woman.

She ran her fingernails lightly down his back. His groan against her breast sent a tremor through her body that ended somewhere between her legs, sparking a sensitivity that made her think she could actually hear the blood pounding low, keeping time with her pounding heart, setting a rhythm for what was to come.

That *what was to come* was not in question. She knew what would happen if she didn't stop them in their tracks right now. Only thing was, she didn't want to stop it.

She was the Wild Woman.

With only his plaid separating them, the length of his shaft pressed against her sensitive folds and the need that had beat at her before became a demanding throb.

Two tugs to his plaid and nothing separated them, his hot skin scorching hers when next he rocked against her.

The hiss she heard when he sucked his breath between clenched teeth could as well have been the sizzle of heat firing between them.

"I doona think I've the will to tear myself away." His voice, low and gravelly, slid up her spine as if he trailed the spot with his hand.

"Listen to me. If you stop now," she panted in response, knotting her hands into the plaid bunched at his waist, "I swear to God, I'll be angry with you for the rest of my life."

"And that I could no live with," he murmured, dropping his head to trail kisses down her neck.

This time when he rocked against her, she lifted her hips to meet him. The tip of his shaft slipped into her folds and he froze, hesitating to make the next move.

She felt a bubble of laughter building low in her chest. The next move was up to her. No problem at all for a Wild Woman.

Sliding her hands down to the firm mounds of his butt, she pushed down as she lifted her hips, grinding against him, feeling him slide just inside her.

His hands cupped her bottom now, holding her in place as he pulled out. Holding her in place as he drove back in, burying his shaft deep inside her.

The bubble that had built exploded from her chest, not laughter but some primal combination of growl and scream.

The Wild Woman wanted more.

He shifted his hold as he pulled out again, one thumb raking over the swollen nub of her desire. Round and round, driving her into a frenzy before he drove deep again.

It was as if stars filled her eyelids and cotton clogged her ears. Every muscle in her body clenched in unison, over and over again until she felt as if she'd plunged off a precipice, flying through the air like some mythical beast.

Once more he buried himself in her, holding her body tightly to his. Deep inside her the throbbing contractions of his release sent her body trembling over the edge again.

He shifted his weight to one side, pulling her over without breaking their connection. They lay together, spent, their hearts beating as one for the longest time.

Was this what Destiny had tried to describe to her that day? The magic of the right man's touch. A touch that curls your toes.

At last, he lifted a hand, pushing hair from her face, tucking it behind her ear. For the life of her, she had no memory of the tie that held it back coming undone.

"Yer an amazing woman, Leah MacQuarrie. I canna say I've ever met yer like before."

"Yer no so bad yerself," she replied, copying his lilting speech.

He stroked a thumb down her cheek and she felt the Wild Woman stir, wondering how long might it take before he was good to go for another round.

"Yer spirit humbles me, woman. I look into yer eyes and I want to hear everything you've been through. I want to ken what makes you you. The story of yer life, from the way you were as a child right up to how you managed to escape MacQuarrie Keep to find yer way to the place we first met."

He wanted to talk?

She traced her forefinger along his shoulder and down his side, feeling the goose bumps that popped out on his skin. Across his stomach, to follow the track of dark hair plunging downward.

A little lower and the object of her interest sprang to life, leaving no doubts as to when he might be ready.

After what they'd shared this evening, she saw no need for secrets between them. She'd gladly tell him all her stories if that was what he wanted.

Later.

For now, the Wild Woman called.

Twenty-three

❧

Leah dreamed of beautiful things, of gentle things, of a butterfly perched on the tip of her nose.

She awoke to find it was no butterfly, but Drew's fingertip resting there. He lay on his side next to her, one long leg resting atop her.

"Morning, dearling. I'd begun to wonder if you might sleep through the whole of yer wedding day."

Her wedding day. She was getting married today.

She smiled into his handsome face, lifting her lips for him to kiss, thrilled when he obliged her.

Mindful to avoid the scar on his chest, she laid her hand on his stomach, allowing her fingers to ripple lightly over the hard muscles there. Over the muscles and lower. His shaft seemed to jump in greeting as she touched it, hardening immediately.

"Mmmm," she murmured, running her hand up and

down his length, delighted when it continued to grow under her touch until he clamped his hand over hers.

Leaning his head over hers, he covered her lips with his. Soft and warm, strong and sensual, his kiss fully awoke the need in her.

"You'll have to rein in that Wild Woman of yers. To my great regret, we've no time to pleasure her now. But you've my oath, dearling, I'll work extra hard tonight to make up for the wait."

Crapola. Way too much story-sharing last night. She'd known the minute she'd told him about the Wild Woman thing, she'd regret it sooner or later.

Sooner, as it turned out.

With a sigh, she flopped on her back and let him go. Not that she had any choice. In truth, it might be just as well he had to go. There didn't seem to be a spot on her body that wasn't sore this morning, like she'd participated in some heavy-duty new workout program.

Come to think of it, that's exactly what she'd done.

He rolled to his side of the bed, stretching to reach his plaid before he stood. With an expert flick of his wrist, he had the plaid wrapped around him.

But not fast enough.

Good holy shit! The scarred injury on his upper leg made the one on his chest seem no more than a silvered stretch mark. This one, with the skin all puckered and misshapen, looked as if someone had hacked a long chunk of meat from the bone.

No wonder he tried to hide it. No wonder he thought less of himself for it.

The fleeting image was burned into her mind, into her soul. She couldn't begin to imagine the pain he must have suffered when it had first happened. Couldn't stomach the mental anguish he carried with him even now.

Whatever it took, she wouldn't add any fuel to that internal fire.

Tamping down her ragged emotions, she met his eyes, seeing the fear there.

"Will I see you again before we leave to go down to the chapel?"

He shook his head, his expression clearing. "Likely no, dearling. You'll go down in the wagon with the other women. I'll ride alongside with the men."

The whole of the ceremony had been laid out for her yesterday. They'd travel down the hillside to the village chapel where they'd stand on the steps to receive the priest's formal blessings on their union. Then they'd return, likely with the entire village trailing along. A good feast was not to be missed.

His shirt slipped down over his head, covering the magnificent chest she'd been coveting only minutes ago.

"I'll send the maids up with a tub for yer bath. That way you can ready yerself in private."

Like that was going to happen. While there was nothing she'd like more than to soak her tired, achy body, she had no doubt that as soon as he opened that door, she'd be beset with the women of his family, each one determined to fix her up for her wedding day.

With a kiss to her forehead, he was gone.

As she'd rightly guessed, he couldn't have been more than halfway down the hall before the pounding on her door began.

"Hold on. I'll be right there." She threw back the covers, realizing as she did so that every stitch of clothing she'd worn had somehow made its way to parts unknown during the course of the previous night.

Untangling the linen coverlet from the bed, she wrapped it around herself before opening the door to what turned out to be quite a parade of activity.

Sallie entered first with Anabella trailing behind, heading up an entire parade of women all intent on some specific part of getting her ready for her big day. Two hefted a large wooden tub while several others carried steaming buckets.

Her bath had arrived.

Anabella laid the dress she'd held on the bed, turning her best imperious glare in Leah's direction after a pointed look around the room. "From the looks of things in here, I'd say you'll no be needing a lecture on how a proper virgin spends her wedding night."

No. She certainly wouldn't be needing anything like that. As a matter of fact, after last night, she was pretty sure she was qualified to be the one giving that lecture.

Not that she'd be rude enough to point that out to Anabella. No matter how much she might like to.

"Leave her be, Mother MacPherson," Sallie rebuked. "They're already married, as you well ken. Obtaining the blessing from the church is but a formality and today naught but an excuse to celebrate with my brother and his new wife."

Maybe that's what today was all about for these people. But for Leah, it was all about getting rid of Moreland so she could convince the MacKiernan laird to help Hugh and Margery.

A purely business transaction, and nothing more. The marriage meant absolutely nothing to her. Absolutely nothing.

Still, a feast was a feast and like everyone else, she saw was no reason not to enjoy a good party.

Or the attentions of a handsome man.

Leah sat as patiently as possible while Rosalyn affixed the circlet of blooms in her hair. Unfortunately, after her morning of preparations, her store of patience for the day was dwindling fast.

For a while there, she'd thought she was going to have to bodily remove the giggling gaggle of women from her chamber in order to have that "peaceful" bath Drew had suggested. Even once they'd left, she could hear them outside her door. Chattering and carrying on like . . . well, like a gaggle of women.

They'd fussed over the dress she wore, picking and adjusting every fold and fall of the garment. The dress was lovely. A pale yellow piece of fluff, with ribbons and actual button closures, the likes of which Leah hadn't seen in years.

She ran her hand across the material now, watching how the soft cloth billowed behind her touch.

"Keep yer head still for a bit longer, lass. I've almost got it." Rosalyn words were muffled as she spoke around the pins she held in her mouth.

Leah tried to ignore the distress she felt wearing the beautiful dress. Ellie had been all smiles as she'd announced it was the one she'd worn at her own wedding. It had been the part about how she was sure Leah and

Drew would be as happy as she and Caden that had gotten to Leah.

A huge lump sat in the back of her throat threatening to dissolve into tears with the slightest of provocations. Whether her unhappiness stemmed from guilt over faking the marriage or disappointment that the marriage wasn't real, she refused to allow herself to dwell on it. Putting much thought to the matter, she knew for a fact, would be all she'd need to send her over the edge of the emotional precipice where even now she teetered.

It was a business transaction. A means to an end and nothing more. Certainly not anything to get all weepy and emotional over.

"There," Rosalyn pronounced, stepping back to admire her handiwork. "All done."

As Leah stood, the long ribbons that hung from the delicate circlet draped gracefully over her shoulders and down her back. Although her dress was borrowed, the women had told her the circlet must be prepared just for her, a keepsake to put away to honor her marriage.

She let out a long shaky breath and looked around at the women who circled her. "I guess I'm ready." The hitch in her voice surprised her.

"Oh, no, sister." Sallie hurried forward, throwing her arms around Leah. "No tears. Yer face will go all blotchy and swollen. You dinna want that, no on a day as special as this."

"Besides, you know those tears are contagious, don' you?" Ellie stepped to her side, putting one arm around Leah's shoulders. "Why do you suppose weddings always make everyone want to cry?" She laughed at her own question, wiping her cheek.

"Joy," Rosalyn said simply, as if the answer should be obvious to anyone. "There's nothing like the joy of realizing you'll spend the rest of yer life with yer own true love. Nothing like the joy of seeing two souls made whole when they're joined together."

Against Leah's will, the tears that had pooled in her eyes began a slow trickle down her cheeks. First one and then another, as if once the path had been forged, the way was open.

For something that was intended as no more than a means to an end kind of business transaction, this wedding was kicking her emotional butt.

This simply would not do. She would not allow herself to behave this way.

A few sniffles, some rapid blinking, and she had the situation back under control where it belonged. Two deep breaths and she was good to go.

As long as everyone kept it light, she'd be fine. It was those heavy philosophical musings about what marriage was supposed to be that got to her. As long as there were no more provocations of that sort, she had it locked down and ready to go.

"Brides," Anabella scoffed. "You'd never have caught me shedding even a single tear, I can tell you. No at either of my weddings."

"I've no surprise at that." Rosalyn handed a soft cloth to Leah to dry her face. "That's what comes of viewing marriage as a business transaction rather than wedding for love. It's a sure path to nothing but misery."

And there it was, winging in from out of nowhere, the final little philosophical provocation she'd hoped to void. It landed like a punch to the gut and vibrated

out. The lump in Leah's throat burst, turning what had
been a gentle drip to a flood, the whole of it totally,
completely beyond her control.

She'd officially dropped over into Emotional Wreck
territory.

Someone took the dry cloth from her hand, replac-
ing it with a cold, wet cloth to hold over her face while
someone else patted her back and made soothing, coo-
ing noises in an attempt to calm her down.

How utterly, completely stupid of her to behave like
this. Consoling herself that none of this was real didn't
help at all. If anything, it made her feel worse, turning
the flood of tears into breath-catching sobs.

A knock sounded at the door and she muffled the
sounds she made by holding the cloth to her face, fighting to control her ridiculous emotions.

"Da says to hurry the hens. Everyone's waiting in the
courtyard."

"Oh, he says that, does he?" Sallie sounded a bit
sniffly herself. "Well, you tell him we'll be down when
we're good and ready and the lot of you can just wait
until then. It's no like there's a wedding to be had without the bride. Now go on with you." A pause and then
Sallie yelled at the retreating footsteps, "Duncan! You'd
best tell yer father I'll be talking to him about that her
remark when I see him next."

Beside her, Ellie chuckled softly. "Ran will be eating
those words for days to come."

The interruption had been exactly what Leah needed,
diverting everyone's attention from her long enough to
allow her to pull herself together.

She dropped the cloth to the table near the fire be

fore taking in a deep breath and slowly releasing it. With all the ridiculous damned tears at last dried up, she was herself again. Back in control.

Ignoring the excited, inane chatter swirling around her, she followed along as they made a type of procession out of her bedchamber toward the stairs, headed to the courtyard where Drew and the others awaited.

Such a silly little interlude back there. A breakdown like that was completely unlike her. All she could think of was that it was a result of being surrounded by all those women, all obviously on total estrogen overload.

Years ago in researching a paper for the advanced science class she'd taken, she'd read an article about how when women lived closely together their bodies would regulate themselves so that, after a while, all the women would have their monthly cycles at the same time. She'd wondered then about the author's assertions that somehow the estrogen passed messages from one woman to another.

Too bad she wouldn't be around in seven hundred years when that article was being researched. She could offer up today's weirdo moment as verifiable evidence of the claim.

They'd stepped outside onto the great staircase by the time Leah was ready to pay attention to her companions again. To her surprise, the courtyard was filled with men on horseback and women and children crammed into wagons, all waiting to accompany them down the hillside to the chapel in the little village.

A general excited murmur wafted over everything, evidence of the festive mood.

Without thought or intention, she sought him out.

Drew stood at the foot of the stairs, freshly scrubbed, wearing finery she hadn't seen before.

His eyes captured hers, his expression so intense she nearly missed her next step and was forced to grab Ellie's arm to prevent herself from falling.

Within a heartbeat he was at her side, taking her arm to the cheers of those waiting.

"Yer holding up?"

She nodded in answer to his question, unable to speak. This close, with his damp hair curling down into the ruffled shirt at his neck, his beauty overwhelmed her. Her mind filled with memories from the night before.

His hair had been damp then, too, but not fresh from the bathhouse. He'd hovered over her, sweat from their mutual exertion glistening on his naked body, sparkling in the glow of the fire's flickering flames.

She shivered as he caught her up, his hands at her waist, to lift her into the wagon.

"Yer the most beautiful bride I've ever seen," he whispered into her ear just before he released his hold on her.

A moment ago she would have sworn there wasn't a spare drop of moisture left in her body, but she'd have been wrong. There they were, buckets of tears pooling, glassing over her vision. Gallons of them, all just waiting for her to tip her head the slightest bit so they could pour down her face.

Blinking hard, once and then again, she fervently prayed she wouldn't embarrass herself out here in front of everyone.

His low chuckle sent a ripple of excitement coursing through her body. The kiss he placed against her ear, his teeth tickling at the lobe, turned the excitement into need, driving away any thought of tears as those gathered around set up a whooping cheer of approval.

"That's better," he whispered before stepping back. With a low bow to her, he turned and mounted his horse, bringing the animal alongside the wagon next to where she sat.

Better? She wasn't so sure. The tears were irrational and stupid, yes, but the pounding need that heated her face now and set her body thrumming with a desire to rip that fancy shirt off Drew's back was hardly an improvement.

She put a hand to her cheek to cool the burn. It was as if a fever had taken her. An illness might explain her irrational behavior. If she were able to be ill. Which she wasn't. Try as she might to deny that part of her, at times like this her Faerie heritage was undeniable.

The only illness she'd ever suffered had been when she touched someone, taking their illness on herself to heal them. And other than that little mishap with the wound on Drew's arm while they traveled to Dun Ard, she'd made sure to avoid using her gift for over a decade.

No, illness wasn't a viable excuse for her bizarre behavior.

But looking up at the magnificent man riding beside her, feeling the tangle of emotions that assaulted her when he was around, she was beginning to harbor a suspicion of what might constitute a viable excuse.

Problem was, with the troubles facing her family, this was no time to be finding her Soulmate. Especially not a Soulmate who descended from Faeries.

Faeries were not to be trusted in matters of the heart, no matter what anyone said. Her father had been Fae and according to her mother, they'd been Soulmates. But that hadn't stopped him from deserting her mother. It hadn't stopped him from breaking her heart.

Suspecting she'd found that one special soul only to have him be Faerie was bad enough.

Worse still was the knowledge she was marrying him with the sole intent of having that marriage annulled within days.

So much for the happy-ever-afters her mom had always promised.

Twenty-four

God's blessings on your union. May His love forever fill your lives together. Go in peace, my children. Greet the world together in God's holy name as husband and wife."

A cheer rose up around them as the priest's words echoed in Drew's ears.

It was done. The step he had long ago given up any hope of ever taking. He was married.

He looked down into Leah's beautiful visage and a grin he thought he might never be able to wipe away broke over his face. She was his, this beauty draped in soft yellow, like dappled sunlight on a spring day.

The expression she returned was almost timid, as if she were unsure of what to do next.

He could take care of that.

Sweeping her up into his arms, he covered her lips with his, deepening their kiss until the sound of the crowd's cheering disappeared, leaving only her in his focus.

Her.

Leah.

His wife.

Caden slapped him on the back, hollering his congratulations to be heard over the noise of those gathered around them. It was enough to break the spell of the moment and bring him back to his senses.

In his arms, Leah blinked rapidly as if she tried to gather her own good senses. She looked up at him with eyes unfocused by her own need and lips swollen and pink from his kiss. He could feel only regret that propriety would require them to attend the feast and celebration awaiting them back at Dun Ard.

He'd much rather beat a path directly to their bedchamber. Even the nearest empty storeroom would do, for that matter. He wanted her that badly.

Instead he carried her to his horse, climbing up to sit with her snug against him, fitting perfectly in his embrace. He urged the animal forward, setting him on a course back up the hillside to Dun Ard before burying his nose in the crook of Leah's neck, inhaling her essence.

The scent of his wife.

He shifted the reins to one hand, dropping the other to press low against her stomach. He'd thought only to pull her closer to him, but her soft moan of pleasure at his touch sent his imagination on a wild journey, conjuring visions of a variety of delights.

It would be so easy to push aside the delicate material of her wedding dress, to reach underneath, to run his hand along her shapely thigh, seeking her heat. So easy to plunge his fingers deep inside her, to tease that sensitive nub of her desire, driving her to the frenzied pitch he knew she would reach, all the while watching the ecstasy take her face.

So vivid his daydreams, he'd grown hard. When she pushed back toward him, her lovely little arse wiggling ever so slightly against his erection, he had to fight for the control not to embarrass himself right here.

His heart pounded in his ears, pounded his need for her.

People everywhere, streaming up the hill ahead of them, behind them, alongside them.

Too many people, too many eyes for him to do what he wanted most.

"Hold on," he warned her, spurring his horse to more speed.

There was no way he'd last until nightfall. He needed her now.

His mount's sides heaved in and out like an old bellows by the time they reached the bottom of the grand staircase at Dun Ard, the exertion of an uphill run taking its toll on the animal.

It was worth it. They'd gotten here well ahead of the crowd that followed. His horse would be fine after a short rest.

He jumped down from the saddle, pulling Leah into his arms and up the staircase behind him.

"What's going on?" she asked breathlessly, but he ignored her.

He needed to find the closest spot.

Into the hallway, beyond Blane's solar, to the small door which led one step down into a storage room.

He closed the door behind them, sealing them in a shroud of pitch black.

"What are you doing?" Leah asked slowly, enunciating each word as if she thought he might have lost the power of speech.

Another minute or two, and he well might.

He backed her up against the door, one hand to either side of her head, dipping his head to capture her mouth with his.

As before, she didn't disappoint. Her lips parted and her tongue dueled with his, giving every bit as good as she got.

By the Fates, he'd needed this. If he'd had the sense of an insect, he'd have passed up his morning workout in the lists and stayed in her bed.

He dropped one hand, lifting her skirt to grasp her inner thigh. Just as he'd imagined earlier, he followed her heat to its source, running his fingers lightly across her opening.

She moaned before pulling her mouth from his, panting already as she spoke. "A quickie? You dragged me into this smelly hole for a quickie?"

"If quickie means this." He rubbed the pad of his thumb over the nub of her desire, feeling it harden under his touch. "I'd thought to have a wee visit with the Wild Woman. Is this acceptable to you?"

One finger, two, he dipped inside her silky depths, continuing to massage the hard little nub with his thumb.

"Oh yeah," she moaned, pressing against his hand. "Oh, hell yeah."

So hot, so ready for him. He wanted nothing more than to plunge himself into her, burying his shaft in the soft, tight pleasure of her body.

Still he waited. Waited until her breath came in sharp, broken little puffs. Waited until she went still against him, her only movement the rhythmic contractions around his fingers. Waited until her hands scrabbled against his legs, pushing his plaid up and out of the way.

She lifted one leg and he entered, hard and fast, grabbing her bottom to hold her weight as she lifted her other leg, locking her ankles behind his back.

He drove into her, pressing her back against the heavy door. Again and again and again until his release took him to the stars.

When it was over, his leg trembled from the exertion, making him grateful for the time he'd spent in the lists this morning. Without it, he wouldn't have had the strength to do this.

"Jeez Louise," she murmured, her forehead against his chest. "I think the Wild Woman could learn to like quickies."

"I as well," he answered. He might even be able to last the whole of their wedding feast without another one. Maybe.

After making sure the hallway was empty, Drew held the door open, allowing her to step out first, his big hand possessively touching her back.

A quick glance down reassured Leah she wasn't a total mess after their storage room encounter. In fact, the soft material of her dress fell properly into its folds as if she'd done nothing more strenuous than riding.

She bit back a giggle as it occurred to her that "riding" had been exactly what she'd done.

Another surprise for her day. A month ago she would have totally discounted any suggestion that she'd be having wanton sex in a storeroom. So much for totally discounting anything ever.

A crowd had already gathered in the great hall, with more people trickling in. A glance out the entryway as they passed showed her people lining the tables that had been placed in the courtyard.

When the MacKiernan clan threw a feast, they really went all out.

Drew ushered her toward the table on the dais just as the musicians began to play at the back of the room. With flute and harp and drum and pipe, their music floated through the room, a delightful toe-tapping background to the hum of conversation and laughter.

As they made their way through the growing throng, Drew pulled her closer, tucking her under his arm protectively.

She'd just about decided her day couldn't get any better when a familiar voice knocked her right off the happy little pedestal she'd roosted on.

"Congratulations, MacAlister. A lovely ceremony, indeed."

Moreland. Would the blasted man never get out of their lives?

"Our thanks to you, Sir Peter," Drew responded with a nod of his head. "I hope you and yer men will enjoy the feast as well. I suppose you'll be leaving us before long?"

"Before long, to be sure," Moreland answered vaguely enough.

With another nod, Drew pushed her forward, away from the annoying knight, all the way to her seat next to his at the table.

People crowded everywhere. So many people, all wanting to introduce themselves or to shake Drew's hand. All of them wanting to offer their congratulations and good wishes for a long and happy life together.

She'd seen nothing like this in her time at Mac-Quarrie Keep.

The serving girl brought two cups to each of them, one the usual spiced wine she'd grown accustomed to. The other was a pale fragrant ale, smooth on the tongue with a touch of sweet. A couple of swallows and one thing became quite clear. Unlike the wine served with every meal, this ale had a much stronger bite of alcohol to it.

One dish after another was served to them, foods of all variety placed on the trenchers she shared with Drew. And always the cup of ale was kept filled.

Her shoulders grew heavy, her mind a bit fuzzed, but still the food and drink continued to come. The constant thrum of conversation filled the hall while the lovely undercurrent of music played on.

Ellie sat to her right, telling her a story about how Caden's family had conspired to play matchmaker for them by encouraging her to sneak away from Dun Ard through some hole under the bathhouse so that he would come after her and bring her back.

Leah wasn't sure she followed the logic of the story, not with all the interruptions as people came up to share their good wishes. It seemed likely that either the tale was made up purely for entertainment's sake or that she'd missed some important detail because, watching Ellie and Caden together, she found it impossible to imagine there had ever been a time when those two hadn't been deeply in love. Just the way they looked at each other was enough to make her blush.

And that was saying a lot for a woman whose first stop after her own wedding had been for a storage room tryst.

True or not, Ellie's storytelling skills had her giggling by the time she excused herself to check on other guests.

Leah took another sip of her ale, biding her time until Drew finished speaking with his brother. Perhaps his version of Ellie's story might make more sense.

If he ever turned around to pay attention to her again, that is. How long could two men drag out a discussion about sheep, anyway? It felt like hours already, though logic told her it hadn't been anywhere near so long.

Maybe it just felt that way because she wanted those deep brown eyes focused on her. She wanted to be the one making him laugh. Like some lovesick teenager with her first crush, she wanted all his attention.

She wanted another drink of that fine, sweet ale.

"Pardon, my lady, but I'd ask yer leniency that I might borrow yer husband for a brief time." The laird himself stood behind her chair. "I've a matter of some import to discuss with him."

"Of course," she answered, doing her best not to sigh. Even she knew one didn't say no to the laird, no matter that she'd been waiting forever to speak to him herself.

Drew stood, leaning down to kiss her cheek. "I'll no be long, dearling. Enjoy yerself until I get back."

She nodded her agreement, but he was already gone.

And just how did he expect her to enjoy herself without him?

"Better get used to it," she muttered aloud, lifting her cup for another sip of the wonderful ale. Before long, if all went according to plan, she'd be back at MacQuarrie Keep. Richard would be vanquished, life would be back to normal. No excitement, no intrigue, no rendezvous in the storeroom.

No Drew.

The thought filled her with an instant sorrow and for a second, she thought for sure the tears were back. She lifted the cup once more but paused as it reached her mouth. Her fingers felt too thick to hold it, her lips too numb to properly feel the rim of the cup.

She'd obviously had enough of the ale. What she needed now was some fresh air.

Twenty-five

Considering how off-balance and lacking in proper coordination her body felt, she was doing pretty well to have located the balcony so quickly.

With a contented sigh, Leah walked to the edge, looking down into the courtyard below where a crowd still gathered around the tables that had been set up out there.

The entire day had been like something out of a fairy tale. An X-rated fairy tale, to be sure, but a fairy tale nonetheless.

Fairy tale. Faerie tail.

She snorted aloud as her mind played with the words, slapping a hand over her mouth to cover her case of giggles.

Just look at all those people down there. How many of them knew they feasted on food served by Faeries?

Most likely none or they'd be hard-pressed to be so happy.

"There's a lot you people don't know," she whispered into the night.

All of them laughing and eating and visiting, seeming to thoroughly enjoy the celebration of her wedding.

If they only knew the truth of it, would they still be carrying on like that? If they only knew that this marriage was a sham? A temporary convenience at best?

Very soon, this part of her life would be over and she'd return to her self-imposed seclusion at MacQuarrie Keep.

Unless . . .

What if Rosalyn had accurately judged her son's feelings? What if the seemingly undeniable physical attraction she felt for Drew was really a sign of something bigger, something that would last forever? What if he truly was the Soulmate her mother had promised awaited each of her children?

Faint strains of music floated to her, bringing with it an old memory, so potent, so powerful, it gripped her heart, refusing to be pushed away.

Her mother, bent over the coffee table in their tiny living room, winding the little key on the music box that had been a wedding gift from her own true love.

Tinny strains of that music filled Leah's mind, as real as if she were back there in that room again. Without thought, her feet moved into the comfortable waltz pattern of old. How many times had she done this with her mother?

It had been her time with Mama. Her time, while Destiny and Chase were away at school. Her time, when Mama would tell her stories and share her secrets. Secrets about life. Secrets about the Fae.

The music would start and Rainbow would clasp Leah's small hands, twirling her around and around, her off-key voice continuing the song long after the music box had gone silent.

"Some—where—my—love," Leah took up the refrain now, dancing alone on the darkened balcony.

She'd been so young then, not yet in school, and even at that age she recognized the sorrow that would eventually take her mother from her.

So lonely. Her mother had been so lonely for the man she'd loved with all her heart. The Faerie who'd left her, taking with him half her soul. The Faerie responsible for the magical gift that had plagued Leah's life.

"No, baby," her mother would say as she'd wound the little key. "Don't be sad for Mama. These are happy tears. It happens like this sometimes. I know I'll be with your daddy again one day. That's how it's all meant to work. We're Soulmates, destined to be together like two halves of one whole. Somewhere, someday, in some lifetime, we'll find each other again and then we'll both be so happy."

"Some—where—my—love," Leah sang. Eyes closed, she danced with the woman in her memory, slipping into her own off-key hum to accompany her steps when the words failed her.

Was she so much like her mother? Would it be the same way for her? Biding her time, waiting for this lifetime to end in hopes she could get on to the next one, that one special lifetime where she and her own Soulmate could finally be together.

Or maybe, just maybe, *this* was her one special lifetime and if she didn't wake up to reality and make the right choices, she risked wasting her one chance at true happiness.

Now if she could only figure out how to determine the truth of it.

"Good Lord, Leah. 'Lara's Theme'?"

Leah's eyes flew open and she grabbed for the railing next to her as her feet stumbled to a stop. Ellie walked toward her, a wide grin covering her face.

"I should have guessed. No wonder Rosalyn's so happy. You really are the perfect wife for Drew, aren't you?"

"Should have guessed what?" Leah's brain felt as though it was wrapped in a big wad of cotton, blurring all her thoughts, making her work extra hard just to think them. It was as if there was something in her sister-in-law's words she should have picked up on, something that needed comment, but she simply couldn't filter it out of all the fuzz right now.

Leah stepped forward and her head spun, forcing her to grab for the railing again.

"I knew the minute I saw you leave the table that I should have thought to warn you about the ale. It might taste good, but it has a mule's kick. I avoid it like the plague, personally, but then I'm not much of a drinker. Come on." Ellie put an arm around Leah's shoulders, leading her to the door and inside. "Let's find that man of yours and get him to put you to bed so you can get some rest."

Ellie wanted Drew to put her to bed so she could get some rest? Giggles overtook Leah again at the prospect.

Ellie sure didn't know Drew very well. "Rest" didn't seem to be something she and Drew were capable of when they were alone. Not anymore. Not since they'd discovered *other* things to do in bed.

"Or in storerooms," she managed to say aloud between fits of giggling.

"Oh, honey, you're going to feel like poop tomorrow. Lucky for you, Rosalyn has the most wonderful herbal concoction to take away the better part of what's going to ail you. Trust me, I should know."

"Herb con . . . cocks." It was as far as she could get without dissolving in giggles.

Her mother had always told her the Fates had a wicked sense of humor. Judging by her life recently, *wicked* had to mean obsessed with penis humor.

First it was a Dick who'd been the reason she'd left MacQuarrie Keep. Then she'd bumped into a Peter, the knight who plagued her life.

"Now herbs with cocks," she managed to say aloud as she fought to catch her breath from all the giggling.

How eighth grade. Penis humor. The Fates had bombarded her with one annoying penis after another.

In fairness, not all annoying. One particular penis had been about as far from annoying as you could get.

"And there it is!" she squealed, overcome with giggles yet again as Drew approached.

"What have you done to her?" he demanded, taking her from Ellie's care into his own. "What's happened to you?"

"Wicked, wicked Fates," she gasped, muffling her words into his shoulder as she leaned against him. Oh, her stomach hurt from laughing so hard.

"It's the honey ale, Drew. You should have warned her or at least told the servers to back off," Ellie answered, sounding as if she fought laughter herself. "I'll bring up your mother's herbs in a bit. If you put the tea on for her first thing in the morning, she'll be just fine."

How lovely! She'd have Drew tonight followed by tea in the morning.

"Cock tea," she giggled into his shoulder, completely unable to stop herself.

Wicked, wicked Fates.

He'd finally had no choice but to pick up Leah and carry her to their room.

"Thank the Fates you've at last come to yerself again." He'd begun to wonder if she'd giggle all night. But, finally, by the time Ellie delivered the little pot of herbs, Leah had managed to get herself back in control.

"Wicked, wicked Fates," she said for perhaps the tenth time from her seat in the middle of their bed.

To his relief, laughter no longer accompanied the words that had set her off on a new round of hysteria each time she'd said them before.

Though in truth, he wasn't yet convinced that this new solemnity wasn't every bit as concerning as the laughter had been.

"Under the covers with you, dearling. You should get yerself some sleep to ward off the effects of the drink."

"Can't," she argued, pointing a hand over her shoulder. "Buttons."

Damnation. It was Ellie's gown she wore. Whatever had possessed his sister-in-law to insist on a line of tiny, hand-carved buttons running the back of the dress to fasten it closed was beyond all understanding. But insist she had. He remembered well the consternation it had caused the old man who'd carved them, his big fingers fumbling to make sure he pleased Caden's intended.

Women.

A simple set of laces would have closed the frothy gown just as well and been a sight more practical.

"Turn around, then."

She scurried from the center of the bed, perching at last on the edge, her hair pulled over her shoulder to expose the dratted buttons. His fingers felt overly large and clumsy as he fumbled to push the wood carvings through the tiny stitched holes. If this weren't Ellie's dress, he'd be tempted to rip the thing apart and toss it into the pit.

As it was, he had a healthy respect for his sister-in-law's temper. Too healthy to risk damage to her dress.

So he continued to fumble, growing more frustrated by the second.

The growing expanse of bare skin that greeted his success was no help, either. If anything, the more the dress opened, the harder it became for him to concentrate on the tedious work.

"That's enough," he announced, rising to his feet. "You can pull it off over yer head now." He hadn't intended his words to sound so gruff, but there was no help to be had for it. A man could only take so much.

With a crooked smile lifting one side of her mouth, she raised her arms above her head. "You take it off for me."

He shook his head and stepped back a pace. No matter what had passed between them before, he wouldn't be accused of taking advantage of a woman who was in her cups. Not even his wife.

"No? You won't even come over here and sit with me?"

The smile on her face grew as she slipped the gown off first one arm and then the other. Pushing the material to her waist, she leaned forward, one finger feathering suggestively over her exposed breast.

"What about now?"

The palms of his hands itched to cover the ripe beauties displayed for him. Again he shook his head in refusal, turning his back to reinforce his will. If he couldn't see what she offered . . .

"Go to sleep," he ordered, his voice raspy as the need took him.

Behind him, her feet hit the floor, a quiet shuffling splat against the stone. A rustle of cloth followed a moment later by a curtain of yellow froth floating down over his head.

"What in the name of all that's . . ."

His plaid lifted and her hand, warm and gentle, stroked up his inner thigh and trailed around his hip, freezing the words in his mouth, cutting off even the workings of his brain which commanded the ability to speak.

Something akin to a gurgle was the only sound he had power to make as she seemed to float in front of him and her fingers wrapped around the base of his shaft.

"What about now," she whispered, stretching up on her tiptoes to run her tongue across his bottom lip.

She stood before him, wearing nothing but the stone hanging at her neck and a big smile.

Not even the strongest of men would have kept their resolution faced with such as that.

He grabbed her, both hands at her waist, and turned to the bed. He had no choice in the matter. Before he could even register his actions, she was wiggling beneath him, bare and wanting, making those contented little noises of hers that drove him wild.

In the next moment, his shirt was off, followed by his plaid. Her hands kneaded their way from his waist to grasp his buttocks even as she locked her legs around his.

"Do you love me?"

Her question caught him by surprise. "Yer my wife," he answered at last, not sure he was able to say more.

"I didn't ask that." She pushed a lock of hair behind his ear and feathered her soft thumb over his cheek. "Do you love me? Am I your Soulmate?"

He could hardly give an answer he didn't know himself. He'd thought it might be possible, but how could he claim to love her when he'd betrayed her?

If she were his Soulmate, wouldn't he have fought harder for that which she wanted so badly? Wouldn't he have stood up to Blane's decision not to send men to help her grandparents?

He wanted her. That much he knew with no doubts. Wanted her in his bed and in his arms. Wanted her ability to heal him. Wanted her to her make him feel whole. Whole in body and in spirit.

Beneath him, she waited, looking up at him, so willing, so trusting, he thought for a brief instant his heart might break with the knowledge of his own treachery.

He could say none of those things. No more than he could bear to tell her that which she wanted most had been denied.

"I need you more than I've ever needed anything."

It seemed to be enough to satisfy her.

"It was the Fates themselves that set us together, Drew. It had to be, don't you think?"

The Fates? Perhaps she was right.

Wicked, wicked Fates.

Twenty-six

*H*ow on earth had Ellie known the name of that song last night?

Leah sipped at the tea Drew had brewed for her before he'd gone. It hadn't even been daylight when he'd kissed her forehead and told her he was off to the lists. She was almost tempted to think he'd left early to escape spending time with her.

Not that she could blame him completely. She'd felt used up and foul when she'd first awakened.

Thank goodness for this tea. Now on her second cup, she could actually believe that her head wasn't going to explode after all.

No more honey ale for her. Not ever. It had clouded her mind and stripped her of every inhibition she had left.

Not that she appeared to have as many as she'd

thought, based on her behavior over the last couple of days.

She laid her head against the back of the big chair, eyes closed, and stretched her feet toward the warmth of the fire. Unbidden, strains of her mother's favorite song drifted through her mind once more.

The damn thing wouldn't even be written for seven hundred years. There was no way Ellie could know its name . . . at least no way unless Ellie had come from the future, too.

Leah lifted a hand to her temple, massaging. The whole thing was enough to give her a headache, if she hadn't already managed that herself with all the ale she'd downed last night.

It wasn't impossible. Look at her. If she'd managed to get here from the future, why couldn't Ellie. The people were Faerie descendants, after all.

Glancing up to the window casement, she noted the sun was high in the morning sky. Surely Drew should have returned by now. It had been hours since he'd left. No one worked out for that long.

Tired of waiting, she pushed up from her chair and crossed the room to the big chest in the corner. A clean shift, a drying towel, and she'd be ready to hit the bathhouse. A nice long soak and she'd feel like a new woman.

And if Drew still wasn't back by then?

She'd find something to do with herself. Maybe she'd hunt Ellie down and ask her where she came from. Or when. That should make for one interesting little conversation.

A contented smile curved her lips as she stepped into the hallway.

Ahead of her, maids bustled back and forth through an open doorway, hauling bundles of bedding in and out.

"Cleaning day?" she asked when she drew even with the door.

"No, my lady," one of the girls answered. "Sir Peter has taken his English arse back where it belongs."

"Agnes!" another rebuked sharply. "You shouldna be saying such as that."

"True," the first replied, smiling. "As I've no proof he's gone back to England, only that he's left here."

The two of them giggled, heads bent as they continued their work.

Moreland was gone?

Oh, this was already shaping up to be the best day she'd had in a very long time.

Bath taken, light lunch delivered to her room and finished, and still Drew hadn't returned.

It was almost enough to make a girl think he was avoiding her. But why on earth would he feel the need to do something like that?

Because Moreland was gone? Now that would make sense. She'd agreed to wait until the knight had left before pressing the issue of going to help the MacQuarries.

And yet . . . according to Rosalyn, Drew had already presented her case to the laird.

She paced, back and forth in front of the fireplace, her thoughts struggling to find a possibility that worked.

Unless . . .

What if Drew had already received the laird's word on the matter? Word that he didn't want to pass on to her.

But would he hesitate because the laird's decision had come down against giving his help or for it?

Whatever the case, Drew might not want to speak with her, but she certainly wanted to speak to him. Even if only to put her uncomfortable suspicions to rest.

She stepped into the hallway to find Ellie hurrying in her direction.

"I was just coming to get you." Ellie grasped Leah's hand as she reached her side. "I want to show you something."

"Show me what?" Now that she'd made up her mind to hunt down Drew and confront him, she really wasn't up for a distraction.

"Puppies! The most wonderful little squirming balls of love you'll ever lay eyes on. They're just precious. And though they're only three days old, Missy assures me they're ready for visitors."

Puppies? Okay. Maybe a short delay would do her good. Give her time to cool down a little so that she wouldn't be quite so confrontational when she found Drew. Confrontational could be bad. Especially if she'd simply made a big deal in her mind out of nothing. Besides, she'd wanted to talk to Ellie anyway.

"Let's go."

She followed quietly alongside Ellie as they left the keep and headed toward the outbuildings, but held back a step or two when she noted one of the stable boys out in the courtyard.

Confrontation might be a bad idea but simply knowing where Drew had gone off to shouldn't be a problem.

She veered her course, stopping just behind the boy.

"Excuse me. I was looking for Drew. Have you seen him?"

The boy appeared startled at first, then glanced up at the sky, one eye squinted, before answering.

"This time of day, it's likely he's in the lists, my lady. Should I take word yer looking for him?"

"No, thank you. I'll wait until he's finished." She turned from the boy, hurrying to catch up with Ellie.

"Is something wrong?" the woman asked as she joined her.

"Not really. It's just that I haven't seen Drew since early this morning so I thought I'd ask around to see if anybody knew where I might find him."

Ellie smiled and reached for her hand again, pulling her forward as she started walking. "No need to worry. This time of day he'd likely be in the lists."

But he'd gone to do that just as the sun was rising. Nobody worked out that much. Okay. Maybe professional soldiers who made their living fighting for whatever lord would pay them most might spend that much time practicing. But Drew wasn't a professional soldier.

He didn't even condone fighting. His mother had confirmed that herself.

They'd entered a small building off the side of the main stable and there, toward the back, stood the huge beast of a dog Ellie had sent to keep her company in the garden. If Leah didn't know better, she'd swear the animal guarded what looked like a padded box, where an alert-eyed little terrier and several squirming bundles of fluff lay.

"Hey, Missy. This is my new sister, Leah. She's the one I told you about. I brought her out to admire your beautiful babies. May we hold one?"

Was she serious? Leah found her head swiveling between the woman at her side and the dog at her feet. Ellie behaved as if she were actually having a conversation with the animal. More amazing was that the dog looked intelligent enough to be answering!

"Thank you, sweetie." Ellie bent, touching each little ball of fur in turn. "You did so good on these babies, Missy!"

Weird. Maybe that's what living in a nest of Faeries eventually did to you, set you to talking to animals.

"Ellie, I've a question for you. I may be totally off base but . . ." She paused trying to think of a subtle way to ask, realizing at last there was none. Maybe she could work her way up to asking what she really wanted to know. "You're not from around here, are you? I mean, not originally."

Ellie looked up at her, smiling as she rubbed one of the little furballs against her cheek. "No. I was born and raised just outside a little town called Prairieland."

"Uh-huh." Certainly didn't sound Scottish. Or medieval. "And what would you say if I were to ask something totally off the wall, like, have you even been born yet?"

The other woman laughed, handing the bundle she held up to Leah before standing with another curled in her hand. "I guess I'd have answer by saying, technically, no. No more than you have, am I right?"

"You are." At least she had her explanation as to how Ellie had known the name of that song.

"Believe me, Leah, it's a whole lot easier if you don't put a lot of effort into trying to wrap your brain around it. The Fae have their own reasons for everything they do. And while those reasons may not make any sense at all to us while we're in the middle of whatever's going on, once you get on the back side of it, the view is altogether different." Ellie snuggled her face into the puppy she held and smiled again. "Aren't they precious?"

The dark ball of fur in Leah's hand wiggled and a tiny pink tongue touched her finger. No wonder people loved puppies so much. They tugged at your heartstrings and made you happy no matter what your troubles, a living, breathing distraction from the concerns of the world.

Maybe she should bring Drew out here to try petting puppies for a while instead of spending all his time with that sword stuff.

Too bad the concerns of the world had a way of creeping back in.

"Don't you think it's strange that Drew spends so much time in the lists? He's always out there."

Two or three times a day ever since they'd arrived here, it seemed. How a man as thoughtful and caring as Drew, as opposed to fighting as he was supposed to be, could be so obsessed with participating in the violence of practicing swordplay was beyond her ability to comprehend.

"Of course he is. He has to be."

"I don't understand. It's not like he's a mercenary or anything. Why does he have to? Why the constant practice to build his skill with a sword?"

Ellie tipped her head, smiling quizzically. "It has nothing to do with skill. You've seen his injuries. The exercise he takes in the lists is the only thing standing between him and the debilitating pain that threatens to make an invalid of him. Surely he's told you. He's spent years searching for some other relief, some miracle cure, but until he finds one, this is all he can do. If he stops, he'll end up confined to his bed in no time at all."

Leah's throat tightened as she listened to the words. As if she'd taken a punch to the stomach, a wave of nausea washed over her.

He'd found his miracle cure. Her. No wonder he was so kind, so accommodating. No wonder he'd insisted that they should marry. It had nothing to do with loving her. Nothing to do with thinking she was his Soulmate.

He only wanted to be healed and thanks to one careless moment, he knew she had the ability to make that healing happen.

Twenty-seven

No more excuses. Time to face doing what needed to be done.

Drew gathered his dirty shirt and plaid into a bundle and left the bathhouse, headed for the bedchamber he shared with Leah.

His wife.

He'd done everything in his power to avoid the conversation he must have with her, even going so far as to borrow a change of clothing from Caden.

But now, as the sun sank low in the horizon, it was time to put aside the actions of a coward and tell her.

If only it wouldn't hurt her so much to hear that Blane had decided against helping her family. He'd give anything to avoid being the one to cause her pain.

Liar! His guilty conscience pounded in his brain, over and over as it had all day.

If her pain means so much, why didn't you fight your laird's decision? Why didn't you throw the full force of your support back in his face when he said no? Why did you agree he'd chosen the right path, like some pathetic bootlicking vermin?

Across the garden and into the kitchens, he listened to the accusations he was unable to shut out. Up the stairs and to his own doorway they followed, their indictment beating at him.

"No more," he whispered, his hand pressing on the door.

He hardened his mind to the argument. Steeled his heart for the confrontation to come. Refused to even consider at what point the voice of his conscience ringing in his head had become Leah's voice.

She sat quietly staring into the fire, her hands clasped in her lap. Nary a single candle was lit against the growing gloom of evening.

"Good evening, dearling." He forced the cheerful greeting in advance of the conversation to come. "Did you no want the candlelight to chase away the dark?"

He busied his hands, touching a twig to the fire to carry to the candles.

Stalling. *Be a man for a change. Tell her the truth.*

Her eyes bore into him when he turned. His traitorous imagination tried to convince him disappointment and accusation already swam in those depths. But that couldn't be. There was no way she could have learned the truth already. Blane had assured him he would be the one to break the news to her in his own good time.

The time that lay heavily upon him now.

"Our laird has advised me of his decision regarding yer request for aid to MacQuarrie Keep."

She didn't move, nor did her expression change. He wondered briefly if she even blinked.

"And?" she asked quietly when a time had passed uncomfortably long between them.

"Our laird has fully considered yer request but regrets he canna offer his help. Any attempt to save yer grandparents would result in a battle with the English who hold yer family keep and he canna justify exchanging the lives of our people for yers."

He waited. Waited for her response; waited for her eyes to soften.

Neither came.

"I ken yer upset, dearling, but yer bound to respect the decision of yer laird."

"Your laird, not mine." Slowly she pushed up out of the chair, her arms crossed over her breast. "All these days of waiting, for nothing. You've wasted my time. Wasted what little time my grandparents have."

"He's yer laird as well since we've married." He moved close to her, placing a hand on her shoulder. "You've no a need to worry over what's to happen to you. As my wife, this is yer home now."

He babbled, carrying on like some serving wench with good gossip, unable to stop his own blether, until she ducked her shoulder away from his touch. Backing away, she stepped behind her chair, placing it between them like a shield in battle, her hands clutching the wood.

"I didn't marry you to find a home for myself. I married you to get rid of Moreland so that I could get help to go to my grandparents. I was clear about that from the beginning."

As if her reason for marriage was important to him. "It's of no matter why we wed. We're wed. That's all that matters now."

"It's not all that matters. I was honest with you. You knew I agreed to the marriage because it was the only way you'd take me to the people who could save my grandparents. But you?" She shook her head, her fingers tightening on the chair back until he thought the blood might cease to flow. "You were only interested in what would benefit you."

She blamed him for Blane's refusal? "I took yer request to our laird. I'm the one who spoke on yer behalf." At least until Blane refused to help. Then, when it might have done some good, he'd been silent.

"That's not what I'm talking about and you know it. Why'd you agree to marry me?"

Did her disappointment make her daft?

"You ken the reason well enough. If we'd no wed it would have brought the wrath of Moreland down on my people. Him and the soldiers who amassed at our gates."

"You lie!" she yelled, her eyes flashing with what could only be anger.

Daft or no, he'd had enough.

With one arm, he swept the chair from between them, sending it toppling out of his way to land on its side. He grabbed her wrist and dragged her close. He wouldn't be accused of something he hadn't done.

"We've covered this ground before, you and I. I told you then, I'm no a man given to falsehoods. I've no ever lied to you."

"Why did you marry me?" she demanded again, as if she'd never heard his answer the first time.

"Because Moreland—" he began, stopping in surprise when she slammed the side of her fist into his chest.

"Lies! You married me to use me. You said yourself you knew what I was. I should have paid more attention, but I didn't. I was too stupid. I'd been careless enough to heal that damn cut on your arm and you wanted me to heal all that afflicts your body." She jerked her hand from his hold, rubbing at her wrist as she backed away from him. "You married me to use me. Deny that if you can."

Of course he couldn't deny it. They both knew that well enough. So he stood there staring at her, his face a hardened, emotionless mask that might as well have belonged to a stone carving.

It hurt. She'd known it was true before he'd ever opened his mouth. Confirming it as he did with his silence cut her to the bone. She wanted only to have it over with. To end this miserable episode and move on.

"Moreland is gone. We should speak to your laird immediately and start proceedings to have our marriage annulled."

"There can be no annulment for us." He turned his back to her, leaning one hand against the mantle as he stared into the fire.

That's what he thought. Of course there could be. "You married me for something I have absolutely no intention of ever giving you so there's no point in hanging on. The whole thing is a farce. It has been from the beginning. We fill out papers or something and it'll all be over."

"There can be no annulment," he insisted stubbornly, turning his head to capture her with his eyes. "We presented ourselves as married to all we encountered, which on its own is enough to make it so. We said our vows on the steps of the church in full view of all, sealing our fate. We *are* husband and wife."

"No," she denied. She wouldn't accept it. She couldn't. Spending her life married to a man who only wanted to use her? Whether it was using her to breed babies or using her for her Faerie gift, it was still using her. No. She wouldn't be used. That was what she'd risked everything, *everything*, to run from before. "There has to be a way to end this."

His eyes, dark and sad, bore into her. "The marriage has been consummated. There can be no possibility of annulment."

Yes it had been. But that had been when she'd imagined he might love her. "No one has to know about that." She wouldn't tell.

"I'll know." He shook his head, taking another step closer. "You'll know. You are my wife, Leah. I warned you it would be forever once we set foot in Dun Ard. You accepted those terms. You agreed to pay that price."

He reached a hand to her shoulder but she slapped it away, backing up another step.

"A price I agreed to pay to save my grandparents, which isn't going to happen now. Not to mention that I agreed before I knew what the price really was. Before I knew that all you really wanted me for was to use me as the magic cure you've been hunting for years."

"You'd refuse to use yer gift to help yer own husband?"

Oh, but he had that incredulous tone down just perfect.

"I won't use that damned, blighted Faerie curse for anyone, least of all someone who thought to trick me into it." She paused at the hitch in her voice, but only long enough to gather her control. "You've no idea what you ask of me. You don't know anything."

Without another word, he walked away, stopping only when he reached the door.

"I may ken little, my lady. But one thing I do ken is that I'd do all in my power to aid my own wife. My honor would demand it."

"You and your honor can just get the hell out!" she yelled, though in truth, her words were lost to him in the slamming of the door. He'd gone before she'd had the chance to demand he leave.

She'd wanted so much for it not to be true. Prayed it would all be some big mistake he would explain away when she confronted him.

Instead, he'd acted as if he were the injured party when she'd refused to heal him.

"Honor, my ass," she seethed, squatting down in front of the fire, her head in her hands.

Just last night he'd said he loved her. How could it turn out like this?

Because he'd never said any such thing.

He'd never said those words. She realized now it was only that she wanted so badly to hear the words, she'd accepted what he had said.

He'd said he needed her. About that he absolutely had not lied. He wanted to use her as much as Lord Moreland had. He wanted her for her gift. Just like the Nuadians had.

And using her against her will was something she'd determined long ago no one would ever do again.

Twenty-eight

❧

A stray moonbeam washed across the floor. It shone through the shutters Leah had neglected to close against the night. She watched unmoving as it slowly crept closer to where she sat.

Sooner or later, she'd need to get up off her miserable butt and get started if she were really going to do this thing.

"Sooner," she whispered, the sound seeming to echo off the walls of her empty room.

Drew hadn't returned after their fight. Not that she expected he would. Not that she wanted him to. It would be more than fine with her if she never saw the sneaky, selfish bastard again as long as she lived.

Now if she could just get to a point where the thought of never seeing him again didn't hurt more than the knowledge that he was a sneaky, selfish bastard, she'd be just fine.

"I'll be fine anyway. I don't need him."

She would be. It wasn't like she didn't have a purpose to keep her going. Hugh and Margery were depending on her. She might have been sidetracked for a bit, but she was back on the job now. They needed her help and she wouldn't fail them, no matter what it might cost her.

With the MacKiernan laird's refusal to send men to the aid of MacQuarrie Keep, their rescue fell squarely on her shoulders. She'd had the whole of the evening to think on what she could do and though her plan was little more than a half-jelled worm of a thing, it was the best she could come up with on her own.

She pushed to her feet, then crossed to the bed and picked up the small bundle she'd prepared earlier. It consisted of the things she'd originally brought with her, along with the rolls, meat, and cheese the cook had sent up for her and Drew to share for their evening meal.

He could damn well find his own food or do without, for all she cared. She would need this.

Since her cloak had been lost, she decided taking one of his plaids would be no great loss. She'd figure out a way to return it later, just as Drew had returned the horse he'd borrowed from the priory. What was good for him was good for her. Granted, he'd asked permission, but it wasn't like that was an option available to her.

Oh, by the way, I've decided to go back to MacQuarrie Keep to offer myself in marriage to Lord Moreland in exchange for control of the keep being returned to Grandpa Hugh.

Yeah. That was likely to go over well with this crowd.

Likely they'd get all ruffled up about the fact that she was already married.

A minor detail she wasn't going to let ruin her plan, such as it was.

It wasn't like anyone had a really efficient way to look things up. Lord Moreland would drag her back to England, so it wasn't as if she'd ever run into any of these MacKiernans. And if she eventually had to face Sir Peter again? It should be easy enough to convince him she'd obtained the annulment she had wanted.

Not a perfect plan by any means. She'd still end up getting used.

But it would be at her choice. *Her* choice. Something she'd willingly offer up to save Grandpa Hugh and Grandma Mac, not something someone had forced her into doing. Or worse, tricked her into doing.

Her breath caught in her throat and she clenched her teeth until she thought they might crack.

She was done with tears. Done. And even if she wasn't, she wouldn't spill another single drop over Drew MacAlister.

Stepping into the darkened hallway, she pulled the door quietly shut behind her.

Her plan would work. It had to. It was all she had left.

The only thing that could hold her back was if she couldn't find that hole under the bathhouse Ellie had spoken of in the story she'd told at the wedding feast.

Accuse him of lying, would she? What about her? It was she who'd refused all along to even admit she had the power to heal.

Drew felt beside him in the dark, dragging his hand through the hay littering the stable floor for the flask of whisky he'd taken from Blane's solar.

And what kind of a wife would refuse to heal her own husband? The man she'd vowed before God and everyone to honor for all her days.

He should put it out of his mind and end the pain but he couldn't. Instead he dredged up every memory of every conversation he'd had with Leah, every moment he'd spent in her presence, every touch, every word, much as a child might pick at a scab on his knee.

Tipping back his head, he drained the last drop of amber liquid from the flask.

Too bad it would do no more than slake his thirst.

"Damned Faerie blood."

What he needed was a good blanketing of his mind. He wanted to be so arse-faced he'd not be able to find a coherent thought with both hands.

Because the coherent thoughts he was finding at the moment were not his friends. And no matter how he might attempt to skew them, they didn't point to his being the good guy here.

Deny as he might, he had lied. To Leah and to himself. Not about the healing. He wouldn't deny he still wanted that from her.

No, his lie went much deeper.

Last night she'd asked if he'd loved her. She'd wanted to know, as any with Fae blood might, if she'd tied herself to her Soulmate.

And him, like the lying coward he was, he'd used every excuse he could find to avoid the obvious answer.

It couldn't be true or he never would have let Blane come to any decision other than the one she wanted, not without a good fight.

It couldn't be true because.

"Because, because, because," he whispered. Because why? Because it terrified the hell out of him, that's why.

How could he claim his one true love, his Soulmate, when he was but half a man? When he feared one day the pain would send him to his bed and he wouldn't get up again? When he feared any woman he loved would be forced to spend her days nursing him as she might an overgrown babe.

He'd lied to them both because it frightened him too much to tell the truth. Because he wasn't man enough to tell the truth.

He loved her. She was his Soulmate.

And it was naught more than foolish pride and hurt feelings that kept them both from embracing that truth.

First thing tomorrow morning, he'd march into the keep and up to their room and tell her so. Come tomorrow, the worries that plagued him now would be but a memory.

Exactly as Ellie had described, the tunnel was there.

Leah crawled out from under the bathhouse and looked down the slope. Not much light to travel by, but it was good enough. If she put a serious foot to it, she could be well away from Dun Ard by morning.

She more or less remembered the map Mairi had drawn for her; she only had to backtrack to the begin-

ning. It helped that this time she didn't need to worry
about avoiding roads. Sir Peter and his men had gone
on to search out the rebels they hunted, so he was no
longer a problem.

And if her uncle had sent more men to search for
her? That wouldn't be a problem either since their
intent would be to take her back to MacQuarrie Keep
and that was exactly where she wanted to go.

She was on her way. Nothing would stop her now.

"You're certain it was her?"

Peter Moreland slapped his glove against the mail
covering his leg. What the hell could she be up to?

"Yes, sir. I watched from the trees as she scrambled
down the hillside and headed onto the road."

Withdrawing his men had simply been a ploy to
allow those inside Dun Ard to make their next move.
He'd stationed men all around the perimeter of the castle to watch for anything unusual until such time as he
could lay his hands on Leah MacQuarrie.

"She's headed south, you say?"

"Yes, sir."

Was it possible she thought to return home?

"Saddle the men up. We'll find her and follow along
to give her time to distance herself from Dun Ard before we take her. No point to provoke a battle we've no
time for."

Not that his men weren't more than a match for the
pitiful Scots he'd met at Dun Ard. Oh, there were a few
who had worthy skills, but his men were well trained to
take them first.

And why risk his men when the prize he sought was his for the taking with only the smallest exercise of patience?

He was a man who understood the virtue and the rewards of patience well. He'd had years to practice the art.

Leah MacQuarrie would be his by noon tomorrow and he'd be that much closer in his campaign to become the next Lord Moreland.

Twenty-nine

❦

Leah dipped her hand into the shallow water, bringing it up to her dry lips. She'd gone out of her way to find a safe spot exactly like this. No deep running water for her this time. She was taking no chances.

Drowning wouldn't do much to help Grandpa Hugh. Assuming she was still in time to save him, that is.

Her thirst quenched, she crawled back from the water's edge to the tree where she'd left her bundle. After the hike she'd had, that bread and cheese was calling her name.

Two bites later, she could deny no more that exhaustion was as much her enemy as hunger. Though it might have been smarter to have made her escape after a good night's sleep, her chances of getting out in the daylight would have been next to nonexistent.

Still, traveling at night was just plain stupid. If she kept that up, she'd end up so lost she'd never find her way to MacQuarrie Keep. She had to be smart about this. What she needed to do was get herself straightened out. Just keep moving through today and then she could have herself a good rest tonight, waking up fresh to start off tomorrow.

She could do that. It would only be staying awake for something like, what? Thirty-six hours, maybe? She could do that.

Like hell she could.

Her legs felt like wet noodles already. She had to be smart, yes, but she had to be reasonable, too. A short rest here, maybe an hour or two, and then she'd be on her way. Just a short nap and she'd be good to go.

Her eyes had barely closed when somewhere out in the surrounding forest, she heard a crackle, like a stick breaking.

Oh, that was just dandy. She searched her memory for any mention her grandpa Hugh had ever made about wild animals. She felt pretty safe ruling out lions, tigers, and bears, but that still left more than enough to worry about.

She pulled the stone hanging at her neck outside her shift, running her thumb over it for comfort. Wolves, maybe? Or wild boar?

Dropping the stone, she rummaged in the pocket hanging from her belt and pulled out the little dirk Maisey had given her and held it up in front of her.

Might not stop a full-grown animal, but that animal would soon find out it hadn't gotten hold of something completely defenseless if it attacked.

She leaned her head back against the tree, knowing as soon as she closed her eyes she wouldn't be able to sleep. Not now that she'd gotten her imagination all worked up.

Rest, then. Just until she felt she could get back up and start moving again.

Another noise and she her eyes flew open in time to have a stray whiff of wind blow her hair across them, blocking her vision until she pushed her curls back behind her ears.

Of course. That was probably it. The wind was blowing through the trees, making the limbs rustle. Nature at its best.

Another reason she wasn't particularly fond of nature. Give her a nice, safe castle any day. One with high walls and archers to keep the predators at bay.

Noises rationalized, she closed her eyes a third time, hoping it would be the charm her mom used to proclaim it only to hear the noise again, closer now.

This time she sat bolt upright, eyes opened, dirk at the ready.

"Did I wake you, Lady MacAlister?"

"Crapola," she breathed, barely aware she'd said the word aloud.

Moreland. Apparently her fears about a predator were well founded.

"Or should I say, Mistress MacQuarrie?"

Double crapola.

She pushed up to her feet, holding the little dagger in front of her. "Be on your way, Sir Peter. I won't hesitate to protect myself if I have to."

He strode toward her, not appearing the least intimidated by the dirk she brandished. Not even when he grabbed her wrist and twirled her around, slamming her back into his hard chest as he knocked the dirk from her hand.

"None of that, my lady," he cautioned, his breath skirting over her cheek as he leaned in to speak into her ear.

No, she had no intentions of making this easy for him.

She threw her head forward, then slammed backward into his chin with all the force she could muster, at the same time stomping her foot onto his ankle.

He grunted, letting go his hold on her and she took off at a run, praying she'd actually hurt, not just startled him.

Barely two steps and the ribbon at her neck yanked tight, sliding around her throat, cutting into her skin. Her head wrenched back and tears filled her eyes as she choked, the whole of it bringing her to her knees in a coughing fit.

Moreland stood over her, the stone and ribbon she'd worn around her neck dangling back and forth from his hand a second before he tossed it to the ground. His fingers tightened on her upper arm and he dragged her to her feet, her face ending up inches from his as she teetered on her tiptoes.

"Don't ever try anything like that again. I'd not enjoy hurting a woman, but taking your body back to Lord Moreland serves my purpose equally as well as delivering you healthy and sound." He released her, stepping back as she dropped to her knees. "Do we understand each other?"

She nodded, the pain at her throat intensifying as she touched it.

Blood smeared her fingers when she pulled them away.

"Here, take this." Moreland held out a long strip of cloth he'd dipped in water.

Whether or not he'd torn it from his clothing she couldn't say. No more than she could account for how long his men had been gathered around. She'd been too distracted by the realization that she was actually injured. Injured and bleeding.

An injury that would be gone in the next day, leaving her no earthly way to explain its disappearance.

Thirty

—◦—

Dreams so fitful they'd felt real plagued his sleep, culminating at last in the all-too-real sensation he was drowning.

Drew awoke sputtering, soaked, to his brother's laughter. He wiped at the water dripping into his eyes, realizing as he did so, the bucket in Colin's hand was the source of the water running down his face.

"What in the name of the Fae has taken yer good sense that you'd think to do such as this?" he demanded of his younger brother.

"*My* good sense? I'm no the one sleeping in a pile of hay when I've a perfectly good wife waiting in my bed." Colin prodded at Drew's shoulder with the toe of his boot. "A wife, by the by, that I'd no had the decency to tell my own flesh and blood about. You couldna tell me you planned to wed? You let me go off with no a word of warning so that I missed yer wedding celebration?"

"It's no like that," Drew groaned, pushing himself up to sit. He could now say for a fact that sleeping on the floor of the stable was definitely harder on his body than anything else he'd tried. "It was more sudden than what you might think."

"I suppose it must have been. Else I'd have to think you'd no wanted me here for it."

"As if my marrying would have kept you from yer determination to seek our ancestor in the glen? Did you find him, by the way?"

Anger sparked briefly in Colin's eyes, turning them the blue of a frozen lake before he spit on the floor at his feet, a clear indication of his disgust.

"Neither the great prince himself nor any of his blighted underlings deigned to answer my call. Foul bastard Faeries."

Not surprising. Had the Fae ever responded to a male descendant in the glen? Drew thought not.

"You could always speak to Mother. Perhaps she'd be willing to travel to the glen with you and—"

"No. I've no desire to drag her into this. Besides, you ken she always tells us the Fae have no interest in the minor concerns of men."

"True." Drew leaned his head against the stall behind him. "You look like hell. When was the last time you slept properly?"

"I'd intended to be sleeping now. But once Caden told me all you'd done over these last days, I decided to drag yer troublesome arse back up to the keep where you belong."

"My troublesome arse? I'm no the one parading about in the glen, shouting to the heavens to demand the attention of the Fae."

"Aye? Maybe no, but you were the one dragged home a new wife and an entire English army. Of the two of us, which would you say was stirring a more worrisome pot?"

Most times it was impossible to get more than five words in a row from Colin. Drew was beginning to think that just might be for the best.

He took the hand his brother offered and struggled to his feet, relying more than he'd wanted on Colin's strength.

"Come on." Colin slapped his back, urging him forward. "Let's go have a look at this new wife you felt the need to keep as such a great secret."

At last his brother had said something that he could agree with. Leah was the very person he needed to see. As he'd resolved the night before, there were things he'd left unsaid between them for too long.

She wasn't in their bedchamber when he pushed open the door. He'd guessed as much when she didn't answer to him calling her name. The bed had been straightened and the frocks his sister and Ellie had given her lay in a neatly folded stack in its center.

"Like as not, she's out in the bathhouse. And, no!" One look at his brother's quirked eyebrow was all he needed to put an end to the question he saw in Colin's eyes. "You'll no be having yer first meeting with my wife in the bathhouse. What say we spend an hour or two in the lists? She'll be back and presentable by then."

Colin's smile evaporated. "I dinna believe that's for the best, Drew. I'm worn down and I couldna guarantee to hold back my weapon."

"Yer no to blame for that." Damn the Fates! Even after all these years, Colin still held himself responsible for the accident that accounted for the scar running the length of Drew's chest. "No more than I am."

Colin shrugged as if he didn't care, but Drew knew him too well to accept that. Still, there would be no discussing it. There never was.

"Caden and Sim were headed down there earlier. You'll find the match you need with them. For myself, I've no desire to do anything but lay my head down for a bit."

Drew watched his brother's retreating back with sorrow. They'd been so close growing up, best friends who'd shared everything including their deepest secrets. Perhaps more than anything, he hated the distance between them now. A distance grown larger thanks to their own personal demons.

Faulty perceptions and doubts that they had allowed to rule their lives for far too long.

While he could do nothing to change the way Colin dealt with his demons, he for one intended to put his own to rest, one blasted demon at a time, starting this very day.

With a last glance to the bed, he left the room and closed the door behind him.

First he'd work the stiffness from his leg and then he'd seek out Leah. He'd start by slaying the demon of fear that had prevented him from telling her what he should have when she'd asked.

She was indeed his Soulmate and he'd never let her go.

"Leah?"

Drew pounded on their bedchamber door. After an entire day of having missed her at every turn, he wouldn't have waited for her to answer at all if his brother weren't standing there with him.

"Whatever you did that bought you a night in the stables must still have her angry with you."

"Leah?" he called again, louder this time, ignoring Colin's smirk.

This was unlike her.

"Leah!" he demanded once more. Deciding her rights to privacy were now forfeit, he slammed open the door and stormed inside.

The room was unchanged from his first visit this morning. Nothing had been touched. No candle lit, not even a fire burned in the hearth.

She was gone.

He knew it, deep in the empty spot in his soul, he knew it, even as he raced from the room to question every person he could lay hands on.

She was gone.

"Calm down, Drew," Caden ordered for the hundredth time.

As if he had the ability to be calm with Leah missing. He had to find her. Now. The sick feeling in his stomach urged him on.

Next to him, Ellie jumped to her feet, her head cocked to the side as she listened to the voices only she could hear. "Missy's found her scent. Out at the bathhouse."

"She's no there. I looked."

Ellie shrugged, shaking her head as she made for the door. "I'm telling you, Missy is saying out at the bathhouse."

Though he no longer doubted his sister-in-law's ability to communicate with animals, he did doubt her mangy dog's ability to track. He'd checked the place himself, as he'd said, twice at least.

But hope ran deeper than doubt and he found himself rushing along with the others, hurrying out to spot where the dog waited.

"It's empty," Caden announced, popping his head out of the bathhouse.

"I told you I'd checked there before. Yer damn dog canna smell for shit. I knew she'd be no be found inside."

And yet he'd hoped. Hoped he'd somehow been wrong about her being gone. He had to be wrong. There was no way she could have gotten through the gates to leave Dun Ard. They were too well guarded.

"Missy says not inside. Under." Ellie pointed to the place where the stream ran under the bathhouse.

"Under" led to outside the walls of Dun Ard. That was how she'd managed it.

Colin touched his palm to Drew's chest and then walked a short distance away. When he turned his face upward to the moon, Drew could almost swear he saw light shining from his brother's face, not down onto it.

The illusion lasted for less than a heartbeat and then it was gone.

Gone like Leah.

"South," Colin announced. "She travels south."

"Then I travel south as well." South? It could mean only one thing. She headed for MacQuarrie Keep. *Damnation!* What did the foolish woman think to do against a castle full of English soldiers?

He broke into a full run, headed toward the stables, unaware of the men who followed him until he led his horse from its stall.

The three of them, Colin, Simeon, and Alasdair, all readying their own animals as quickly as he.

He caught Colin's eye and his brother smiled. "You dinna think we'd let you go alone to yer fun with the English, did you?"

Thirty-one

Leah stiffened her back, refusing to allow the men's laughter to deter her.

"I'd have the courtesy of your answer, if you please." She lifted her voice to be heard over their noise. "It's a perfectly reasonable barter I offer."

"If you had any ground from which to barter it might well be," Richard offered. "But you haven't any."

They'd been at MacQuarrie Keep less than half an hour and already she wished everyone in the room dead. Well, almost everyone. She felt almost grateful to Sir Peter, in spite of his having captured her. He, at least, did not laugh.

Immediately upon their arrival he had brought her here, delivering her to these buffoons, where she'd offered up her bargain. She'd marry Lord Moreland so that he might have his precious sons and in return Richard would leave Scotland and never come back again.

The knight had warned her it wouldn't work when she'd informed him of her plan on their return journey. Still, it was the only hope she had for helping Grandpa Hugh and Grandma Mac.

The sound coming from Lord Moreland at the moment was more of a wheeze than a laugh, culminating in a fit of dry hacking coughs before he could add his thoughts on the matter. "You've no say in the matter, girl. What's to become of you is your uncle's determination, none of your own." He waved a shaking hand toward the door. "Get my page! I need my potion."

Sir Peter stepped outside the room and returned shortly accompanied by a young boy carrying a flask, which he handed over to the old lord after removing the stopper.

The old man sipped from the flask before handing it back to the boy to replace the stopper.

The knight had mentioned his uncle's dependence on the "potion." From the looks of the old man, she might well be saved the trouble of marrying him if she could only drag things out for a week or two.

"So she wed herself a native barbarian, did she?" the old man asked once he'd managed to catch his breath again. His voice was as crackly as his skin and he spoke at great volume, as those whose hearing had deserted them often did.

"An annulment should be no problem, my lord."

Obsequious, kiss-ass toady. Dick.

"Peter!" Lord Moreland wiggled his thin fingers in his nephew's direction, urging him to approach. "Find the man. That Scot. Kill him. I've no time to waste on an annulment. A widow will serve my purpose as well as a maiden."

"No!" The protest burst from her, beyond her control, but no one really seemed to notice she'd even spoken, though Sir Peter had moved to her side.

"Rather than rushing into this, Uncle, perhaps we should take the time to make her husband's death appear an accident. No point in rousing a landed family to battle. We've no idea who in the court they might have alliances with. You'll want a waiting period before you take the woman anyway. To make sure any offspring of your union are from your seed."

"Good God, Peter. Excellent point." The old man's head wobbled back and forth as he spoke, almost as if he'd lost all control of it. "Very well. I'll leave it in your capable hands to determine when and how to dispose of the man. As for you, girl . . ." He peered at her with glassy eyes, as if he couldn't quite bring her into focus. "I'll give you a month, maybe two to prove you're ready to breed, but no more. I'll not be cuckolding another man's spawn."

Disgusting old man.

"All settled, then?" Richard beamed at the man next to him, rising to his feet with a parchment clutched in his hand. "I've the document here for your seal, authorizing me to act as guardian for any children resulting from the union between you and my beloved niece."

Next to her, Sir Peter tensed, his head slowly swiveling up to focus on his uncle.

"We'll see, we'll see," the old lord consoled, his glassy eyes darting around the room like those of a man watching an insect. "For now my nephew remains as my designate."

"But, your lordship." Richard sat back down heavily, the parchment still in his fist. "I've proven my trust and fidelity in giving my only son to be your page. Surely that has to influence your decision. Your nephew is but a soldier."

"A soldier, yes." The old man repeated the words, his head bobbing back and forth again. "With a good head on his shoulders. A soldier, as you say. But my designate nevertheless. For now at least. We'll see, Hawthorne. I had a great fondness for your wife's father. That he left his title and properties to you speaks well for you. We'll see."

None of this was getting Leah any closer to the resolution she'd imagined. She'd been ignored long enough. "And what of my offer of bargain? I'd have my answer now."

Her words were once again greeted with howls of laughter from the two men at the table in front of her.

"Take her to the rooms where my parents are held," Richard ordered, completely ignoring her demand. "In order that she might make herself presentable before dinner."

One of Richard's guards stepped closer, giving her a little push forward.

"I'll see her delivered to her grandmother's keeping," Sir Peter offered. "Perhaps my lord's page would be able to show us the way?"

After a nod from his lord, the child ran to Moreland's side, a grin covering his face. "Thank you, Sir Peter," he whispered, hurrying on ahead of them.

"Her bargain," the old lord cackled as they left the room. "I do like a woman who tickles my humor."

Humor? If the old bastard found that funny, just wait until he tried to get her alone in a bedchamber. She'd do her best to kill him with laughter.

The child led them up the staircase and toward the back of MacQuarrie Keep, to the little-used rooms that had once been set aside for Hugh and Margery's boys. Now, it appeared from the guards stationed at either side of the corridor, it served as their prison.

"So you're my cousin," the boy said out of the blue.

This child was the page Richard had mentioned?

"If Richard's your father, I suppose I am," she answered. "I'm Leah. What's your name?"

"Edward," the boy offered at last, stopping to turn and study her, his sharp eyes missing nothing. "I have no other first cousins. I didn't think you'd be so old."

What a delightful child. Not.

"Well, she is," the knight interrupted. "So best you mind your manners, boy, and take us where we need to be. Quickly."

"Yes, sir," Edward agreed with an infectious grin. "This way, sir." He took off at a run, racing down the hall ahead of them.

For a bad guy, Peter Moreland wasn't turning out to be so awful. Or maybe, it was just that he didn't look so bad in comparison to the "good" guys she'd spent time with.

By the blood of the Faerie Queen herself.

Drew sat back on his haunches, his fist clutched to his chest cradling the treasure he'd found at his feet.

"My gut tells me it's the English who camped outside

Dun Ard that we're following now." Sim stood above him, his nose lifted, scenting.

From a short distance away where Dair crouched, his finger tracing a footprint, he confirmed Sim's assertion. "The markings here tell the same story. English soldiers."

"And yer wife," Colin added.

"Aye," Dair agreed. "I'd bet my life she was here, too."

"A safe bet," Drew managed at last to force out around the fear lumped in his throat. He held out his hand, offering his evidence for the others to see.

"Leah's necklace. She never took it off. Moreland found her. Out here alone. Defenseless. He and his men found her."

Colin took the necklace, examined it front and back before passing it on to Sim.

"Bloodstains the ribbon," he growled, his hard eyes masking any emotion he might feel. "And signs here of a struggle. And here." He pointed with his toe.

"Aye," Dair agreed, dropping a hand to Drew's shoulder as he stepped close. "But nary a drop of blood on the ground. What stains this ribbon is no enough blood to bring yer lady permanent harm."

Permanent harm? Death, his friend meant, too kind to say the word aloud.

"Permanent or no, they'll have me to answer to for any harm she's suffered."

He swore it. By the blood of the Faerie Queen herself. If they'd hurt Leah, he'd carve them open with his sword and roast their innards in the nearest firepit.

"She's family, Drew." Colin reached down a hand to help him stand. "They'll answer to all of us."

Thirty-two

∘

"Run down to the kitchens, sweetling, and tell cook that I said you were to have a sweetcake. If she refuses, you tell her she'll have me and Maisey to deal with on the matter, aye?"

Margery kissed the top of Edward's head and sent him on his way.

"He's the spitting image of Robbie at that age, is he no?" Maisey shook her head as she stared at the closed door. "Exactly like yer father, Leah, right down to the wee pink cheeks I always loved to squeeze."

Margery sighed, brushing at the wrinkles in her skirt. "Gives me hope that Richard hasn't wasted his life after all."

Leah clamped her jaws together to refrain from saying anything. If getting to spend a little time with her grandson made all this any easier on Margery, well then, so be it. After all, she couldn't heap blame on a child who looked hardly a day over seven, if that.

His father, on the other hand?

For her money, Richard was still in the running for the biggest dick on the face of the planet, even if his little boy was a sweetheart.

"Why are you wearing this old thing about yer neck? It's no a complement to yer frock, lass."

"Leave it." Leah pushed away Maisey's hand as the old woman reached toward the scarf she'd wound around her throat. Though it wasn't the fashion of the day, it hid the thin scabbed line left behind when Sir Peter had broken her necklace.

Rather, it hid where the line should be. Under the scarf, her skin was as clear and unmarked as it had ever been, but only Grandma Mac knew that. She'd told her as much when she'd confessed to losing the stone.

She glanced up to meet Margery's eyes, the guilt of having lost the stone the woman had given her weighing heavy on her heart.

"I like it," her grandmother declared, turning to dig through the chest behind her.

With a satisfied smile, she held up the item she'd sought, another of the scarves Leah had made when she'd first learned to knit.

"There." Margery draped the scarf around her throat, a match to the way Leah wore hers.

With a shake of her head and a resigned sigh, Maisey pulled the comb through Leah's hair one more time, pronouncing herself satisfied at last when she laid the comb down.

"That's it then, my ladies. Yer ready for yer grand appearance at dinner."

Ugh. An evening with the ogre and the Dick.

"I'd give anything not to go. I can't think of a single thing less appealing to my appetite that sitting in a room with Richard and that old prune Moreland."

"Now, Leah," Grandma Mac began, but stopped with a sigh. "Yer grandpa Hugh will be there. Do you no want to let him see you've returned safe and sound? He's fashed himself something awful over yer being gone."

It had been the only thing even resembling good news she'd had since her return. Once Richard's son had arrived, his mood had improved and he'd had Hugh brought to the children's wing along with Margery. They were kept separately—apparently the Dick feared his parents might plot against him if they were left alone together—but at least they were both in a warm, secure place.

"All right, fine." She'd go without fuss for her grandpa Hugh's sake. "But I can't guarantee I have it in me to be the least bit civil to either Lord Moreland or your son."

"Nor can I, sweetling," Grandma Mac retorted, taking her hand as they opened the door. "Nor can I."

"The portcullis is in place and they've archers posted along the perimeter of the wall walk. Gaining entry will be a bit of challenge, I'd say." Sim scratched his chin as he studied MacQuarrie Keep in the distance.

The four of them crouched in the forest outside the castle walls. They planned to take their rest here until nightfall.

"Their guards are of no concern," Drew answered. "We need only wait for moonrise. We'll enter the same way Leah got out in the first place."

Thank the Fates she'd told him the story of her harrowing escape.

"Moonrise," Dair repeated. "And how will that aid us in finding our entry?"

"At moonrise, we'll make our way to a hidden entrance at the back of the castle."

"You do ken that there's naught but a loch surrounding three sides of the castle, do you no, Drew?" Dair squatted in front of him, looking from him to the castle in the distance and back again. "Three sides including the back where you say you plan to gain entrance."

"Aye. That's why I said it's a *hidden* entrance we'll be using."

"From the sound of it, lads, we're in for a wee swim this night." Colin scrunched down, propping his head against a tree trunk. Eyes closed, he stretched out his legs, apparently settling himself in.

Not for the first time, Drew marveled at his brother's ability to sleep anywhere, at any time.

"A swim, eh?" Sim asked, his attention still focused on the castle and the surrounding countryside.

Indeed. According to Leah, when the water rolled out to sea and reached its lowest point in the loch, the entryway and tunnel would be open to them. They'd have until the water rushed back in to find their way into the bowels of MacQuarrie Keep. And from there?

From there they'd rescue his wife.

There'd be no sleep for him. Instead he rested his back against a nearby trunk and dug into his sporran until his fingers closed over the carved stone Leah had worn around her neck. He lifted it from his bag before knotting the ribbon where it had been ripped apart and slipping it down over his head.

The stone slipped inside his shirt, smooth and hot against his skin.

They'd find her. He could not bear to think otherwise. Find her and take her home to Dun Ard, where she belonged.

Seeing Richard sitting in Hugh's spot at the table ground on Leah's nerves. Thankfully Grandma Mac had warned her about it. Still, it took more willpower than she'd given herself credit for to keep her mouth shut.

"She's decent enough table manners, I'll give you that about her, Hawthorne. And pleasant on the old eyes as well."

Leah's ears rang from Lord Moreland's incessant shouting. If she actually ended up married to this old relic, she'd have to work on seating arrangements so she didn't occupy the chair next to his like she did now.

Maybe she could arrange for them to eat in different castles. Or different countries.

Next to her, he coughed again, sending the food he'd just stuffed in his mouth drooling down his chin. With his fingers, he wiped it away and then dug down into the trencher that sat between them scooping up another bite.

Their shared trencher.

She allowed the stew-laden piece of bread in her hand to drop to the table untouched. She'd starve before she'd eat off of the same platter as that pig again. Him with the conceit and gall to comment on her table manners!

Another coughing fit next to her, followed by an ungodly loud shout at poor little Edward. "Potion, blast it!"

The boy ran forward, handing over the flask, eyes to the ground, but not even his subservience saved him the back of the old man's hand.

The resounding smack snapped the child's head back, causing him to stumble and bringing his father to his feet.

But only for a moment. As soon as Richard realized himself, he sat back down.

Coward.

Was no one going to protect this child? If someone had dared do something like that to her when she was his age, her older sister Destiny would have been all over the culprit like a wildcat. What this poor little kid needed was a Destiny of his own and it sure didn't look like his dad was up to the job.

"You've been warned to have my flask at the ready," the ogre beside her yelled. "You're to wait on me, you stupid cur. I don't intend that I should have to wait on you!"

Lord Moreland drew back his hand to strike the boy again and Leah's choice seemed clear. She grabbed his thin wrist, easily holding it in place.

The eyes he turned on her were fevered. "Don't be

fooled, girl. I'll warn you only once. Being my wife won't save you from the same as I've given him."

"Then I'll grant you the same courtesy, your lordship," she hissed, digging her nails into his wrist. "Be warned that, unlike that child, I'll hit back."

She released his wrist to reach for her cup, irritated beyond measure to find her hand shaking. No matter that it was anger and not fear that fueled the movement.

Next to her, the old man laughed, irrationally. Almost hysterically. Whatever was in that potion he drank to control his cough, she'd be willing to bet it would be very expensive and very illegal in about seven hundred years.

The remainder of the meal passed uneventfully. Uneventful if she ignored the old man beside her, head lolled back against his chair, snoring. When those around them began to stand, two of Lord Moreland's guards stepped forward and lifted him to his feet, all but carrying him from the hall.

Oh, there was something to look forward to in a husband.

She stood to make her way to Grandma Mac's side, only to feel a small hand slide into hers.

Edward waited, looking up at her as if he feared she might reject him.

No chance of that. She squeezed his little fingers reassuringly and dropped to her knees to face him, running her forefinger softly over his swollen cheek.

"He's not doing that to you anymore, baby, you understand me?"

"I'm not a baby. I'm a page."

"And if he does," she continued on, ignoring his half-hearted protest just as she ignored that she sounded exactly like Destiny had sounded when lecturing her as a child. "Listen to me. If he does? And I'm not there when it happens? I expect you to tell me immediately. I'm not letting that old bastard hurt you again. Not ever."

The child's eyes rounded and he nodded his understanding, but he stepped quickly back when he realized his father stood over them.

"You didn't have to do that." Richard reached out as if to touch his son, stopping at the last minute and clasping his hands behind him. "It won't always go so well for you if you repeat your actions. Lord Moreland isn't a particularly patient man. He's a man who likes to have his own way."

As if she cared what that asshole liked.

"First off, I didn't see anyone else doing much about it, Richard. And second, I'd say that old bastard's got a long way to go to actually qualify as a man. Men, real men, don't hit defenseless children." She glared at him as she rose to her feet. "And they don't let anyone else get away with it either."

She'd like to say more to the spineless jellyfish who was supposed to be her uncle, but it wouldn't be fair to Edward. One look at the child told her he worshiped his father. She couldn't, however, resist a parting shot once Edward raced to hold the door for Margery.

"You should try harder to be the man that little boy thinks you are."

She followed along with Margery and Hugh to the corridor where they were being confined, the guards trailing only steps behind them. Next to her, Edward kept pace, his little hand snugly fit in hers.

From the moment Richard had arrived, nothing had worked out as she'd planned. Not getting help from the MacKiernan laird, not trying to bargain for the Mac-Quarries' freedom, and certainly not her misguided love for Drew.

But perhaps there was a greater reason why it hadn't. Maybe the Fates had determined it was time for her to pay back the kindness that had been shown to her in her time of need. Maybe it was her turn to help someone and she'd been directed back to MacQuarrie Keep to do exactly that.

She squeezed Edward's little hand.

If this was payback time, she didn't intend to let the Fates, or Edward, down.

Thirty-three

❧

They were in!

Knee-deep water swirled in the tunnel. Currents, like invisible fingers, pulled at their legs, making each step an effort.

Drew braced a hand against the slimy wall, giving himself a moment to regain his strength. If the damned tunnel were only large enough to allow them to stand upright, it would be so much easier.

Behind him Dair slid to a stop. "I say we opt for a boat the next time we try such as this."

"Bothered by yer wee swim, Maxwell?" Simeon pulled up the rear.

"It's no the swim I mind, so much as the waters that want to drag me back out to sea. And I'll no even mention this smell. It would make a fishmonger proud," Dair grumbled from behind.

"Quiet!" Ahead of him, Colin hissed the command and all talk ceased.

His brother was right, of course. They had no way of knowing what—or who—might wait in the darkness that loomed out ahead of them.

As they worked their way forward, Drew realized the water level was continuing to drop. It hadn't felt as if they'd gone uphill and a quick glance over his shoulder confirmed as much. It was the natural effect of the waters in the loch draining toward the sea.

"If we'd waited a bit to start our swim, this tunnel would have been a sight drier." Dair echoed his own thoughts.

"Mayhap," Sim countered. "But the last thing we'd want would be to get caught in here when the waters return."

He was right. It would not be a pleasant way to die.

Ahead of him, Colin stopped abruptly and his own feet slid on the slimy floor in an attempt to avoid falling against his brother.

"The ladder's here."

Just as Leah had described. If everything else was as she'd said, the ladder would take them to a storage room and from there they could easily make their way into the keep.

"Lend me a shoulder," Colin ordered from his spot ahead of him on the ladder.

Clutching the edge of the slimy metal, Drew shinnied up beside his brother until he could reach up to feel the impediment they'd encountered. Water-soaked wood, it was without a doubt the trapdoor to the storeroom.

"On my mark," Colin whispered. "One, two, push!"

Drew braced himself against the wall and, in unison with his brother, pushed up with all his might. Above them, the wood gave way, and the trapdoor opened, allowing them access to the room above.

One by one they lifted themselves up, exchanging the wet dark for a dryer version.

"Mind the barrels," Colin cautioned in a whisper. "Find the door."

The minutes felt like hours as they worked their way around the room, Drew's heart pounding with excitement.

Not long now. Not long at all until he'd have her in his arms, proving to himself at last that she was safe and unharmed.

And if she wasn't unharmed?

The nagging voice of doubt ate away at his confidence as it had since the moment he'd laid his hand on the bloodstained necklace.

He couldn't think on it now.

"Here." Dair's voice echoed in the dark and within minutes they stepped into a wide hallway.

A small torch burned at the far end of the passageway, but after the oppressive darkness of the storeroom, even that pitiful light hurt his eyes.

"Be still," Colin ordered next to him, reaching out to place his palm over Drew's heart.

Drew waited, watching as Colin closed his eyes, tilting his head as if he listened for something far away while lifting his other hand, palm extended.

"This way," his brother said at last, heading off down the passageway.

"But how—" he began to ask, only to have his brother cut him short.

"Trust me. We'll find her this direction. I feel it."

Trust Colin he would. However his brother did it, whatever it was he felt, the only thing that mattered to Drew was that he *did* feel. And if Colin could *feel* his way to Leah, it had to mean that Leah lived.

Not only was Dick a jerk and a coward, he was just plain stupid, too. Three grown women sharing a single room meant for two little boys?

Leah jammed her fist into the lump of blankets under her head. Grandma Mac and Maisey had each taken one of the small cots against the far wall, so she'd laid her pallet here in front of the fire.

Honestly, the forest floor had been more comfortable than this cold stone.

She pulled at the covers once again before lying still, staring into the fire.

On every night of the journey she'd made with Drew, he'd taken his blankets to floor just like this. The pain in his leg must have been excruciating after a night of the cold seeping into his damaged muscles.

No wonder he did yoga in the middle of the night! To fight off the pain. He'd said his sister-in-law had shown him the movements.

Had to be Ellie. Since she'd come from the future, it was only reasonable that she would have been the one familiar with the exercises Drew practiced.

Reasonable? Leah turned her face into the blankets to stifle her snort. How many people in the world would consider anything about time travel to be reasonable?

Drew's family, certainly.

Of course, at the moment, they were technically her family, as well. At least until her marriage was ended.

Leah rolled to her back, jerking her covers over her chest.

She had to do something about that. Lord Moreland had ordered Drew's death and that was something she absolutely could not permit. He might have wanted to marry her for nothing more than her ability to heal, but she knew, to the depths of her soul she knew, he meant much more than that to her.

He was the Soulmate her mother had predicted she'd find one day. That she couldn't be with him was hardly a surprise. Look at her mom and dad.

She'd have to find a way to speak with Sir Peter. He might be an arrogant English knight, but she believed there was more to him than that. It had, after all, been his stalling which had prevented someone from being on their way to kill Drew at this very minute.

Argh! Her thoughts simply circled round and round, always ending back with Drew. Would it be like this forever, with the man haunting her every waking minute for the rest of her life?

Maybe she had turned into her mother.

With that less than comforting thought jangling around in her head, it was officially useless to lie here any longer. Tossing aside her covers, she sat up, scrubbing her hands over her face. Through the little window high on the wall she could already see faint traces of light brightening the eastern sky. Since there was no chance she was getting any sleep anyway, she might as well get up.

The fresh air coming in that little window carried a

nip with it, so she padded over to the chest where she'd placed her things and pulled out Drew's plaid to wrap around her shoulders.

No. She would absolutely not get back on that merry-go-round thinking about him again. Absolutely would not.

Leaning down, she jammed another log into the fireplace and reached for the little kettle sitting on the hearth. Some herb tea might do the trick to soothe her mind.

The pot bumped against the stone hearth, but any noise it might have made was lost in a crash of sound coming from the hallway outside her door.

"What was that?" Behind her, Grandma Mac was already out of bed and on her feet, shaking Maisey's shoulder to awaken her.

Before Leah could answer, the door to their bed-chamber flew open, crashing back into the wall as it swung wide.

Her mind was still playing tricks on her. It had to be.

Drew strode toward her, his face dark with his emotion. "Come on. We're getting you out of here."

Was he insane? What was he doing here? If Moreland or any of Richard's men caught him, it would be all over.

"You have to leave. If they find here, they'll—"

He cut short her warning, crushing her body to his, covering her lips with his own.

The kiss drove all thought from her mind. Not even the desperation and fear she'd felt for him stood a chance against the overwhelming rightness she experienced in his embrace.

By the time he broke the kiss, he'd drawn her to the door.

"My grandmother," she managed to blurt out, breathless and still enthralled.

"All of you!" he barked. "Now. We've no time."

The shouts coming through the open doorway reinforced his words.

Grandma Mac and Maisey followed on her heels as Drew led her into the hallway where two of the men she'd met at Dun Ard, along with a third she didn't recognize, already guarded Grandpa Hugh and Maisey's Walter.

"They're coming," the man she didn't recognize warned as he started forward. "There's no way out now but to carve our way through. We'll clear a path down the stairs and hold them there as long as we can. You get her to the storeroom. Barricade the door and wait until the tide goes out again."

"I'm fighting at yer side, Colin. No matter what you believe, I can be a help. We fight our way out together."

"I dinna question the value of yer sword, brother. Only the need to save yer wife. Think to her safety. We'll join you when we can. We've managed through worse."

Drew tightened his hold on her hand, pulling her after him as they hurried down the hall toward the stairs and uplifted voices.

Metal clanged against metal as her rescuers' swords crossed those of the English soldiers. Men shouting, servants screaming, all assaulted her ears.

Drew shoved her against the wall, behind him, using his body as a shield while he fought what appeared to her to be a never-ending supply of men, all intent on seeing her husband and the men fighting at his side dead.

She looked up in time to see Richard standing at the head of the stairs. Sir Peter appeared at his side, drawing his sword on the run, his expression wiped of all emotion like a true hardened warrior. Richard followed behind him, weaponless.

The air around her seemed to shimmer with violence as Moreland's sword crashed against the one in Drew's hand.

She covered her ears against the sound and still it reverberated in her lungs, as if the stone walls around them magnified the battle sounds. Unable to tear her eyes from the weapons, she watched as sparks shot away from the impacts.

If only Drew would step away from her. He could take this man. She knew it. She'd seen him that day in the lists.

But he didn't. He fought instead like a man whose only concern was her protection. His moves were purely defensive.

Her chest tightened, as if in premonition, and she looked to the top of the stairs.

She'd read once that in times of severe emotional distress, all that happens around you speeds up and blurs.

That author had been wrong.

For her, the next few minutes felt as if they lasted a lifetime, each image crystal sharp in its intensity, but beyond her ability to prevent.

Edward stood at the top of the stairs, calling to his father. His little face was a mask of fear and in his hands he held a sword that was taller than he.

Richard turned toward his son as the boy started down the stairs at a run. Off-balanced by the weight of the weapon, the child lost his footing and fell.

One bounce and then he tumbled, head over foot to the bottom of the stairs, where his body lay crumpled, impaled on the sword he'd tried to get to his father.

An unearthly howl shattered through the room and Richard threw himself over his son's body. Around them, fighting ceased, the English who followed Richard waiting to see what their lord would do next.

Even Moreland held his weapon, as if he too were immobilized by Richard's grief.

Richard pulled the sword from his son's body and tossed it to the ground. Clutching the child to him, he rocked the boy back and forth, his inhuman wail of sorrow echoing off the stone walls.

"Leah?"

Margery called her name on a pleading breath, but it was enough to snap her out of the spell that had held her motionless.

"Yes," she answered. Of course she would. How could she do any less?

Slipping past Drew, she ran to the huddled father and son, dropping to her knees beside them. "Give him to me," she ordered.

The pain in Richard's eyes when he looked up at her brought tears to her own. It was impossible for her to feel hate for a man who'd lost his whole world, even one such as Richard.

"Wait!" Margery was at her side. "She can save Edward's life, but first you must give us yer oath that when she does, you'll take yer men and leave here. That you'll leave us unmolested and you'll never return to Mac-Quarrie Keep."

"My only son's lifeblood spills out on your floor, Mother! Your grandson. He breathes his last as we speak." Richard's voice cracked, and tears spilled from his eyes. "It's too late for any to save him now. I am lost."

"It's not too late. Show him, Leah. Show him yer throat."

Kneeling next to Richard, Leah pulled the plaid from her shoulders, exposing her neck to his view.

"I saw the wound there with my own eyes." Sir Peter spoke from behind her. "It's not possible for it to be healed."

"Give me yer oath and send yer men from the room," Margery insisted.

"Go!" he screamed, turning his tortured gaze to his mother. "You have my oath. Everything I have is yers for my son's life."

"Now, Leah."

Margery gave the go-ahead, but Leah had already reached for the child. Oath or no, she'd no intention of allowing her trusting little cousin to die. She blocked out everything but Edward, ignoring the sounds of the soldiers leaving, the hushed voices behind her, even the knowledge of Drew's presence.

Nothing mattered at this moment but the boy in her arms.

His eyes were open but unfocused. Blood burbled from the wound in his little chest with each forced breath.

"Don't be frightened, baby," she whispered to him as

she covered his body with her own. "I know it hurts but I'm going to make it better real soon. I promise."

She held Edward, concentrating on his wound, seeing him in her mind, his cheeks pink and healthy, his strong legs carrying him down the corridor ahead of her.

How the gift worked, she had no idea. She'd been perfectly honest when she'd told Drew that. She knew only that when the moment came, the magic would fill her completely with a heat like no other.

The magic took her when her fingers grazed over the wound, stiffening her body and all but robbing her of her senses. Her muscles pulsed with it, the burn building until she felt as if her skin would melt off her bones.

A second wave of magic followed the first, blanketing her sight in a cocoon of green waves just before the pain of Edward's injuries shot through her chest. She thought she heard a woman scream but she had no time to wonder who it might have been, for in that instant the third wave of magic smashed into her, robbing her of all conscious thought.

On Richard's order, the soldiers had vacated the hall. Dair, Colin, and Sim remained at Drew's side while Leah's grandparents hovered near the stairs. The knight, Sir Peter, waited with an arm around Hawthorne's shoulders. All of them, every soul in the room, silent, awestruck by the tragedy playing out in front of them.

Helplessness such as Drew had never known tightened his chest as he watched Leah cradle the dying child to her breast.

A low hum filled every corner of the room and a sudden wind howled through the hall. As if they'd been caught out in the frenzy of a vicious storm, the wind tore at their hair and loose clothing, whipping against them like tiny lashes to exposed skin. Its intensity built until furniture in the hallway began to shift and tumble in its path.

The air between him and Leah shimmered, engulfing her and the boy in a quivering sphere of green.

A curtain of Faerie magic.

He'd seen its like only once before. It had engulfed his cousin Mairi and her Ramos and when it had shattered, they were both gone, sent back to the future from where they'd come.

Her body convulsed as if she'd been shaken by a giant invisible hand and he threw himself at the sphere, beating against the impenetrable wall of magic with his fists, desperate to get to her. Desperate to be with her if the magic took her away.

"Leave her be," Margery yelled over the howling wind.

From inside the sphere, Leah screamed, her body arching over the child before falling limp. He dove at the shimmering green wall once more, just as it shattered in an enormous crash. Like an explosion of thunder indoors, it shook the very foundation of the hall, knocking them all from their feet.

Closest to the sphere, Drew took the full blast of the magic that sent him flying through the air. His back slammed against the wall, knocking the breath from him. His head pounding, he struggled to get to his feet.

He had to get to Leah. Had to protect her. Had to keep her here.

Flipping to his stomach, he fought the wind, crawling, digging his fingers into the stones of the floor to reach her.

Around him, sparkling lights of all colors shot through the air, twisting and pitching, diving at his head like shards of living flame gone wild.

Ignoring it all, he made his way forward. His vision tunneled only on the woman ahead of him, her body limp on the floor, a growing pool of blood seeping from beneath her.

He gathered her body into his arms, turning her over to discover the front of her nightdress soaked in blood.

Not the child's blood, hers. Fresh, pumping from a wound in her chest. The wound that had been Edward's.

She lay limp in his arms, blood gurgling from the corner of her mouth with each ragged attempt her lungs made to fill with air.

He hadn't known. It should have been obvious to him when the scratch that had been on his arm had transferred to hers. She'd tried to tell him. She'd claimed that he knew nothing.

She'd been right.

"How could you let her do this?" He screamed the words, to no one. To everyone.

His sweet, gentle Leah, his Soulmate, had given her life to save that of the child and he could only watch helplessly as her grandmother directed his friends to carry her away.

Thirty-four

❧

Peter Moreland ran a hand through his hair, wishing he could push away the memories plaguing him. He stared into the night sky, contemplating the stars in the heavens in a way he never had before.

The mysteries he'd witnessed in the past week could be nothing less than miracles. Miracles sent to convince him he needed to alter the course of his life before it was too late.

Behind him, the sound of his uncle's wracking cough shattered the silence as it had throughout the evening.

His lord lay cushioned on pillows in the opulence of the tent he insisted on setting up each night. He behaved as if he were an important member of the royal family on tournament instead of what he really was. An evil old, dying man.

"Sir Peter!"

Young Edward ran toward him, his face radiating the healthful glow befitting a child.

"My father says I should give this to you."

He held out the leather-covered flask containing the potion his uncle relied so heavily upon in his illness.

Though Hawthorne and his son traveled back to England under the protection of Moreland and his men, he had severed all ties with Lord Henry after the incident at MacQuarrie Keep. Richard seemed to have realized at last that his only son was too precious a treasure to entrust to Lord Henry's keeping.

"It's most important you remember the chatelaine's instructions for his lordship's medicine," the boy warned. "No more than three times each day. She made me swear to it."

Peter didn't doubt that she had. He'd watched the chatelaine herself prepare the potion for his uncle, a dangerous mixture of briony and honey, opium and henbane, all tossed together with a splash of hemlock juice.

Though not a student of the healing arts, even he understood that what was contained in the flask would not cure his uncle, but merely dull his pains. And while a small amount of the addictive mixture might ease his uncle's suffering, too much would serve to hasten his end.

It was no wonder the chatelaine had instructed the child to withhold the flask save the three times. And of no concern to the old crone how many times the boy's ears would be boxed for that withholding.

"I shall remember, Edward." As he remembered many things.

He accepted the flask the boy offered, ruffling the child's hair with his other hand. "You've been an excellent page, boy. I'd be honored if you'd one day consider applying as my squire."

He'd miss having Edward at Moreland Manor. His smile, rare though it had been of late, had been a boon to the gloom of their home.

"Thank you, Sir Peter." The child started away, stopping with a deep practiced bow before running back to his father.

Edward's life should be much improved now and Peter found he was grateful beyond measure for that.

"Where is he? Send the damned brat with my potion!" His uncle's shout rang out from the tent, his next words lost in another fit of coughing.

Peter passed through the flaps and kneeled at his uncle's side, extending the flask as he did.

"Your page is no longer with us, your lordship. Perhaps, to make things easier for you, you'd like to hold on to the flask yourself."

"Yes, yes," his uncle agreed, taking the flask from his hands and tipping it to his lips.

Once, twice, and a third time before Peter stood and made his way back outside.

Memories assaulted his thoughts as he strode away from the tent. Too many of those memories ones he could only hope to one day forget. Too many he'd give his very soul to purge from his mind.

Memories of the sweet smile Henry's wife, the gentle Elspeth, had offered to everyone she encountered. Memories of the fear in her eyes each time her husband had entered the room or of her screams, muffled behind the door of the chamber she'd shared with his uncle. Memories of her body after her fall from the tower, broken and bloodied but still clutching her lifeless babe.

Perhaps it was the more recent memories that would haunt him longest, like that of his uncle, deep in the throes of the opium, reliving those last moments with Elspeth on the tower.

These were the memories that wracked him, bringing with them guilt because he'd been blind to the danger, blind to the evil that was Henry. Guilt for not having acted in time.

Whether his uncle had pushed her from the tower himself or ordered it done by another, Peter might never know. Which one made no difference, her death was on his hands all the same.

Behind him, for the first time tonight, all was silence. Above him, a streak shot through the sky, blazing a brief and glorious trail before it disappeared.

By his ignorance and oblivion, he had failed to help the gentle Elspeth when she'd needed him. Perhaps by his actions now he had at last given her soul the peace she deserved.

Tipping his head once more to the heavens, he sent up a prayer for the recovery of the woman left behind at MacQuarrie Keep. It was through her sacrifice he'd come to know the miracles that would forever change him.

He'd witnessed the warning of the miracles. Witnessed and heeded, sending up with his prayers an oath never to be the man his uncle had been.

Thirty-five

⁓

*C*haotic dreams assaulted Leah as she floated somewhere outside her body in a gloriously color-streaked void. Even in this ethereal state, Leah recognized the severity of the shock her physical body had suffered.

She'd never healed anyone so close to death before. Even her sister's husband Jesse had more life left in him when she'd healed his gunshot wound than poor little Edward had. Her only attempt at anything even close to this had been when the Tinklers had brought Robbie back to MacQuarrie Keep, but the seal of the old magic encasing his wounds had protected her even as it had prevented his healing.

Your gift is strong, but not without limits, daughter.

Words spoken into the chaos by a beautiful man with her sister's eyes. He claimed to be her father, this apparition floating next to her in the river of mist.

When the waves of mist had first licked up around her waist, lifting her from her feet, she'd panicked. Fear that she'd drown pummeled her until voices, thousands of voices, had reassured her. The mist itself swirled with every color of the rainbow, heaving and seething like a thing alive, holding her aloft, gently carrying her through the currents.

A ragged streak of light had split the colors around her and she'd felt a cool touch to her forehead and heard her mother's voice.

You are stronger than you know, my Lee-Lee. Let it go. Release the negative. Embrace love.

Hallucinations. There could be no other answer. Just as she'd hallucinated Drew sitting at her side each time she'd tried to awaken.

She'd swear it was him sitting there, wringing out a cold damp cloth to place on her forehead, holding her hand, tears tracking down his cheeks.

Hallucinations, all. Drew would never cry, least of all over her.

But hallucination or not, she wanted to be with him. More than anything in her entire life, she wanted to be at his side, as his wife, no matter what it took.

Around her, the mist rose up in mighty waves as a putrid slime oozed from her body and into the beautiful swirling colors. Like whitecaps in an angry ocean, the waves swept over her, washing against the ooze that tried to steal the color from the iridescent river until, at last, all that remained was the sparkling mist, clear and exquisite as a rainbow of liquid crystal.

How long she'd floated in the joy of that mist she couldn't say, but as suddenly as it had appeared, it was gone. The beautiful apparition that claimed to be her father, the blinding white light with her mother's voice, the soothing fingers of the mist itself. All of it gone.

All except Drew.

She opened her eyes to find him sitting at her side, his head resting against the back of his chair, eyes closed. His hand, large and warm, encased hers.

After so long in the void, her body felt as if it weighed a thousand pounds, pushing down into the bed. No hallucination, this, there could be no doubt.

She was back. From where, she had no idea, only that wherever it was, she was back from it and next to her, the man she loved slept in a chair, his hand clasped around hers.

Drew's dark lashes lay against purpled hollows reminding her of the black lace fan she'd coveted as child in the costume store down the street. As she watched, the lashes fluttered and lifted and, slowly, his velvety brown eyes focused.

"Thank the Fates!"

He was on his feet in an instant, gathering her in his arms.

"I thought I'd lost you."

Please don't be a hallucination. But if it was one, she didn't ever want it to end.

"Yer grandmother swore you'd recover, vowed it had not been such as this the last time you'd used yer gift."

No, this had been a new experience, even for her.

"I'd never healed someone so close to death before. I guess it took a little more out of me. And Edward? Is he all right?"

"Yer wee cousin was fine within moments after the . . ." He shook his head as if he grappled for the words. ". . . the event. Yer never to attempt the like of it again, do you ken? Never."

Such a bossy man, her husband, but surely he didn't mean his words. After all, they both knew he'd married her with the full intent that she'd use her gift to heal him. A healing she'd told herself would never happen.

But now?

He'd risked his life for a second time for her. First in the churning waters of the loch when he'd pulled her from the clutches of death and then again when he'd come to MacQuarrie Keep to save her from Richard's plan for her.

She wouldn't refuse him the gift that would make his life better. Especially not if healing him was what it would take to keep him in her life.

She lifted her hand to stroke his cheek but he grabbed it, placing his lips to her palm.

"As soon as yer fully healed, I'm taking you home to Dun Ard, where you'll be safe."

"This is my home, Drew. MacQuarrie Keep." Her responsibility as well as her home with Richard gone.

"As my wife, you belong at Dun Ard," he insisted stubbornly.

"As your wife," she repeated, the awe of his words filling her heart.

She could point out that he belonged here, taking his rightful place as the next laird if he truly meant to be her husband in more than name only. If he wanted her as his wife for more than her gift alone.

She had to know the truth.

"I don't need to go back to Dun Ard with you to heal the injuries to your body, Drew. My gift works anywhere. I can do it right here."

Right now, if that was what he wanted. She was ready. Both her body and mind fully recovered. What she'd been through in healing Edward had shown her she had no reason to fear her gifts. Healing Drew would be simple. Knowing she was capable of that and so much more had lifted all desire to deny her blood right.

It was like being a child again, feeling the wonder of the gift coursing in her veins.

"No!" He all but shouted the word, clasping her hand to his heart. "I meant what I said, dearling. Never again. When I asked it of you, I'd no idea that in order to heal me, you'd have to take on the injury yerself. Watching the woman I love fight for her life these last days was something I dinna want to do again. You'll no ever put yerself through that again. No for me. No for anyone."

The woman he loved! Her. He wanted her for her, not for her gift. The knowledge sizzled through her blood, making her want to spring from the bed and scream it to the heavens.

"I'll no allow it."

Allow?

That one word burst her celebratory bubble quickly enough. She'd tell him what he could do with his *allow*, all right.

But looking into his eyes, seeing to the depths of his soul and the sincerity of his love for her, she bit back the words she would have said. She could well continue this bickering long into the night, but arguing with him wasn't what she had in mind. The years stretched out ahead of them for her to educate him on the error of his word choice. For now, she felt much too good for either arguing or educating.

Rolling to her side, she pushed up to sit, slapping his hands away when he tried to stop her.

"You need yer rest, dearling. Yer injuries need time to heal."

How little he understood.

"They are healed. Completely."

In reply, he arched a disbelieving eyebrow.

"Seriously. That's how it works. Once it's gone, it's as if it never happened."

His look of utter skepticism said more than any words could.

Fine. Two could play the silence game.

Reaching up, she loosened the ribbons holding the neck of her nightdress, sliding one shoulder out to free her left arm.

"What do you think yer doing?" he demanded, rising to his feet at her bedside.

She smiled her reply, edging the other shoulder down until her right arm was free as well. Her next move was to push the gown to her waist and remove the bandage from her rib cage.

"I'm simply showing you that there's nothing left to heal."

His hand lifted and his finger traced the spot where the wound had been.

"Just hours ago," he whispered, as if he couldn't believe his eyes. "You . . . you need yer rest," he stammered, like a man who hadn't yet accepted the reality confronting him.

"I don't need rest," she corrected, urging his hand up from her unblemished ribs to cover her breast. Her breath caught in her throat at the contact, her body instantly heating with desire. "What I need is you."

And then he was there beside her, his lips moving from her face to her neck, his strong hands holding her close to him as he whispered in her ear.

"In that case, dearling, you've my oath as yer husband. You'll always have what you need."

As he would, if she had anything to say about it.

His shirt and plaid disappeared in record time, not that she was keeping track of time, really. Time didn't matter. It was her ally. She needed only to have her wits about her when he lost his.

Hanging from his neck, her stone.

When she reached up to touch it, he pulled it off over his head, dropped it down over hers, tracing its marking as it lay between her breasts.

"Where it belongs," he whispered.

He made love to her slowly, sweetly, taking his time until she thought she might scream from the beauty of it all.

When the time came, after he'd sent her cascading over the edge of her own need and brought her back again, she was ready.

As his back arched into his release, she slid her hand from his abdomen down, digging her fingers into his damaged thigh, latching onto the scar he thought to keep her from healing.

He shouted when the magic hit, driving deep inside her with the force of the magic behind him. The power sparkled behind her eyes, ricocheting from her body to his and back again, melding them together until at last it shattered around them into a billion glittering shards.

Her highlander was healed.

Epilogue

Wild Woman! Bring yer man some tea!" Drew propped his head on his arms, watching the emotions dance across his wife's face as she made her way toward him.

Her ties hung loose and open, allowing him a lovely view of the stone she always wore, gently swaying back and forth between her breasts, enticing him to crawl back under the covers.

"Sorry, my sweet. The Wild Woman's got things to do today and so do you."

It was undeniable fact she spoke.

"And so I do," he answered, pushing himself up to sit on the edge of the bed. "Dispute Week."

It was all he could do not to groan with the knowledge of how his day would go.

First week of each month was set aside at MacQuarrie

Keep for the hearing of disputes. As new laird, it was his responsibility to pass judgments and settle petty problems to keep the people happy.

With each complaint he heard, he had a greater understanding as to why Hugh had "done him the honor" of naming him laird right away. It left crafty old Hugh all the time in the world to sit in a boat with Walter, fishing and tilting back a jug of whisky while he was the one sitting in a dank hall listening to whiners.

"Maybe you'll get lucky and everyone will be happy with each other for a change."

"Maybe." He took the steaming mug she offered and set it on the table next to the bed, reaching out quickly to catch her wrist before she made her escape.

She squealed as he pulled her back down on top of him, but there was no fight in the woman, only giggles.

"Drew! There's no time. They'll be waiting for you in the Hall."

"Let them wait," he countered, burying his nose in her hair. She smelled of spices and herbs, like some exotic dish he couldn't get his fill of. "I find I canna leave my bed just yet."

"You're a spoiled, spoiled man, Laird MacQuarrie," she teased, biting her way up his neck.

Yes, he was. Spoiled and happy beyond belief. He had a home and a loving wife and one day, if the Fates saw fit, MacQuarrie Keep would be filled with all the little MacQuarries Margery nagged about regularly.

"Are you happy, Lady MacQuarrie?"

In response she smiled, covering his hands with hers. "Ecstatic, my laird. And you?"

"Beyond happy, dearling."

On that first night they'd spent together at Sallie's, he'd held Leah as she slept and he'd known then she would be the instrument through which he would reclaim the future the Fae had stolen from him.

What he hadn't expected was the manner in which that future would be returned to him.

Leah had given him so much more than the Fae had taken away. She hadn't just healed his body; she'd healed his heart as well.

With her at his side, for the first time in his life, his soul was complete.

POCKET BOOKS
PROUDLY PRESENTS

A Highlander's Curse

Melissa Mayhue

Coming soon from Pocket Books

Turn the page for a sneak peek of
A Highlander's Curse . . .

Prologue

This hardly looked a proper cottage at all, let alone the home to a seer of Thomas the Rhymer's fame.

Colin MacAlister hesitated a moment to survey the ruined shack confronting him before dismounting.

Not even his own mother's claim that his actions were those of a brash, untested youth had prevented this quest, so certainly he wouldn't allow something as minor as the unwelcoming appearance of this abode to deter him.

False bravado, she'd accused. Have a care for the Fae, she'd warned. Respect the danger they represent.

He'd show her. His bravery was real. And as for the Fae? It was contempt he felt for them, not respect. He'd seen them with his own eyes this past year when they'd all but killed his brother. Drew's body might have survived, but his heart, his spirit, they'd shattered that part of him.

There was nothing to fear from the Fae in this place anyway. They were too entrenched in their own arrogance to inhabit a place such as this. No, if the seer was here, he'd be alone.

Colin filled his lungs, slowly and with purpose, before forcing the air out again and with it, the doubt that plagued him. His determination bolstered, he tossed his reins over a low branch and headed for the door of the little hovel.

Perhaps the old man he'd spoken to back in the last village had been mistaken. Why would a man such as Thomas Learmonth leave his manor at Ercledoune for a heap of crumbling sod such as this?

No matter the appearance of the hut, he still had to try. He must find Thomas. He'd ridden too far and risked too much to give up now.

He'd but lifted his hand to knock on the door when it opened. A woman so old she looked as if her skin wrinkled in on itself stood before him.

"I seek Thomas of Ercledoune. Is he within these walls?"

She moved toward him, forcing him to take a step backwards.

"What is it that a strapping lad like yourself would have of poor auld Thomas?" She scratched her chin, staring at him with one eye squinted shut. "Not that I'm saying he's here, mind you."

"My business is with him and him alone. I'd warn you no to be playing games with me, woman. I've no the time or patience for it." He hadn't the luxury of time to waste on some lonely old crone.

"You've some nerve about you, lad," the old woman

cackled in her oddly accented voice. "Lonely old crone, you've pegged me, have you? And after the grand sum of no more than a mere moment's acquaintance? You base that assessment on your vast years of experience and hardship, do you?"

A chill raced the length of Colin's backbone as he at last met the old woman's eyes. A green as dark as the hidden depths of the forest stared back at him, capturing him, holding him immobilized.

He'd not spoken those words aloud. He'd only thought them.

"You're all too easy for me to read," she murmured, the color in her eyes swirling as she spoke.

"What takes you from me, my love?" a man's voice called from beyond the door, breaking whatever power had bound Colin's attention to the woman.

"Out of my way," he muttered, the impetuousness of youth bolstered by need allowing him to push past her and into the room beyond.

What he found when he entered was in stark contrast to what he'd seen from the outside. The room itself was bathed in a warm glow of light coming from a large fireplace off to one side. Nearby, an old man sat in a richly cushioned chair, his hands resting on a polished table next to a stack of the finest, whitest paper Colin had ever seen.

The old man held a quill between ink-stained fingers, dipping it first into a little pot and then touching its tip to the sheet in front of him.

"Thomas of Ercledoune?" Colin demanded, his tongue suddenly heavy in his dry mouth. It could be no other than the great seer himself.

"Aye," the old man answered slowly, turning a watery gaze in Colin's direction.

At last! Joy sparked in Colin's heart.

Legend had grown around Thomas of Ercledoune, a seer who had accurately predicted the death of Alexander III. A man who, if those legends were to be believed, gained the gift of sight from the Faerie Queen herself.

"You must tell me, True Thomas, will Edward the Longshanks be pushed back or will all of Scotland fall to his armies? Is there any hope for our freedom? I must know."

"Leave him be," the old woman ordered, stepping around Colin to place a protective arm over Thomas's shoulders. "Your petty concerns of this world are of no consequence. Can you not see he's exhausted and ill?"

"All the more reason I must speak to him now, before it's too late." This might be his last chance to learn what the future held.

"I order you to leave him be," the woman stubbornly insisted.

"Away with you!" Colin yelled, surprising even himself with his outburst. Whoever she was, she had no right to give him such orders. He wouldn't be denied the knowledge he sought. Not now. Not after all he'd gone through to find True Thomas. "I must know my destiny. I'd hear it from his lips!"

In front of him, the air around the old woman glowed green and her form shimmered as he watched. He rubbed his eyes, unable to believe what he saw as her shape shifted from old woman to child to maiden.

"Neither crone nor maiden, young upstart, but a queen who confronts you now."

Colin leapt away, grabbing for the sword on his back as he did so. To his amazement, he found himself unable to move, as if his hand had frozen to his weapon, his feet firmly stuck to the floor. He could not move any part of his body. He could, in fact, do nothing but watch the shimmering beauty draw close, her anger pulsing around her like a living rainbow.

"It's your destiny, you'd have, is it?" Her eyes flashed as her hand slammed down on the table beside them. "So self-important you are, you'd not even take care for feelings and health of an old man? So self-important, you'd be rude to a helpless old woman? You should be ashamed of yourself."

She didn't understand. It wasn't really like that. He wasn't really like that. He'd explain it all if only he could make his tongue work.

Her eyes widened as if in surprise when she came close and placed her fingertips against his chest, directly over his heart.

"And you, with the blood of the Fae coursing through your veins. Your behavior would be bad enough from a Mortal, but from one of my own?" She shook her head in disgust. "Well, pup, you'll receive more this day than you bargained for. If it's destiny you want, then by all means, it's destiny you shall have."

The air he breathed went cold, his nose stinging like he'd stumbled into the glen on a snowy day. Around him, the room shimmered and wavered and his eyes tinted over with a green film as if he were trapped within a colored, pulsing sphere of light. He heard the woman's words reverberating from somewhere outside that sphere.

"You ask after the destiny of Scotland, but that's not what you truly want, boy. No Fae's destiny can ever be complete without finding his one true love, his other half, his Soulmate. Surely you've learned that much of your own people."

She was wrong! He was a warrior by nature and training. A warrior by choice. All he'd ever dreamed of was defending Scotland. By sheer force of will, Colin fought the Magic binding him, managing at last to move his lips.

"No!" His voice was little more than a whisper. "Dinna need love." Love was for women, gathering like hens in a warm solar, not for warriors like him. He had a much higher calling.

"Oh you think so, do you, my rash child?" The Faerie Queen's laughter tinkled around him, bouncing off the green sphere and echoing inside. "Well, we'll just see about that higher calling of yours. Seems to me you're but a youngling Fae in need of a lesson. And a lesson you shall have, a history lesson of your people. In the long ago, in the battle that split Wyddecol from the Mortal plain, soul pairings were ripped asunder, leaving each soul a jagged half, crying out for its missing piece until it could once again find its own match. Only when the two halves are once again joined will a Fae feel complete. That finding is the true destiny of all Fae. A destiny you'd deny as you stand here before me."

Lifting her arms, she placed one hand on either side of his head. "I call on the Magic lying dormant in your blood to rise up and I give you this gift, young Fae: from this day forward, you'll feel all those souls, each and every one. You'll feel their sharp, jagged edges, seeing their anguish in your mind's eye. You'll feel their pain as they blindly call out for one another, even as your own need calls out, the need you deny exists. You'll see the souls which fit together. All of them. All except your own, that is, since you claim your own need is of no importance to you."

"I ken yer anger, my love, but such a burden as you put upon the lad will drive him mad." Thomas's voice, floated through the haze. "Can you no see yer way clear to provide an escape from the millstone with which you weigh him down?"

"Very well, love, for you." The queen's tone, caressing and warm, chilled as she turned her attention back to Colin, the green of her eyes swirling like a boiling cauldron. "Only by joining with your own Soulmate will you cease to feel the horror and pain of the great wanting."

The Faerie Queen's voice seemed to pierce his body, as if her words dove through his skin and into his very bloodstream. When at last she stopped speaking, the silence echoed in his head, beating against the inside of his closed eyes as loudly as the anxious pounding of his heart.

She released him then and he fell limply to the floor, lying there as weak as a newborn babe when she walked away.

"Come, my beloved," he heard her say over the scraping of a chair against the floor. "I've indulged your desire to stay in this world long enough. It's time we returned to Wyddecol where your youth and vigor will be restored."

Just as he thought himself alone, he felt her close, whispering in his ear. "I granted you an escape only to please my Thomas, and though you've angered me greatly with your impudence, I feel the need to tell you the whole of it, youngling. Since you swear you've no need for your own missing half, it should come as no serious disappointment to learn she'll not be found in this lifetime. Perhaps my gift will allow you to learn the true importance of your destiny before your paths cross again."

And then she was gone, the sound of his own shallow panting his only company in the stillness of the room.

How long he lay there, unable to lift even a finger, he had no idea. Perhaps he slept, but he couldn't be sure. At last, his eyes flickered open and he pushed himself up to sit.

The room around him was dark and dank, smelling of animal dung and wet hide. The table and chair he'd seen earlier had disappeared, a roughly hewn wooden bench setting in their place.

He rose to his feet and stumbled outside into the light of afternoon to find his horse exactly as he'd left him, his reins still draped over the low branch.

With one last glance back at the little hut, he hefted himself up onto his mount and turned his horse away, back toward the village. Disappointment in his failure to find the answers he'd sought closed in on him, shrouding his thoughts.

Whether he'd really found Thomas of Ercledoune or only imagined the entire incident, he might never know. For the moment, he wanted to believe it had all been some bizarre nightmare brought on by sleepless nights and lack of food.

He had almost convinced himself that was the case.

The first twinges hit him just outside the village proper, sharp pains cutting against his consciousness. Jagged impressions of brightly shining lights, like broken sunbeams gone horribly wrong, they flittered through his mind. So many of them, one piling in after another until he lost count of the different shapes battering inside his mind, each of them pulsing, seething with the unrelenting agony of their own unabated loneliness.

He kicked his horse's sides, demanding speed, through the village and beyond until at last the images began to fade.

It was then he knew the truth of it.

Those shards of light had been the souls of the villagers. Just as the Faerie Queen had said he would, he'd felt every single one of them calling out for their missing half. He'd felt their desolation and pain.

His meeting with Thomas of Ercledoune had been no trick of his imagination. Nor had his encounter with the Faerie Queen been a fantasy. They were all too real.

As real as the "gift" she had given him.

As real as the curse he'd bear for the rest of his days.

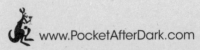